Antiques, Industrial Archaeology and Heritage Conservation have all played a role in the professional career of Tawny de Cypher. However, since moving to Portugal in 1989, translation for cultural institutions has brought the author into contact with the fascinating story of Anglo-Portuguese relations.

Investigation into local history already produced a non-fictional work, published in 2006, whose first edition sold out in four weeks. This research was extended to provide the foundation for GRIMPIL'S RETROGRESS: PORTUGAL. It is hoped that the public will derive as much enjoyment from reading this first full-length novel, as the author had in writing it.

GRIMPIL'S RETROGRESS
~PORTUCAL~

GRIMPIL'S RETROGRESS
~PORTUCAL~

TAWNY DE CYPHER

ATHENA PRESS
LONDON

GRIMPIL'S RETROGRESS
Portucal
Copyright © Tawny de Cypher 2008

All Rights Reserved

No part of this book may be reproduced in any form
by photocopying or by any electronic or mechanical means,
including information storage or retrieval systems,
without permission in writing from both the copyright
owner and the publisher of this book.

ISBN 10-digit: 1 84748 119 1
ISBN 13-digit: 978 1 84748 119 1

First published 2008 by
ATHENA PRESS
Queen's House, 2 Holly Road
Twickenham TW1 4EG
United Kingdom

Printed for Athena Press

FOREWORD

Portugal, one of the oldest nation states of Europe, became an independent kingdom under the hand of its founder, Dom Afonso Henriques, in 1143. The process of independence was launched from Guimarães, which owed its existence to Countess Mumadona, the wife of the first governor of the *condado portucalense*. Afonso Henriques extended the county's original frontiers, based on the area between the rivers Douro and Minho, as far as the Moorish kingdom of Al-Garb in the south. His son consolidated the boundaries of the national territory, which have been maintained ever since.

Portugal is also signatory to the oldest international treaty still in effect, the Treaty of Windsor. Signed by Britain and Portugal in 1373 to strengthen Portugal against Castile, it was renewed by Dom Joao I, formerly the Mestre de Avis, when he reasserted Portuguese independence and strengthened the second dynasty by marrying Phillipa of Lancaster.

However, at no stage was the destiny of the two nations more closely interwoven than during the Napoleonic Wars. Napoleon's plan for imposing his will on continental Europe involved closing European ports to British shipping, a demand which the Portuguese Prince Regent, Dom João VI, was unwilling to implement. With French influence already paramount in Spain, a secret treaty between the two countries sought to invade and dismember Portugal.

This plan was initiated in 1807 under the leadership of Junot. To thwart French intentions, the British evacuated Dom João and the court to Rio de Janeiro. The French took possession of Lisbon and proceeded to extract a war indemnity and demobilise the standing army. Resentment against these policies was reinforced by the revolt in Spain, causing Spanish troops to return home. Starting with Oporto, city after city proclaimed Dom João restored to the throne and a Committee of National Salvation was formed, presided over by the Bishop of Oporto, which sought arms and financial support from Britain. Junot sent General Loison to suppress the uprising, but he was turned back by opposition from popular forces.

An expeditionary force commanded by Arthur Wellesley (later Lord Wellington) was despatched and defeated the French at the battle of Vimeiro. A French withdrawal was negotiated by which their troops were transported back to France, taking all their booty with them. Napoleon however was less than satisfied at the turn of events and went in person to direct the pacification of Spain, on whose throne he had placed his brother Joseph. Britain sent another expeditionary force under Sir John Moore to pursue the cause of Spanish resistance, but a series of strategic and tactical errors led to the disastrous retreat and evacuation from Corunna.

A revolt in the Tyrol obliged Napoleon to abandon Spain, leaving Soult in charge of the plans for the second invasion of Portugal. Although the Portuguese were able to frustrate his attempts to cross the Minho, they did not have forces sufficient to stem the tide of the French advance, which occupied Oporto in March of 1809. Soult, however, was unable to exploit this victory for lack of support from his fellow commanders. The inactivity of Marshall Victor on the Spanish Tagus condemned the invasion to failure.

Wellesley landed once again and advanced on Oporto at the head of a combined Anglo-Portuguese army. He himself considered the retaking of the city as one of his greatest triumphs, succeeding in dislodging an enemy of superior numbers from a well-defended position with relatively little loss of life. Wellesley continued to prosecute the peninsular campaign until he eventually carried the war inside France's borders, leading to Napoleon's downfall.

The price that Portugal had to pay to maintain her independence was to become a virtual British colony, with political and military power concentrated in the hands of the British Commander in Chief, Beresford. This situation continued after the end of the war, until a military uprising in Oporto in 1820 expelled Beresford and obliged the court to return to Lisbon. Seven years later, the death of the old king lead to a crisis between his successors; Dom Miguel, schooled in the absolute monarchy of Vienna, and Dom Pedro, advocate of constitutional monarchy.

This situation eventually led to civil war, from which the Liberal Army, with ample assistance from France and England and despite being besieged in the city of Oporto from 1832 to 1833, emerged victorious. The sweeping reforms of the Liberals, however, produced as much resentment as repression by the Absolutists had done. Successive rebellions troubled the country, through attempts to restore Dom Miguel to the throne, whose forces were lead to final defeat by MacDonnel, and by popular uprisings such as the revolution of *Maria da Fonte* (1846), or by political movements, such as the *Patuleia*, in favour of a more radical constitutional settlement.

-1-

Horace Grimpil opened the leather briefcase on his lap. It contained two diaries: that of his grandfather, full from marbled end-paper to marbled end-paper, and his own, incomplete. Although it had been his intention to maintain a faithful account of his travels, his purpose had faltered. He could no longer remember how much of the events had been recorded. Opening his diary at the last entry, he read the only words written on that page: *I wish to possess her love as much as my love for her possesses me.* The words startled him. He snapped the book shut. He recalled the breathless night. He could remember crossing the room to the already open casement, throwing aside the shutters in the hope of letting some fresh air into the room, but the night air outside had been no cooler than the suffocation inside. The sky had been studded with stars, but the corner of the sky where the comet had been was devoid of the fiery exclamation mark written by the hand of God.

On the eastern horizon a star appeared in the heavens, burning with greater intensity than all the others. Among all women she was like that star, more brilliant than the countless others surrounding her. How he wished to get closer to that distant sun, feel its warmth, bask in its clarity. He was like the comet, that after millennia of wandering through empty space, finally entered the orbit of its home planet, its frigid mantle of ice transformed into an incandescent plume more resplendent than Lucifer's fiery mane.

How he wished to be able to show the intensity of the flame that burned in his breast. He had wondered how it would be if their lives were joined in matrimony; if she were here with him in the intimacy of their bedchamber, a cascade of dark hair flowing freely over the white pillowcase, her breath passing between parted lips as she slept... Placing the paraffin lamp beside his journal on the desk at the foot of the window, he had picked up the pen and written the only words he had been capable of phrasing: *I wish to possess her love as much as my love for her possesses me.*

-2-

When Argenton entered the room, Nicolas Jean de Dieu Soult, Duke of Dalmatia and Marshal of the Imperial Army, was studying his handsome features in the mirror. Soult was displeased at being interrupted in his reflections.

'Argenton, send for the barber, would you. I need a shave.'

Alone again, he continued to appreciate his mirror image. Worthy of a Roman consul, he thought. He noticed that, despite his evident youth, he was greying at the temples. The effect pleased him: the vigour of youth melded with the sagacity of years. He turned his head sideways; how excellent his profile would appear stamped on a coin. He remembered the countenance of his emperor cast in gold, wearing the laurel wreath of victory. But for the revolt in the Tyrol, Napoleon would be here now, guiding the destiny of his armies and bending the fate of nations to his will.

Before leaving, Bonaparte had drawn up a very precise timetable for him to follow: Oporto occupied by 5 February and Lisbon by the sixteenth of the same month. It was 25 March 1809, and he was seriously behind schedule. In fact, he had only left Santiago de Compostela on 8 February, and his attempts to cross the River Minho had been frustrated. On the very day scheduled for his triumphal entry into the nation's capital, his forces were being repulsed at Vila Nova de Cerveira, an obscure river-crossing with a few hundred inhabitants.

Argenton, meanwhile, picked his way through the confusion of military accoutrements: the stacked muskets, the knapsacks, the cauldrons, the sprawled soldiers taking their rest. It had been a frustrating outset to the campaign, with the interminable march through northern Spain, only punctuated by a brief respite in Orense, before entering Portugal by Chaves. The frontier fortress held out for three days, but General Silveira's army was too small to offer any sustained resistance. After recognising the inevitability of a French victory, he had withdrawn his forces, leaving the road open to Braga.

The roads, however, were almost non-existent, and the only attempt to bar their passage came at Carvalho de Este, a few leagues beyond Braga. Despite their tenacity, the forces of the *Leal Legião de Lusitania* not only lacked front-line troops but everything else as well – munitions, artillery, horses. After the break-up of the standing army, there were few experienced commanders left in the country. Worse still, their only able commander, Freire de Andrade, had been slaughtered by the revolting townspeople of Braga for deciding not to defend their city. When the French finally marched into the City of Archbishops, they found it deserted; the populace had melted away. At least it provided them with a few days' respite.

Argenton returned to the Commander-in-Chief's quarters to find Soult explaining the disposition of the various divisions to his generals. He had obviously forgotten about the need for a shave. Argenton and the barber waited in an antechamber. Pointing out the objectives on the map before them, Soult ordered Heudelet north to Ponte de Lima to open the road to Valença, where their heavy artillery and baggage train were waiting. Lorges was to go east to Barcelos, Franceschi to proceed south to Guimarães, while La Hussaye would advance on Famalicão to seek out a crossing over the River Ave at Trofa. They were finally drawing close to their objective: the city of Oporto. It was with a certain sense of satisfaction that Soult contemplated the completion of the first part of the mission entrusted to him by Napoleon Bonaparte, Emperor of the French and the undisputed master of continental Europe.

-3-

Grimpil's mind returned from reflecting on the past to remembering more recent events. Although the scene had only occurred a short time previously, he was already uncertain as to how to reassemble the images retained by his mind into their correct chronological sequence. Was the image of the outstretched arm from the moment before or after her body had struck the water? She had broken the calmness of the water when she fell in, but he couldn't remember any turbulence resulting from someone struggling for life. The water had quickly calmed with the complete absence of any sound beyond the original splash. Had she struck her head on the stone parapet as she overbalanced? He could recall bubbles of air breaking the surface, but had they simply been caused by air trapped in the folds of water-logged cloth? Why had he not acted? Had he deliberately failed to act because he wished her dead, or had he simply been unable to intervene against the will of fate? What was important now was to focus on something other than the sight of the drowning girl.

He shut his mind to the scene and opened his journal at the first page.

Monday, June 20th, 1854

We set sail from Falmouth on the afternoon tide, bound for Oporto, on board the good ship Flora, commanded by Captain Chapel.

His prevailing memory of the voyage was the odour of sea salt, pitch and wet hemp. Captain Chapel had considered conditions of wind and sea so highly favourable that he had spread more canvas. The vessel ploughed the waters of the Bay of Biscay with such vigour that the sensation of nausea never completely passed. Only after drawing towards the Portuguese coast and entering calmer waters was it possible to return to making his diary entries.

-4-

'We're fanning out, lads,' said the barber, reporting the latest intelligence from headquarters to his comrades-in-arms from Gascogny.

'You might be fannying about,' said Jacquot, who had little time for non-combatants, 'but we don't mess around on duty.'

'I said fanning out, not fannying about,' replied the barber, somewhat chastened by the lack of interest in his news.

'So what's in for us?' asked the sergeant, always pleased to know what orders they were going to receive before being told by the officers.

'More fighting,' replied the barber laconically, now less enthusiastic about imparting his intelligence.

'Thanks for the news,' responded another contemptuously.

'*Famalicão*,' stated the barber, no longer interested in withholding information.

'Family what?'

'*Cão*' answered the Barber, stressing the last syllable, which meant 'dog' in Portuguese.

'Yeah – that would be about right for us dogs!'

'Well, at least you've got a kennel to sleep in tonight,' the barber retorted as he went on his way.

After the endless nights of sleeping in the field, a bed was the infantryman's greatest luxury. No one knew of the hardships of a military campaign better than he; the constant need to arrange something hot to fill his stomach, something to stuff into his boots to save his feet from blisters and somewhere to rest his head at the end of the day. Keeping his ammunition pouch full and his powder dry were secondary concerns. Battles were singular events, almost a relief to alleviate the tedium of marching, even if the infantryman got the worst of those as well.

Soult, as he rose to positions of command, had learnt that

prudence was the better part of valour. Having achieved the rank of field marshal, he realised that the task of a commander was more like that of governing a small state, relying more on careful organisation than bravado. If this was not sufficiently complex a task, it had to be performed on the move, travelling through territory that, if not overtly hostile, was totally uncooperative. His prime concern of the moment was to maintain his lines of communication. He had not received any news from León or Badajoz. How far would he be able to proceed without support from the south? Then there were the generals under his command. To what extent were they loyal to his person? As Napoleon used to say, 'You can always rely on the enemy.' To which he would add, 'Hélas! The same cannot always be said for one's allies.' What inducements could he extend to secure their adhesion to the common cause?

The two most important allies in any enterprise were Master Gold and Mistress Silver, but Junot had depleted the country of virtually all its resources. Without metal coin there could be no government. Nor could there be government without the consent of the people. He would have to make it clear that the old monarchy was gone for ever, as well as showing the benefits of entering the French sphere of influence: progress, trade and security. After all, had not Afonso Henriques, the founding father of the nation, been the son of a Burgundian nobleman? The very existence of Portugal derived from the well-spring of French military prowess; it was only natural that the renaissance of the country should come from the same source.

−5−

Thursday, June 23rd, 1854

I was gratified that my first sight of Portugal should be none other than the town in which my grandfather was born. The first work of man to emerge on the landscape was a series of giant arches, striding across the flat fields, which Captain Chapel informed me was the aqueduct carrying water to the Convent of Vila de Conde.

My satisfaction was diminished, however, by the prospect of entering the bar of the Douro, especially when embellished by the Captain's litany of shipwrecks and disaster occasioned by unsuccessful attempts at negotiating these treacherous waters, swollen by a heavy downpour of a few days previously. Our pilots came on board and took command of the vessel, but the force of the current seemed to resist their attempts to penetrate the natural barriers placed in our way. On one side lay sandbanks and shifting shallows, waiting to run us aground, while on the other pointed rocks and granite reefs were ready to tear out the entrails of the ship. We had to sail as close to the wind as possible on a seemingly disastrous heading until, at the last moment, the skilled hands of our pilots brought the helm round so that we passed through these perils and entered the calmer waters of the pool.

On one side, the city of Oporto is piled high on

the Cathedral Hill, houses cascading down its flanks to the waterfront. On the other lies Vila Nova de Gaia, overlooked by the Serra do Pilar and its imposing monastery. With fears of shipwreck still fresh in my mind, I was alarmed to see a submerged vessel on the Gaia side of the river, with water covering her decks. The Captain tried to assuage my apprehension by informing me that the St José had been scuttled deliberately for carrying yellow fever, an explanation that left me no less disturbed than previously. Indeed, we would not be allowed to leave *The Flora* without first being submitted to an inspection by the health authorities. Therefore, our first day in harbour was spent in expectation of the doctor's visit. We waited in vain, while the sailors brought our baggage out of the hold, until the afternoon of the following day when an individual hailed us from the shore, informing us he was the doctor's assistant, the doctor himself being unable to attend us. Either for fear of contagion or simply from professional negligence, he remained on the quayside and ordered the crew and passengers to line up along the rail, carrying out his inspection from a safe distance. I would have argued with such lax practice if I had not been so desirous to get ashore. Therefore, as soon as we received our clearance, I sent word to Smith & Woodhouse that we were landed, requesting they send a carriage.

−6−

Spread out around the improvised defences around the city of Oporto, Soult's army of 24,000 men was poised to attack the capital of the North. The nation's second city would soon be in his power. Junot's attempt to impose his governance the year before had proved that to conquer the country it was essential to first master the provinces between the Douro and Minho. That was exactly what Soult intended to do. He hoped the *preudhommes* of Oporto would prevail over the warmongers who agitated the masses with thoughts of armed resistance. His network of spies reported a state of virtual anarchy within the city, where the fury of the mob descended on anyone being suspected, rightly or wrongly, of pro-French sympathies. The most sensible policy would be to surrender so as to avoid loss of life and property.

Ever since the first days of the revolt against French rule, the Bishop of Oporto had become the leader of the northern provinces – 'General Mitre', as he had been dubbed. Soult thought back to the names of clerics resonant in the annals of French history – Mazzarin and Richelieu – men who had wielded more effective power than the kings they served. It was better that prelates reserve their preaching to questions of Christian salvation. The time for bishops in politics had passed, and indeed, for that matter, the time for monarchs, too. The affairs of Europe were now in the hands of men enlightened by rational principles and governed by the guiding spirit of the brotherhood of man – liberty, equality and fraternity; men of destiny – like himself, like Napoleon – capable of rising to the highest ranks on no other basis than their own innate qualities.

While he was perfectly ready to impose his will by force, he had, of course, made the usual promises to safeguard the city if it surrendered, along with the usual reminder of the consequences of resistance. 'General Mitre' had placed his head in a noose. Having incited the people to resist, would he now risk his own neck to negotiate terms of surrender? He was the prisoner of his own rhetoric. It was all well and good to swear undying loyalty to the House of Bragança, but Dom João was basking in tropical splendour on the other side of the Atlantic. He had forfeited his throne, even to the extent of advising his people to accept the French as their new governors. So be it. He would assume the reins of government on behalf of his emperor.

While he was waiting for a reply from the Bishop to his request for the city to surrender, his secretary was reading aloud a text for publication: 'There has to be a king, but a king with an independent spirit. One who can preserve the nation against English captivity. There are no doubt many who would like to see the House of Bragança restored to the throne – but how can this family return if the English, who took them away, will not bring them back?'

Once installed, they would need a mouthpiece through which to address the citizens of Oporto and all the province of the North.

'Argenton,' he said, turning to his Aide de Camp, 'we shall need to find a printer sympathetic to our cause.'

-7-

Apart from being one of the finest streets in the city of Oporto, Rua Nova dos Inglezes was the centre of British trading interests. At ten in the morning it could be mistaken for any commercial artery of Bristol or Liverpool, so thick was it with the conversation of British merchants. The talk was mainly about the impending war with Russia and there was much exchange of opinion as to the best way to prosecute campaign. Amidst the high politics there was also opportunity to discuss more local details: the remarkable transformation in Carlos Whitehead and speculation as to what could have changed an inveterate waster into one of the most assiduous merchants on the street.

'So the lad needed to sow a few wild oats. Perfectly natural. But with such a fine upstanding father it was inevitable that one day he would settle down to serious business,' opined one of the merchants.

'If you ask me, only the influence of a woman can make such a transformation,' replied another, and immediately conversation turned to speculation as to which fair face had turned the head of the young scion of Whitehead's.

Further along the street, another pair of gentlemen were greeting each other.

'By all accounts, young Grimpil has arrived,' informed the more elderly of the two, who sported an impressive pair of bushy whiskers. 'He is lodged with Woodhouse.'

His interlocutor was in his early forties, whose accent denounced North Country origins and his broad forehead intellectual capacities. 'Grimpil... Grimpil' he said, as if searching his memory. 'I'm afraid, Mr Naylor, I don't know the person in question.'

'No, I guess his father's days were before your time. By all accounts he's a Fellow of St Botolph's; selecting some vintage for High Table, no doubt; youngish chap. You might care to meet him, Mr Flower, and catch up with the latest from England.'

Mr Flower received the suggestion by pressing his already narrow lips together in a gesture of distaste. He resented these intrusions on his time and found the social responsibilities of living in a foreign colony irksome. 'Dealing with Smith & Woodhouse then, is he?' he inquired.

'That's right. Oh, look! Here comes Graham. I'll leave you two gentlemen alone. Good day, Mr Flower: Good day to you, Mr Graham.'

The newcomer greeted Flower cordially. 'I say, Flower, have you heard? Dunlop has taken up his commission and is to join the expeditionary force to the Crimea.'

'Is that a fact? No, I hadn't heard.'

'I'm surprised Old Man Naylor didn't tell you. What were you talking about, then?'

'Oh, apparently there's a pup in town; Grimble, I think he said; academic. I just hope to steer clear of him. Listen, I'm meeting Forrester for lunch. Would you care to join us? If you're interested in listening to our tedious conversation, of course.'

'I should be delighted, William. There is no finer pastime to be had in all of Oporto.'

'One o'clock, then, at the Factory.' And, tipping his hat, bade farewell to his friend.

-8-

From his palace next to the cathedral, the Bishop could see the gun emplacements on the hill overlooking Gaia. He failed to understand why the cannons appeared to be pointing directly towards the Episcopal palace. Surely they were supposed to be directed towards the enemy. He had to confess that he understood little of the technicalities of war, although as Chairman of the Committee of National Salvation he presided over the city's military fortunes.

Sitting around a table with him, studying the map of the city's fortifications, were the Brigadiers Parreiras, Barreto and Vitoria, to whom the task of defending Oporto had now fallen, along with Baron Ebben. The systematic construction of a defensive network proposed by Captain Joaquim de Almeida had never been implemented. How could he have found the physical and financial means to realise a project on such a princely scale?

The men now looked at the thirty-five redoubts that constituted the only barrier between the city and the French army. The Bishop was not convinced these positions were an effective barrier. He imagined that the defence of the city would be secured by placing men on the battlements of the city wall, much as he had seen in the pictorial representations of the glorious feats of arms of antiquity.

'What we could really do with is some 12-pounders,' said Vitoria.

Most of the artillery at their disposal were only 6-pounders and therefore of much shorter range. In some cases old cannon, which had served as bollards on the quaysides, had been uprooted to be recommissioned. Inevitably these were completely unserviceable.

'What we could really do with,' rejoined Parreiras bitterly, 'is a goddamn army!' adding hastily, 'Begging Your Eminence's pardon, no offence meant.'

'A chain is only as strong as its weakest link. The important thing is that we keep the French at arm's length and not let them overrun any of these positions,' observed Barreto.

'Quite so,' replied Parreiras dryly. 'We shall divide the line between us. Barreto, you take the northern sector from the Castelo do Queijo as far as Prelada; I'll take the centre, and, Vitoria, you take the southern sector from Aguadente as far as Freixo. Ebben, you keep your men as mobile reserve. How many pieces do you have?'

'Four' replied the Austrian.

The three brigadiers eyed each other. Finally Parreiras broke the silence. 'It will have to do.'

'But will it be enough?' asked the Bishop.

'Do you have faith in God?' Parreiras queried.

'Of course I do.'

'Then, in that case, I suggest you pray for us all!'

–9–

The premises of Smith & Woodhouse did not differ significantly from those of any other Port wine shipper. From an undistinguished entrance at street level, a stone stairway climbed to the first floor where, on entering a small waiting room furnished with a pair of high-backed chairs, one could admire a rather lifeless portrait of the founder, dressed in his robes of the Lord Mayor of London. On the other side of a darkly stained wooden counter lay the counting house, where the bookkeepers sat at their ledgers at desks ensconced in the only window, which faintly illuminated the rest of office. The centre was occupied by a partner's desk, covered with a profusion of letters, bills and documents of all kinds. At this moment neither of the partners was seated at it, but instead a young man, who was entertaining the clerks with a story that had reached its ribald conclusion.

'My friends, you had to be there to believe it. If only you could have seen the expression on his face.'

'So what did he say?'

'Say? He didn't *say* anything! He was so incapable of speech that he just opened and closed his mouth like a freshly landed fish on the quays of Ribeira. Gesticulate, yes; he was able to gesticulate, wagging his finger until it was fit to fall off. But speak... no!'

'You scoundrel! If I had been there...'

We will never find out what the clerk would have done had he been there, for, at that moment, footfalls were heard on the stair, heralding the arrival of Mr Woodhouse. The clerks immediately buried their noses in their ledgers, and the young man moved towards the door to take the coat from Mr Woodhouse as he entered.

'Good morning, gentlemen,' greeted the new arrival. 'Alfredo,' he said, addressing the raconteur, 'I want you to take this letter to Senhor Sousa, in Gaia, and make sure everything is ready this afternoon for Mr Grimpil. Return immediately if there is a reply from the lodge. Understood?'

Alfredo nodded.

'Very well, then; be on your way.' And, turning to the elder of the clerks, he continued 'Senhor Fernandes, I shall need the stock books of our vintage wines from '47, '51 and '53, and later we shall need to look at prices. Have you prepared the figures?'

'Yes, sir,' replied Fernandes, and, without needing to read the gold lettering on the spines of the registers, his hand went automatically to the place where the information that his master had requested was registered.

-10-

The Bishop had never imagined that one day he would assist at a battle, and the first thing that struck him as he surveyed the horizon was the apparent lack of any armies. He was expecting some kind of head-on collision between two bodies of men, but either the battleground was elsewhere or both armies were hiding from each other.

He returned to his quarters to fetch a telescope and arrived breathless at the top of the steeply inclined ladder that gave onto the platform beside the great brass mouth of the Cathedral's main bell. Sweeping the horizon, he could make out faintly adumbrated concentrations of colour almost a league away that he took for the French encampments, but at this distance what threat could they offer?

As it to answer his thoughts, flashes of light were repeated at close intervals all along the horizon with incredible rapidity. Without warning the air was rent by the sound of the cannon, each as ominous as the crack of doom but repeated with such frequency so as to make one endless peal of deafening thunder.

'Holy Mary, Mother of God,' uttered the Bishop instinctively. 'Save us now and at the hour of our death.'

He could see more sporadic isolated replies from the batteries closer to the city, but they lacked the speed and intensity of fire as those coming from the French side. At this distance, the sound was infernal. How could it be supported at the much closer range? From what he could see, the enemy action was more intense on the flank than the centre, but the amount of smoke from the cannons was beginning to obscure the view.

He dropped to his knees to pray.

'O blessed Virgin Mary, Mother of God, Protector of the Kingdom of Portugal, come to the aid of your beleaguered sons. You who gave victory to Afonso Henriques against the Moors and King John against the Castilians deliver us now from the hands of the infidel, who seeks not only to eradicate the House of Bragança but also the House of God; desecrate the sanctuaries of our Mother the Church and pillage your holy relics. Against your enemies raise your hand to succour your faithful, so that we may redouble our worship of our Holy Mother. Mediatrix of all graces, intercede for us with your blessed son, our lord Jesus Christ.

The Bishop interrupted his prayers to scrutinise the battlefield. The view was more chaotic than ever. Dense palls of smoke rolled over the landscape, alternately revealing and concealing detachments of troops, galloping cavalry, and the incessant roar of cannon vomiting forth sound and fury. Perhaps Our Lady wasn't entirely the right person to whom to address his prayers. What he needed here was the wrath of the Old Testament God: an irate, vengeful God, ready to castigate his enemies with fire and brimstone.

He began again, 'O Lord of the Prophets, you who raised your hand to smite the Egyptians when they pursued your chosen race, who guided David's hand to conquer the giant Goliath, strengthen the hand of your faithful servants so that we might, too, vanquish the invader and restore the kingdom to the peaceful worship of your holy name…'

He looked over the parapet again. The intensity of the combat on the flank seemed to have diminished. Had his prayers been answered? Had God worked a miracle to deliver Oporto from the claws of the Imperial Eagle? His hopes were dashed, however, as he could see rank after rank of blue uniforms advancing towards the centre of the line, bayonets lowered, advancing with steady pace to the pounding of the regimental drums.

An occasional crack of musket fire could be heard, but it was ineffective to stem the tide. The front lines were now running forward towards an emplacement when the sudden eruption of the cannon obliterated the sight from view. He leaned his back against the sun-warmed stone and looked towards the heavens. He realised with sickening certainty that the heavens were empty; there was no help from there or any other quarter. He turned to look back towards the battlefield. The Portuguese position had been overrun; the defenceless militiamen were fleeing in the direction of the city to save their lives. Hot on their heels rode a squadron of dragoons, the blades of their upheld sabres glinting in the sunlight. Down they came in vicious arcs, cutting into the backs of the retreating soldiery, hacking them down as they fled.

'Stop!' cried the Bishop. 'Stop!' But there was no one to hear his cries, and, even if they had been heard they were completely in vain. A tide had been loosed, and now there was no force that could prevent it from running its course.

-11-

The most important building on the Rua Nova dos Inglezes was the Factory House, built by the Shippers' Association in the Palladian style. It served as the focus of the commercial and social life of the British community in Oporto. On this day, at this hour, in the upstairs kitchen above the ballroom, the cooks were preparing the luncheon of the day, the most highly regarded of all Portuguese specialities – Bacalhau, or dried salted codfish – to be served with boiled potatoes and cabbage, dressed in a sauce of olive oil, vinegar and crushed garlic. The main dish would be accompanied by a White Monção wine, light and slightly sparkling, whose delicate bouquet served to counterpoint the dryness of the fish. The dessert was to consist of baked pears stuffed with walnuts and figs, doused in brandy.

Great copper cauldrons already stood on the range, with water just beginning to boil, ready to receive the fillets of cod which had been soaking in water for the last few days. The kitchen boys were peeling potatoes and the head cook was leaning out of the window, shouting instructions to a messenger down below to arrange bread from the bakery. Down in the dining room, other staff were covering the great table with a specially made linen tablecloth and polishing the silverware.

-12-

The Bishop entered the vestry with unusual haste. Before the Sacristan could comment, the Bishop told him to find a portmanteau and join him in his private chapel. When he had done his master's bidding, he found that the Bishop had already assembled a collection of church plate – candlesticks, chalice, ciborium, monstrance, altar cross – spread out over the large oak table, which he now tried to load into the bag.

'It's not big enough,' he complained. He tried lifting it. 'It's too heavy.'

He withdrew the heavy velvet covered bible with its gilt clasps and ornamental corners.

'Try it now,' he instructed.

The frail sacristan, who was not accustomed to lifting anything heavier than an incense boat, could barely raise it off the floor.

The Bishop studied the contents and took out the candlesticks. Putting them aside, he was struck by a fresh idea. Taking the stole from the vestments chest, he tied the sacred vessels, knotting the foot of each one by one, until he had produced a type of bandolier of religious silverware. He was more satisfied with the solution and summoned the Sacristan to experiment, the result a type of bizarre ordination.

The Sacristan bowed under the weight.

'Excellent,' exclaimed the Bishop. 'Now walk.'

The Sacristan obeyed, the vessels striking against each other, producing a sound similar to that made by a herd of goats in movement.

The Bishop threw a large cloak over the Sacristan's shoulders and said, 'Follow me.'

The Sacristan did as instructed, the sound of the silverware now muffled under the heavy woollen wrap.

As the Bishop walked, he unbuttoned the soutain and threw it aside. He took the ring from his finger and shoved it in his waistcoat pocket. Before leaving the vestry, he took the Sacristan's hat, which he thrust on his head. Turning up the collar of the Sacristan's greatcoat, he seized a pasteboard portfolio and headed for the stables, while behind him the Sacristan tried to accompany the Bishop's vigorous pace.

Keeping the brim of his hat pulled low so as to avoid being recognised the Bishop set out on horseback, pushing his way through the crowded streets, calling out in a stentorian voice, 'Make way! Urgent government business!' The Sacristan trotted behind, following as best he could. When they emerged beyond the walls onto the waterfront, a long line of miserable humanity slowly filed its way across the narrow pontoon bridge. On the other side, the Bishop could see the high walls of the Convent of Serra do Pilar and the protecting muzzles of the cannon. Now he understood. He must get inside those walls without delay.

With redoubled energy he shoved aside the lesser mortals who appeared in front of him. 'Make way! Urgent government business!' he bellowed, batting the leather portfolio from side to side as if swatting insects.

When they finally reached the Gaia side of the bridge, there was a number of militiamen on guard duty.

'Guards,' he called out authoritatively. 'Open the hatches!'

The men looked at each other uncomprehendingly.

'You must sink the barges! Open the hatches! Orders of the Junta!'

'We can't do that; the bridge is full of people,' said one of the soldiers.

The Bishop took the man by the shirt front and hissed in a low voice, 'The city is about to fall into the hands of the French. We must prevent them from crossing the Douro at all costs. Orders direct from Beresford!'

'I don't know nothing about that,' replied the militiaman truculently. 'I need orders from my corporal.'

'Corporal? Don't give me your pissing insignificant corporal! These are the orders of the Supreme Marshall General of the Armed Forces of the Kingdom!'

The man was visibly cowed but far from convinced. He

couldn't imagine how anyone so highly placed could even be aware of his existence, let alone be giving him orders. He looked to his comrades for support.

'Who are you to be giving us orders, any road?' asked one of them defiantly. 'If you've got orders, then show 'em us.'

The Bishop thrust his hand into the portfolio and brought forth a sheaf of papers. He wasn't sure what they were, but it was extremely unlikely that any of them could read. The soldiers eyed each other nervously as the Bishop brandished the papers triumphantly.

'Well, if you've got orders, best show 'em to the Corporal. He's in the billet at the top of the road,' said the militiaman, indicating the house in question with a grimy forefinger.

-13-

In the cool obscurity of the wine lodge Senhor Sousa went about his business with calm deliberation. Here time was measured in decades, not in years, and he was completing the work of his forefathers in the same way as his successors would complete his. The wine lay dormant in row upon row of great oak casks, ageing in silent reverie. The wine from those years in which nature had been especially benevolent, when the sun had blessed the grapes with high sugar content and the summer rains swollen their pregnant skins to bursting point, was kept apart. After seven years in the wood, the precious tawny liquor was transferred to the dark green bottles that were stacked in rows as high as a man's head within alcoves closed by iron grilles and securely locked away. Senhor Sousa kept the keys to these cells and, once in a while, would open the cages to gently rotate the bottles by a few degrees, as one might visit a child in the night to adjust the bedclothes. While they slowly collected dust on the outside, alchemy was taking place inside. In its slumber the wine dreamed of the great silence that spread over the terraced valleys, the heat of the midday sun and the scent of wild aniseed on the early morning air, and from these memories distilled Port wine.

Sousa was disturbed from his labours by the entrance of Alfredo. He was always disturbed by the presence of Alfredo, for not only did the lad suffer from the more forgivable failings of youth, but he was also indifferent to the things that Sousa considered important, while giving importance to things that Sousa considered worthless. He doubted the wisdom of his master's decision in hiring the lad and feared that Woodhouse was getting too old to run the business. If only he had handed over the administration to Flower, a man with all the qualities to give continuity to their endeavour.

Alfredo delivered his message and almost at once stepped outside in the hope of importuning a passing maiden, but the street was quiet and no unsuspecting young ladies were to be the subject of Alfredo's attentions that morning. The lack of sport bothered him, so he went back inside to 'help' the cellar-keeper. Sousa was making the necessary preparation for the afternoon's wine tasting and was attempting to impress on Alfredo the importance of this event.

'The gentleman has come a long way to sample our wines. He is the representative of a very venerable institution, which has always honoured this house with its custom. Not only must we offer him the best wine, but also the best service.'

Alfredo said nothing. Perhaps his mind was so agile because it was relatively unburdened by any intellectual baggage. From under half-closed lids he followed every detail of the old man's movements, retaining all the steps Sousa had taken. At that moment a cooper came in, asking for the foreman, and Sousa left with him to attend to some aspect of repairing casks. Left alone, Alfredo surveyed the scene before him: a table spread with a white cloth, on which stood three decanters, indistinguishable one from the other but for the brass tags they wore around their necks, each engraved with a number. The first thought that passed through Alfredo's mind was to swap the tags around, but he rejected the idea as being worthy only of a schoolboy's prank. He needed something more subtle, richer in possibilities. Acting with decision, swiftly but without haste, so as not to leave any telltale signs that might denounce him, he returned the contents of two of the decanters to their original containers and refilled them with wine the same as the third.

-14-

The remainder of the residents – those who believed the city could resist at least for a few days in the hope that help might still be on its way – hastily threw together a few essentials and pressed their way down to the waterfront to get across the river before the soldiery invaded the city. The street leading to the Water Gate was packed and the bridge crammed with people, especially women and children. Each one sought to hasten their own progress, pushing and shoving their neighbours as if they were any less anxious to get across the water to the safety of Vila Nova de Gaia.

From behind them came the sound of musket fire. The men were making their last-ditch attempt to halt the French. A sizeable force in the Bishop's Palace laid down a tempest of musket shot, creating an ambush for the advancing cavalry. Behind them came the infantry with their fixed bayonets glinting in the sunlight; no quarter would be given.

Captain Duras led his unit of cavalry at a slow trot. He did not want to risk falling into an ambush in the narrow streets, which, although apparently deserted, could still hide militiamen or even just furious civilians, ready to defend their city in any way possible. Fighting on the open field was honourable combat, but as he rode down the cobbled street, in full view of countless empty windows, he felt himself more of a target than he had ever been in any battle. This was the new war, the war without uniforms, where any individual, young or old, could equally be a civilian or a combatant. This was a war where stones were as effective as bullets, trees as cannons; a war without confrontation, only sudden death by an unseen hand, from an unseen quarter. There was no glory in this.

An intense volley of musket fire came from the direction of the Bishop's Palace to his left. He considered the possibility of going to support the action, but as the unit gathered pace as it descended Rua das Hortas, musket fire also broke out from ahead. He had no option but to lower himself against his horse and lead the unit in a charge forward. With the sound of iron against stone ricocheting off the granite walls, along with the stinging flight of lead, his unit erupted onto the waterfront at full gallop, trampling all who lay in their path.

Panic spread through the mass of people. The shock wave travelled forward to those on the river bank, a surge of pressing humanity forcing its way forward onto the bridge of boats. The pressure was too great to resist. Those still massed at the mouth of the bridge were forced into the water. They clung to the ropes and stays, screaming to their families and friends for help, but anyone who attempted to come to their rescue was also impelled into the water.

No sooner had he emerged on the quayside, Duras found himself faced with a cannonade from the defenders on the other side of the river, which greatly increased the confusion and desperation that reigned. The great surge of humanity was more than the bridge could sustain. The parapet gave way as the narrow deck could no longer contain the multitude, plunging an ever growing number of people into the Douro. Struggling under their burdens, or even just the weight of their waterlogged clothes, they desperately tried to remain afloat, or spent the last of their forces trying to save the lives of their loved ones. The water was filled with struggling bodies and the air with cries of anguish.

As if this affliction was not sufficient, an ominous groan issued from the bridge itself, followed by the snapping of chains. The structure had broken free of its restraints, slowly snaking away as the pontoon gained new life under the river currents. Those caught at the far end were immediately precipitated into the fast-flowing river, some being able to clutch hold of planking from the deck of the bridge to save their lives, others disappearing instantly into the waves. These were followed by many others who, deprived of their footing, were hurled into the river. Those who moments before had been pressing forward now sought to reverse their direction; all to no avail. Unable to prevent themselves from being propelled forward, a continuous stream of people was being cast into a watery grave. The waters of the Douro were thick with the bodies of the drowned or drowning. The firing from the far side ceased, and Duras, moved by the magnitude of the tragedy which unrolled before his eyes, ordered his men to dismount and come to the aid of the hapless victims who could still be rescued.

–15–

Immediately to the right, on entering the Factory, was the newsroom, to which visitors were admitted and where the ship captains met to gather the latest intelligence. It was here that Woodhouse had arranged to meet Grimpil at half past twelve. With the punctuality with which the British conducted their business, renowned among the Portuguese, who generally paid less slavish respect to hours, the two men shook hands and settled over a pre-prandial Port to discuss their affairs.

'I trust you slept well, Grimpil?'

'Indeed I did, sir. My first night on dry land and, if I may praise you on your hospitality, a most comfortable bed.'

'I ordered the servant not to wake you.'

'Most considerate of you, Mr Woodhouse; a courtesy greatly appreciated I can assure you.'

'Very well, now; let me see. I have arranged for you to visit the Entreposto this afternoon. I trust you feel sufficiently recovered from your journey to undertake such a visit.'

'Thank you for your concern, Mr Woodhouse. I am not only fully recovered but most anxious to attend to this part of my business.'

'I have laid aside two excellent vintages for you to choose from; the '42 is sweet and full-bodied, the '47 is rich and well balanced. However, I strongly advise considering the '51, which, although still young, is most promising, some say as good as that of 1820. So your task may not be easy. But you can consider that at your leisure after lunch. What news from England?'

'We shall have both war and taxes, and I fail to see how England is well served by either. I'm afraid Mr Russell's ears are deafened by Palmerston's belligerence. Neither Mr Gladstone's nice moral judgement nor his even better political economy has prevailed. My friends in the Exchequer are quite dismayed and fear we may return to the days of the national debt.'

Woodhouse looked inquiringly into the depths of the Port wine as if an answer might be found there. The turbulent nature of local affairs and the constant effort to maintain the smooth running of the business had left him with progressively less notion of events in the world beyond the Douro valley. What was more, there was now the problem of oidium to deal with!

'And what, then, of your personal plans? Shall you be going to Vila de Conde?'

'Indeed. It was my late mother's dying wish that her ashes return to her native soil. She always said that she had left her heart in Portugal, even though England had given her safe haven. It could not have been an easy transition for her to make.'

Woodhouse's own recollections of life in Great Britain were a distant memory, almost as if they belonged to some other being rather than himself. 'In any case, you're welcome to stay as long as you wish, my boy. As they say, "My house is your house". And what of Sir David? Is he well?' Woodhouse inquired, drawing himself from his reverie.

There was a moment's silence until Grimpil replied, 'I'm afraid our much esteemed master is very debilitated; the doctors are very reserved in their prognosis.'

'Indeed,' said Woodhouse quietly, and silence fell while he digested the news. The comings and goings in the hall now increased as the hour for lunch approached. A servant came over to advise them that the table was set. 'I'm sorry to hear that,' said Woodhouse, his mind still on the previous topic of conversation. 'Yes, let us go upstairs, Grimpil; our luncheon awaits.'

-16-

Alfredo stepped back to admire his handiwork. The only problem now was if the old man called him back to the office. The best thing to do was to make himself scarce and come back after lunch. It was too late to catch any kitchen maids on their way back from the market, so he decided to go down to the river front. There was always movement there, and he might find someone from whom he could cadge a free lunch. He was not to be disappointed, for hardly had he got to the river front did he hear a familiar cry – 'Ahoy there, *Ginga-mocho*' – a name of endearment used only by a cousin of his who worked the river, on board a Rabelo.

The Rabelo is a craft especially designed for navigating the shallows and rapids of the upper course of the Douro, which is the main thoroughfare of the Minho region. It is a shallow draft vessel whose deck is given over to its cargo, having a flying bridge to the stern where the pilot stands, steering the craft with a long paddle-shaped rudder, whose length, combined with the height of the bridge, provides the helmsman with the leverage necessary to guide the boat through turbulent waters.

'Ahoy there, *Verdugos*' replied Alfredo to his cousin, who invited him to come and join him. The sailors had stretched an awning over the area between the bridge and the stern to provide shelter while the crew were eating their lunch. Alfredo did not delay in accepting the invitation, crossing the narrow board that joined the Rabelo to the jetty.

-17-

By the time the bulk of the army entered the city, it had been virtually abandoned by its citizens, except for the prostitutes and the lowlife scum who saw good prospects for revenging themselves on their social superiors under the cover of a foreign occupation.

For the soldier, sack was the only real benefit that life in the army had to offer; after the weeks of hardships, discomfort and scarce meals, he would be recompensed with soft beds, endless feasting, all the fanny he could swive and all the loot he could carry off. Best of all, for a day or two he would be free of his superiors. The officers maintained a safe distance between themselves and the licensed indiscipline of their men. In the euphoria of victory, with a generous measure of adrenalin in the bloodstream, the soldiers would be keen to consummate their triumph in the time-honoured fashion. A city could be occupied, but full possession could only be taken after penetrating its innermost passages.

The honest womenfolk, irrespective of their age, had all fled. Even a city the size of Oporto could not produce the number of whores sufficient to completely satisfy an army of 24,000. However, a prostitute knows a man's shortcomings better than anyone. They knew that the first wave of elation would pass quickly, if tempestuously, and their bodies would have to support the price of defeat with stoicism. The tangible benefits would follow later. Having sated his lust, the soldier would move on to more enduring pleasures. In a city whose main activity was the wine trade, the soldiers were not hard pressed to find the primary ingredient to fuel their celebrations. Wine abounded, brandy was plentiful. The festivities began in the tascas, where food and drink were waiting to be had with the minimum of effort, later to spill onto the street. In a very short space of time, the otherwise well-ordered ranks of an army can dissolve into disorganised bands of undisciplined revellers. By this time, most of the men had drunk themselves into a state where they could accrue little benefit from their female companions. Bands of drunken soldiers aimlessly roamed the streets into the night, lauding in song what they were no longer capable of doing in deed.

> *Alouette, gentille alouette*
> *Alouette, je t'enculerais*
> *O la bite*
> *O la bite*
> *O le cul*
> *O le Cul*
> *Alouette, je t'enculerais.*

-18-

The dining room, decorated in the style prevalent at the beginning of the century, opened from the main landing, its length occupied by a long table capable of seating fifty people. Flower, Forrester and Graham were already seated at the end nearest the door. Forrester was the eldest of the three, a shock of black hair piled on the left side of his head. The frank and open expression on his broad features spoke of great reserves of energy and a vigorous, if not impulsive, nature. He was without question the outstanding figure of his time. He had earned much praise by the production of his map of the Douro valley and its wine-growing area, and a second has been published. Flower was quite the opposite. His ascetic features suggested a more reserved and a more cautiously scientific nature. He had been out since 1834, originally in the service of Smith & Woodhouse, but his abiding passion was calotype photography. The two men were united by this common interest. Graham was the youngest of the three, scion of a family with business interests in textiles but which had accepted payment of a debt in Port wine, thereby becoming shippers. The three friends dispensed with dessert and, as soon as the main course was cleared away, Forrester produced a portfolio, which he laid on the table with the flourish of one who lays a trump.

'I've got something to show you, Willum.' And, opening it, he took out a sheet of fine white paper. 'Now take a look at that, my boy.'

Flower picked it up and examined it. It was of high quality and consistent texture, and, by holding it against the light, he observed that the watermark had thoughtfully been placed at the foot of the sheet.

'I say, J J! This is extraordinary.'

Graham laughed. 'Only you two could be transported by a simple sheet of paper. What secrets does it hold?'

'This is no ordinary sheet of paper; this is a specimen of Turner Patent Talbotype Paper and probably the only one to be found this side of the Bay of Biscay,' Forrester replied.

'It leaves me none the wiser,' remarked Graham dryly, 'but I detect the name Talbot in there, which can only mean it has to do with your precious photography.'

'Excellent deduction, my friend,' said Forrester and, turning to Flower, who was still lost in admiration at the smoothness of the bond, continued, 'Henneman has finally convinced Turner of Chafford to take the matter seriously. And this is the result.'

'But is the quality consistent? I mean, this sample is excellent, but can they maintain the same standard throughout?' queried Flower.

'They promise they will not rest until even more has been accomplished,' Forrester said portentously.

'So enlighten me,' interposed Graham. 'Is one of you going to explain?'

'You see, in order to record a photographic image, a sheet of paper is impregnated with light sensitive chemicals, so that, when exposed to direct light an impression is registered and retained.' Flower explained. 'This image can be spoilt by imperfections in the paper; imperfections that one would never notice if one were using the paper for writing. But to register a photographic image, even something as apparently undetectable to the naked eye as uneven fibre distribution can seriously prejudice the quality of the results.'

Flower continued. 'Well, J.J., if they can promise to exclude these impurities and guarantee quality, then there is no doubt about it: it is vastly superior to Whatman's.'

-19-

In the shade under the awning, the crew ate from the three-legged iron cooking pot that stood in their midst, each one in turn tucking into the stew with a chunk of bread. They were listening to an old sailor, who was recounting the days of his youth, opening doors on long-forgotten memories.

'I was just a lad at the time, sailing on my uncle's coaster. Now, the mouth of Tejo is ample, nothing like the Douro; yet it was so thick with the masts of English frigates that it looked more like the *Pinhal de Leiria*.'

Alfredo insinuated himself into the circle. 'When was this?' he asked.

'Long before you was born, son. In the days of old King John!'

Alfredo had never heard of any King John.

'When Napolião was Emperor – but not here, mind you! When they tried it on here, they got a good roasting. Still you can imagine poor old King John, quaking in his boots, wondering how long he could sit on the throne before the French came to boot him out.'

'So why would they do that?'

Alfredo's cousin quickly filled him in with the part he had missed, while the sailor took the opportunity of the interruption to knock back some wine from a large straw-covered flagon.

'Napolião had ordered all European ports closed to British ships. If King John went with the French, the British would blockade our ports and strangle us to death. If he went in with the Brits, the French would invade and take over the country.'

'So what did he do?'

The sailor wiped his mouth on the back of his hand and continued his account.

'Try as he might, King John could not avoid taking sides. Now, Britain was our oldest ally: Britain, with a sack of sterling silver in one hand for buying Port wine and a sack of Portuguese gold in the other from selling its wares. So he threw his lot in with the Brits, who put him on a frigate to carry him off to Brazil for safekeeping, like a man who puts his valuables in a vault when he knows there's a thief on the loose.'

'So that's what the British ships were doing in the Tejo?'

'Quite so! Britannia might rule the waves, but she doesn't rule the winds. With the French troops marching down the Tejo valley and getting closer by the day, the British fleet was locked in the bay of Cascais, waiting for a favourable wind to set sail. They finally managed to make deep water the day before the French arrived.'

'Lucky devils!'

'That year was a terrible wet summer. It rained so hard that you would've thought St Peter had taken up the defence of the realm, for the *alfacinhas* were incapable of organising any resistance of their own and opened the city gates when the French arrived, like a litter of half-drowned puppies. So Junot set himself up as King and began to decree friendship between the two peoples.'

'But if they were the invader, how could they preach friendship?'

'Because they had already done the people one great favour. They had got rid of the King, the Court, the Ministers and the whole lot of placemen and pensioners, and all the useless hangers-on. It was the best house-cleaning that ever got done. But that's not all, 'cos they were about to do another.'

'Another favour?'

'Well, having reformed the civil service, Junot turned his attention to the spiritual well-being of the Portuguese. He thought the best way to bring the people closer to God was to remove all the gold and silver from the churches.'

'The thieving rascals!'

'Indeed, the people thought so. They started to revolt against the French, and there was many a French soldier who woke in a tavern to discover he had had his throat slit while he was asleep. Finally the British army put ashore, defeated the French in battle and sent them home.'

'Good for them!'

'So they really were our friends!'

'Maybe yes and maybe no!'

'They got rid of the French, didn't they?'

'That they did, but at a price. You see, there was a treaty between them, and the French agreed to leave the country. Now this is the strangest part of all: the British agreed to take them home courtesy of the Royal Navy. All of them; lock, stock and pillage. Much against our protests, for it was our looted gold they were taking with them.'

The story-telling was interrupted by cries of outrage from the assembled company. When these finally subsided, the sailor continued.

'If it had been me, I would have given them a good whipping and made them crawl back on their hands and knees. But it was an agreement between gentlemen.'

The discontent at this injustice continued to rumble like distant thunder, until the sailor said, 'But the story doesn't end there.'

'So tell us more!'

'What happened next?'

'It'll have to wait till the next time.' And, giving a sly wink to the skipper, he said, ' 'cos now it's time for you lot to get back to work.'

-20-

Grimpil placed his knife and fork on the plate and wiped his mouth on the napkin.

'Well, then; was it to your satisfaction?' asked Woodhouse.

'Yes,' he replied politely, but failed to see why such a dish should be regarded so highly. Trout in almonds, for example: now that was a delicacy, but dried salted cod fish? It was a dish for mariners.

'More wine?' Woodhouse proffered the bottle.

Grimpil accepted. Although apparently inoffensive, the sparkling wine had left him rather light-headed. He took a draught to wash away the taste of the fish and looked forward to the dessert to compensate for the rather disappointing first course.

Woodhouse was expounding at length on his memories of the wine trade. 'The important thing is to have character and keep your word. The Englishmen's word is his bond. I remember back in 1820, a particularly dry year with a hot summer. When Mr Warre visited his estates in August, the grapes were already ripe enough to harvest, but so small and parched they looked like sultanas. It was obvious there was neither the quality nor quantity for a vintage. So when he returned to Oporto – and a long, arduous, not to mention dangerous journey it was in those days, on mule back – he informed his colleagues and competitors that he would not be shipping any wine from that year. Little did he know that since he had left the Upper Douro a fine summer rain had been falling day and night, swelling the grapes to vintage proportions. All the other shippers declared the year a classic, which indeed it was, but Mr Warre had given his word that he would not ship, and, despite considerable financial prejudice to the house, would not and did not ship – because he had given his word.'

-21-

On the morning of the following day, Irene woke up beside the stocky Gascon Sergeant, whom she reckoned was the most trustworthy. She had certainly never drunk so much in her life. Her mouth was dry and her head felt like a wooden block. She poured some water from an earthenware pitcher and looked out of the window to try and figure out where she was. The soldier was also stirring. He sat up, scratching his head.

'*Merdouille de merdouille,*' he uttered, 'Give me some water!'

She hurried to dress herself. The soldier might be feeling amorous and she didn't want to waste any time. Today was to be decisive, a make or break day, and she wanted to take full advantage. She went to the kitchen to prepare coffee, although there would be no bread baked for some time. Either the movement or the smell of the coffee aroused two of their companions. One of them staggered to the window to take a prolonged piss out of the casement down into the street below. The four of them sat round the kitchen table to a rudimentary breakfast. They were all clearly suffering from the after-effects of the night before. A still unfinished bottle of brandy was produced and the remaining contents divided between them. After knocking back the firewater, the company appeared more animated. Irene was eager to be off and tugged at the sleeve of the Sergeant.

'Let's go,' she said. 'Church.'

'What!' was the monosyllabic reply.

She made an imitation of someone praying, joining her hands in prayer and raising her eyes to heaven. The others burst out in derisive laughter. It was obvious they hadn't understood her intent.

She took one of the beakers and lifted it ceremoniously in both hands, intoning words from the liturgy of the Mass.

The soldiers looked at each other, the light of understanding spreading over their faces.

'Let's go,' said the Sergeant, slinging his musket over his shoulder. '*Va moosh.*'

Irene led them through the narrow streets until they arrived in front of a church. There was a soldier on guard at the door.

'Bugger off,' he snarled. 'This one's ours.'

Inside, the floor was littered with scattered hosts and the broken heads of statues. She could hear the thud of rifle butts against splintering wood. She tugged at the sleeve of her Gascon and indicated a new direction.

They quickly came to another church, which was still locked. Irene beckoned the men to follow her around the back. There was a small window set high in the wall. The tallest of the men placed himself against the wall and the Sergeant stood on his shoulders. Forcing open the window, he squeezed through the narrow aperture. Within seconds they heard the sound of bolts being drawn and the group was admitted into the sacristy.

-22-

The dining room was emptying gradually as the diners either returned to their business or retired to the drawing room. He noticed a group of three, deeply immersed in conversation, and asked Woodhouse if he knew them.

'The gentleman talking is Flower, and facing him is Forrester. At the moment, his star is in the ascendancy, what with his cartography and all, but a few years back he stirred up a lot of controversy with a pamphlet he wrote. Damn near accused the whole trade of adulterating the wine. It is true that the quality of the wine shipped fell off considerably with the abolition of the Company; the Liberals were too hasty in their zeal for free trade. Although the Company was a symbol of absolutist government, it was also the guardian of the purity of Port wine. Some of his ideas, mind you, were completely wrong-headed; he even suggested that the fermentation of the wine should not be stopped by the addition of brandy. Can you imagine such nonsense? The result would have been a harsh dry wine not just unshippable, but totally undrinkable. Would have ruined us all! The trade fortunately disregarded him, and since then he's settled down to do some serious work. As for Flower, I must confess I've never fully understood him. Deep, you know; never know what's going on inside his head. I had hoped that one day we could have taken him into the partnership. I certainly could do with someone reliable to whom I can entrust the management. I'm getting too old for all this. When you've finished your dessert I'll introduce you. The other chap is young Graham, an amiable non-entity, but he'll do all right. Business is like politics: the less you do the better. The growers know what they're doing, and nature does the rest. The blenders know their job, and the clients know what they want.'

-23-

Two hours later, Irene, along with the others, was beginning to feel hungry, and the weight of their booty was growing cumbersome. They looked for a house that would serve as a base. Having found one that looked promising, they made their way directly to the pantry and emptied the larder of food and drink. After having eaten, Irene went to examine the contents of the linen press and wardrobes. She found some gowns which, although rather old-fashioned, would fit her, along with a fine collection of linen ware, some lace and a bolt of silk. She wouldn't be able to carry it all. She contemplated changing into one of the gowns but decided against it. Now was not the time to attract attention to herself. She wondered where Gilda and Mona could be. She would need more hands to secure the day's gains, although she reckoned that once installed they would probably continue in this house. Her thoughts were disturbed by the sound of boots on the stairs. She hurried to the side of her sergeant and eyed the newcomers suspiciously.

The soldiers were all obviously familiar with each other, greeting each other effusively, slapping each other on the back and laughing and joking. The newcomers also brought with them a sack of loot, which they stacked in a corner. Good, Irene thought to herself. Now that the soldiers had acquired tangible assets, she could start selling her services. The group settled around the table to attack the leg of cured ham.

-24-

The dining room was nearly deserted when Forrester rose to take his leave, and Flower noticed Woodhouse at the far end talking to a young man whom he didn't recognise, but who could only be the fellow that Naylor had spoken of. Only this morning he had been blissfully unaware of his existence. He had entered his firmament like a wayward comet and having entered his horizon was now drawing steadily closer. It was too late for him to follow Forrester, for the newcomer, led by Woodhouse, was already making his way towards him; introductions were now inevitable.

'Good day to you, sir,' hailed Woodhouse. 'I trust all is well with you. Allow me to present Mr Grimpil.'

Introductions were made and formalities exchanged.

'Mr Grimpil is here on business and shall be visiting our lodge this afternoon. Mr Flower, perhaps you would be good enough to accompany him; I'm sure he'd appreciate it enormously.'

Flower pursed his lips; he had never overcome his distaste for social obligations, which formed such a large part of business life. He much preferred the orderly world of invoice and inventory to the random nature of human intercourse. The laws of etiquette, however, would not allow him to refuse, coupled with the fact that Woodhouse tended to forget he was no longer in the employ of the house.

'Take my carriage. I shall return to the office on foot. A little post-prandial constitutional will do me the world of good.' And, so saying, Woodhouse took his leave, leaving Flower and Grimpil to descend the great staircase together and proceed to Woodhouse's carriage.

-25-

The company was jovial and the conversation lively.

'O René, what are you going to do when the war ends?'
'When the war ends? The war will never end!'
'Long live the War!'
'Long live Napoleon!'
'Long live France!'

Irene drew closer to her Gascon. She was getting looks from one of the newcomers whose import was well known to her. She feigned innocence and turned away, resting her averted gaze on the Sergeant's shoulder. She observed the grease on his collar and wondered when he had last washed his jacket.

The Gascon was busily relating a story. 'Anyway, the only place he could find to shelter from the pouring rain was inside an empty barrel. So, he wedges the barrel with rocks and curls up inside like a dog to go to sleep.'

She took hold of the Sergeant's arm, while the beady eyes of the soldier with chiselled features never left her.

'When it was time to change the watch, Jacquot here reckoned it would be a good idea to play a prank and removed the rocks.'

'You should have seen that barrel go downhill, with Didi inside, screaming and hollering,' continued Jacquot with evident delight. 'The *Bifes* thought it was an attack and started firing like crazy, even though they couldn't see nothing. Didi had to spend the night in the bottom of the ravine for fear of being shot to pieces if he tried to move.'

'One thing's certain,' resumed the Gascon. 'He hasn't tried sleeping in a barrel again.'

The company dissolved into laugher, except for the beady-eyed soldier, who arose and spoke quietly into his ear. When he conveyed the message to Irene she pretended to be shocked and even managed a modest blush. She protested her virtue and how she was promised to an apprentice. The two men began to argue with each other. Irene could detect that the tone was still jovial. The Gascon transmitted the soldier's opening bid.

'Oh, no, I couldn't. I don't know how you think I could be able.'

Now that the bargaining process had been started, it was just a question of keeping it going long enough to inflate the price to the maximum, without stretching the man's patience beyond breaking point.

'I don't know what you think I am! I'm an honest working girl, waiting to be married.'

The negotiations continued.

'But what will people say about me? I shall be branded a harlot and a collaborator. I'll never be able to arrange a husband.'

The price was now far in excess of anything she had ever received before. She would play the game just a little longer, so she showed hesitation in rejecting the offer, worrying the ends of her kerchief as if anxiously struggling with her conscience.

The soldier was not going to let go now. The price increased.

'Oh, well, just this once. I suppose no one will ever know.'

They eventually removed to the bedroom, Irene playing her role to the end. 'Oh, but don't breathe a word to a living soul. If my neighbours were to discover…'

Once in bed, she exchanged her reluctances for cries of admiration and moans of satisfaction, while trying to bring the business to a swift conclusion. The soldier left, strutting like a prize cockerel, convinced that the superiority of his person had conquered the scruples of an honest maid. The more the man boasted his prowess to his fellows, the more eager they were to exchange a little of their booty to prove that they were as good, if not better, in the arts of Venus as they were in the art of Mars. Irene was calculating her potential earnings: nine men, once each at least. As long as no one discovered they were being hoodwinked, at least till afterwards, but then it would already be too late.

Back in the dining room, the men were gathered at the window, exchanging friendly insults with another band of soldiers in the street.

When they had finished, the Sergeant turned to the men.

'Brothers-in-arms, we'd better get back on the job, or they'll be no loot left for us to pillage.'

'I'll stay behind to guard our stash,' offered a sandy-haired youth.

'Good thinking, Jacquot; Louis, you too. But look lively, or one of these thieving bands from Alsace will steal all we've got. Come on, lads.'

And so saying, the company trooped out.

Irene shot a coy smile at Jacquot and retired to the kitchen.

'Better go downstairs, Louis, and man the front door. I'll stay up here and keep a look out from the window,' he said.

No sooner had his comrade gone downstairs, he directed his steps towards the kitchen.

-26-

The morning breezes had cleared the skies, and the sun shone with some intensity as the two Englishmen stepped out on the street. As the carriage made its way down the cobbled street in the direction of the river, only the persistence of the wind kept the temperature from becoming uncomfortable. While all the business of the trade was carried out on the Oporto side of the river, the wine itself was stored and blended on the Gaia side. The two banks were now linked by a suspension bridge that had been built ten years previously. Grimpil's fear of being drowned in the Douro were reawakened by this crossing, for the bridge swayed perceptibly in the modest force of the wind, and his relief at arriving at the other side was only tempered by the idea that he would have to repeat the experience on his return journey.

'College man, are you?' Flower asked, calculating that if he were to lead the conversation he would lessen the risk of having to reveal anything of himself to the newcomer.

'St Botolph's.'

Flower was pragmatic by nature and empirical by philosophy. He had acquired all of his not inconsiderable knowledge by discovery and by the experience of putting into practice what he had learnt. He failed to see why so much credit was given to repeating other people's ideas and attempting to apply them, usually unsuccessfully.

'And do you speak the language?'

'I can understand it fairly well. My mother was Portuguese, you see. I have no trouble with the written word, but I have had little opportunity to practise the spoken tongue.'

'So this is your first time out, is it?'

'Quite so.'

'And is Port wine all your business?'

'Not entirely. I hope to be able to pursue my researches while I am here. I am contemplating a biography of Wellington.'

'Is that so, Mr Grimble' remarked Flower.

'Grimpil, actually.'

'Quite so, Mr Grimpil. Was it not Wellington who commanded the forces which expelled the French from the Iberian Peninsula?' For him, the presence of the Iron Duke at the opening of the Great Exhibition was more vivid than that on the field of Vimeiro or Waterloo. He suspected that, in the chaos of war, luck was as important as judgement, a fact that most military commanders strove to conceal.

'You are perfectly correct, Mr Flower, and I would venture to say the greatest general Britain has possessed, rivalled only by Marlborough. For a country with a more naval than military tradition, they are both outstanding examples of how, when Britain most urgently need a commander in the field to rival our continental enemies, our squirearchy has been able to provide men of outstanding personal qualities. It almost makes one believe in Aristotle.'

'So what about Cromwell? Surely he must be Britain's greatest general? After all, he did organise the New Model Army.'

Grimpil saw his wonderful theory crumbling to dust. 'I was thinking of generals with service in the European theatre,' he replied, hoping to salvage something from the ruins of his thesis.

There was a short silence, broken by Flower.

'So how many invasions were there?'

'Three all told. What Napoleon really wanted to achieve was the dissolution of Portugal, returning most of the territory to the Spanish crown, which he controlled. It was the Spanish revolt that undid his scheme.'

'Is that a fact, Mr Grimpil?' commented Flower rhetorically. Talk of Napoleon Bonaparte reawakened doubts concerning his nephew. The transition from second Republic to third Empire had left him deeply suspicious of Louis Napoleon and his intentions. As for involving Britain in a war with Russia, as far as he could see only France would benefit. However odious the Czar might be, how did it serve British interests to turn the Mediterranean into a French lake?

-27-

Soult was not entirely pleased with the course of events. While he wished to be perceived as liberating the people from the twin yoke of feudal bonds and foreign tyranny, his victorious entry into Oporto had been marred by the disaster of the pontoon bridge, coupled with the inevitable sack of the city. No commander can deprive his men of the legitimate spoils of victory. In any case, the principal victims were the Church and the aristocracy, so let it be a lesson to them. Now was the time to restore order. As soon as he assumed governance he would have to adopt measures to prove that he acted in the interests of the people.

'Will you be making your headquarters in the British Factory?' asked Argenton.

To a certain extent, installing himself there would be a clear signal that the French had taken over the reins of the city, displacing the British from their own bastion. It had also been the location chosen by the allied General Balestá while responsible for the city, until his untimely death in somewhat suspicious circumstances.

'No, I don't think so. A new order requires a fresh start. I don't wish to be associated with past failures. I need to find a building befitting my rank and station.' The Factory was in the lower town, below the Cathedral hill and close to the river. 'It would be a good place to set up a department of finances, but it is too small for the gubernatorial palace.'

'Why not use the Bishop's palace? The most recent incumbent has vacated recently, albeit in somewhat hurried circumstances,' suggested the Aide de Camp, with a certain irony.

'Quite so!' Soult, however, knew he would need to show respect for religious sensibilities. In fact, he would need the support of the Church to legitimise and consolidate his hold on power. But take up residence in the Bishop's palace... No! He needed something more civilian: the natural residence for a prince of the realm. In short, a palace.

'Are there no palaces in this city? Surely in a country overflowing with aristocratic titles there must be something that rises above an ordinary mansion.'

'Oporto is a city built essentially on commerce, the major fortunes are in the business sector. However, Oporto is also a city built on seven hills. It's difficult to find a large area flat enough to implant anything above an average mansion.'

'Don't be ridiculous, man! There has to be something. Bring me the plan of the city.'

Argenton fetched the plan and unrolled it on the desk.

'What's this?' asked Soult, stabbing a finger at a conspicuously large, isolated building.

'That's the "Misericordia", sir,' replied Argenton, 'a charitable institution.'

'Indeed! Well, it can serve as a military hospital. And this?'

'It's the monastery of—'

Soult dismissed any further comment with a wave of the hand.

'It'll do nicely for a barracks.' His finger strayed to the north-east side of the city. 'And this here?'

Argenton ran his finger down the key at the side of the map until he found the corresponding number.

'It is the property of the brothers *Morais e Castro*. Recently constructed.'

'And what's it called?'

'It appears to be known as the Palácio dos Carrancas.'

'You see, I told you there had to be a palace here somewhere. What's the name again?'

'Palácio dos Carrancas.'

'Carrancas! Don't like the sound of it; Carrancas… aren't they bedlice?'

Argenton looked for the dictionary. Life as Aide de Camp was full of many and varied services.

'Grimaces.'

'Grimaces!'

'It's what the dictionary says. Grimaces or frowns.'

'Well, no doubt we can change the name. Something like…

'Oporto Palace?'

'No, no! Something more resonant… Palace of the New Order!'
'Rather prolix, wouldn't you say, sir?'
'Let me think. How about Palace of the Triumphant Eagle?'
'Worse still.'
'Well, I'm sure we'll come up with something eventually. Right now, we've got other priorities. Send for Pellerin. I need to know how long it will take to repair the pontoon bridge.'

-28-

Grimpil continued to expound his thesis, evidently in the belief that Flower was accompanying his reflections. 'If you recall, the Spanish uprising occasioned that famous painting by Francisco Goya. It also provided the Portuguese the opportunity to defy the invader and the British the leverage they needed to get the French armies out of Portugal. It is notable that with the transfer of the Court to Rio de Janeiro, Lisbon ceases to be the centre of political organisation. Portugal is returned to its embryonic state and, as in the time of the *Condado Portucalense*, Oporto becomes the capital, seat of the Junta da Salvação led by its bishop. A curious state of affairs!'

His observations were curtailed by the fact that they had now arrived at the quays on the Gaia side of the river. The strand was lower on that side and the current slower, being on the outer side of the curve in the river, close to the point where a lesser tributary joined the main stream. They were now more or less opposite the Rua dos Inglezes and could appreciate the mass of the city skyline, punctuated by the twin bulbous pinnacles on the Cathedral's towers and the baroque silhouette of the Torre dos Clerigos. All manner of craft were moored on the river, from lighters and barges to brigs and schooners. The bright afternoon sun and a natural tendency towards siesta had calmed the endless movement of goods and people around the wooden jetties. Even so, there was still a number of lumbering ox carts ponderously making their way back and forth. So archaic was their appearance, with their solid wooden wheels and elaborately carved yokes, and so laborious was their pace, that it seemed as if several centuries had passed since they had started out on their journeys. To his left rose the lodges of the Port wine shippers. Some were more grandiose, such as the colonnaded porch of Sandeman's. The warehouse of Smith & Woodhouse obeyed the more modest pattern of a single-storey building, constructed in granite blocks, covered by tiled roofs divided into shallow quadrangular pyramids.

Flower turned to Grimpil. 'We are nearly there,' he said.

'Will you do me the honour of accompanying me, sir? I should much appreciate the benefit of your greater experience in these matters,' was the reply.

Flower knitted his brows. He could see he would have to sacrifice his afternoon completely.

-29-

The *Comendador* looked sharply at his nephew. 'Grimpil, you say.'

The name had not been pronounced in his presence for nearly twenty years.

'Horace Grimpil,' confirmed the younger man. 'Too much of a coincidence, would you not say? Difficult to believe that he is not related to…' And he allowed the sentence to fade into silence, for no one ever spoke the name of his uncle's most bitter nemesis.

The *Comendador* stood looking out of the window at the unkempt garden below. The work of nature had obscured the hand of man. The hedges had lost their clipped military straightness. The borders had invaded the paths, and the ornamental plants were now in a minority in relation to spontaneously occurring species. The sight gave the *Comendador* a certain savage pleasure; his country, like his garden, had gone to seed.

'Find out what you can of his reasons for being here, his movements, his contacts.'

'Very well, sir,' said the nephew obediently, for he was familiar with his uncle's brusque manner. 'I shall do as you bid.' He took his leave.

The *Comendador* did not leave his position by the window and watched his nephew as his horse trotted away along the long dusty road that lay beyond the walls of the Quinta. There was no doubt in his mind about Grimpil, but the question which now presented itself was whether *he* was also in Portugal. Certainly not in Oporto, possibly in Lisbon, maybe comfortably installed in some obscure locality. The *Comendador* felt the first stirrings of the hatred that had lain dormant for so many years. For all the misfortunes that he had suffered in life, and the greater misfortunes he had seen inflicted on his father land, the name *Grimpil* had come to symbolise all the wrong that had been perpetrated. His revolt at the injustice of history focused on the Englishman who had crossed his path and had come to personify the enemy against which he had sacrificed all. If he had dissipated his family's fortune, then at least he could take comfort in the knowledge that it had been in defending an honourable cause. If he had lost the position in society that was rightfully his, then it left his mind unburdened by the responsibility of public office, and his soul relieved of the vanity of power. He had seen his country reduced to poverty, subject to foreign powers, its affairs directed from outside its frontiers. Its government had been placed in the hands of adventurers, profiteers, placemen, and procurers. Capital had replaced virtue, and credit, honour.

But why had their venture failed, when everything indicated its natural success? Maybe in the final analysis they would have done better to accept the Duke of Dalmatia as Portuguese King. Had he abandoned his god or had his god abandoned him? If only Dom Miguel had come to the throne twenty years earlier, how different it all would have been.

-30-

The tide of war had passed on. It was some other bugger's turn to get shat on, thought Irene, with grim indifference. 'Look after number one' was her only concern. During the few glory days immediately after the entry of the French, she had accumulated a fair quantity of plate, but things were getting back to normal and she had returned to her lodgings with her treasure trove wrapped in the bolt of silk and made into a bundle with only the linen showing. To all intents and purposes it appeared no more than a bundle of washing that girls of her type could regularly be seen carrying back and forth. She was more concerned now to find a way of cashing in as rapidly as possible on her newly acquired wealth. As those who had fled returned, those who had stayed behind quietly melted away. As soon as the governors returned to the city, they would institute magistrates to punish those found with stolen goods, and Irene had no intention of going to gaol.

She remembered her Gascon had spoken of an engineering corps billeted in the house of the goldsmith. She asked him to take her there, although, when they arrived, the officer in charge was not present. They spoke to the lady of the house, who admitted them to a waiting room while she fetched her master.

'Father, there is a female to see you.' The way she said 'female' and not 'lady' puzzled Tibães. He couldn't recall any contacts with females of any kind. He found a young woman waiting in the reception room, her aspect and manner denounced her as being of a class not usually admitted into respectable family residences.

Irene was accustomed to disapproving looks from those more fortunate than herself. Try being born in the gutter and then see if you keep your airs and graces, she thought bitterly, but nevertheless proceeded immediately to her business.

'I have come to do business with you.'

'I don't imagine we have any business in common, young lady,' he replied coldly.

'Maybe yes and maybe no – all depends on the price. How much will you give for this?' she said, opening her legs.

Reaching inside her petticoats, she drew forth a small silver salver.

'Family heirloom,' she added briskly.

Quite so, thought Tibães, but whose?

There was no need to examine the piece. It was of superior quality, worth at least 5,000 *réis* under normal circumstances. But these were not normal circumstances. In the first place, he was receiving stolen property and should kick the strumpet out of his house immediately. Then there was the problem of money. At the moment he didn't have any cash nor any means of securing any. On top of this, Taboreau had imposed an administration tax in order for the General to be able to live in the luxury he was accustomed to. In fact, the whore would have to pay it as well, for in egalitarian times not even the oldest profession was exempt from tax paying. The truth of the matter was that the misfortunes of war had left them in the same predicament: both urgently needed money and had no licit means of acquiring it. This worried Irene considerably less than Tibães.

'Well, how much is it worth to you?'

'I can't give more than 500 *réis* for it.'

'Come on, it's worth more than 2,000.'

'No. As I say this business is very risky: what's more, it has a family crest engraved on it. It's very easily identifiable.'

'Not after you've melted it down, it won't be!'

Tibães winced. The trollop had spoken the ultimate blasphemy. No one better than he knew of the skill and craftsmanship that had gone into producing such a piece, the hours of patient shaping and polishing. The thought of melting it down broke his heart.

'1,800,' said Irene.

'Maybe I could go as far as thousand.' Tibães knew that he had surrendered to the inevitable. The business had an undeniable logic which would make him follow this path to its inevitable conclusion.

'1,500.'

'1,200.'

'Done.'

'I'm afraid I shan't be able to pay you until next week.'

'That's all right, I'm not going anywhere and Your Excellency had better not have any plans for travelling. The roads are very dangerous at the moment.'

Events had led him to being threatened by a whore in his own house and he had no choice but to ignore her insinuations.

'Do not trouble yourself; I give you my word.'

'Just as well, 'cos I'll be back… with more!'

-31-

From his waterside perch, Alfredo spotted Woodhouse's carriage passing and recognised the figure of Flower seated next to another, who could only be the new arrival, already looking like a boiled lobster in the full force of the sun. He bade farewell to his fellows, as the two Englishmen stepped down from the carriage and disappeared into the darkness of the warehouse. The interior was lit by an occasional skylight, which, by virtue of the industry of generations of spiders and decades of accumulated dust, filtered the incoming light to such a degree that more was rejected than accepted.

Grimpil was glad to be out of the sun and welcomed the coolness of the warehouse. The Monção wine was deceptively innocent; its effect had been magnified by the fact that he was unaccustomed to drinking wine at lunchtime. This, combined with the ride in an open carriage in the full force of the sun, had left him slightly faint and certainly not at his most perceptive. A middle-aged man of low stature, wearing a copious leather apron, stepped forth from the gloom where the weak light reflected darkly off the age-blackened flanks of the enormous barrels, resting their pregnant bellies on the flagstones.

Sousa was more than pleased to see Flower and shook his hand warmly.

'Yes, my wife and daughters are fine, thank you,' replied Flower, 'and business is tolerably good, although it doesn't leave me much time free for my Calotypes. I have business to attend to in Régua and shall pass by Penafiel and Amarante. I will certainly take advantage of the trip to make some photographic registers.'

While they were speaking, Grimpil became aware of the presence of a fourth individual, who now approached the table. Taking advantage of the apparent neglect with which he was being treated, he addressed Grimpil asking him which sample he would like to try first. At this act of *lèse majesté*, Sousa sprang forward, displacing the young man, and began to explain. 'We have three wines for you to try, sir, all of them excellent, but with some difference in their accent. I suggest we start with the '51, which is, of course, still in its infancy, but I think you will find hints of future greatness. Here, let me pour you a little.' And, when having done so, he passed the glass to Grimpil, saying, 'Alfredo, fetch me another glass for Mr Flower, will you?'

Alfredo was not entirely in favour of this new development and, although he obeyed the command, delayed as much as possible in fulfilling the task. Grimpil savoured the wine. As he held it in his mouth, the fullness of its aroma greeted his palette, generous with a slightly nutty aftertaste.

'A good wine to accompany cheese, I would say,' said Grimpil, looking at his companions for agreement. 'Although I suspect there may be those who would prefer a slightly more fruity bouquet.'

'Then let us pass on to the '47. I think you will not be disappointed by its boldness. Alfredo, do hurry and fetch another glass for Mr Flower. This is a wine of strong personality, and, if you permit me to describe it so, a Roman profile.'

-32-

Soult reviewed his options. The General he most trusted was De Laborde, a man of deeply rooted principles and who had an excellent record of service both on the battlefield and as an administrator. He had been Junot's Governor of Arms in Lisbon, but on balance he was probably better deployed at the front. He would bring back General Quesnel to take charge of the civil administration of the city. He had been Junot's Superintendent of Police and knew both the job and the city.

He was less happy about the presence of Loison, and feared he would be a liability. If he was already a man of few attractive qualities, the fact he had lost his hand in a hunting accident hardly made him more so. The Portuguese called him Maneta and he was execrated above any other military commander for the violence with which he imposed respect on the city of Evora. Here in the north, the towns of Peso and Régua also had reason to remember his name.

Soult, however, feared the General for different reasons; one was that he owed loyalty to no one but himself, and another was that he was not lucky. Luck had to be earned from the graces of the most fickle of mistresses – fortune. Fortune could only be won by systematically and consistently making the right choices. A successful commander needed to keep his options open, choosing whether to fight or not, and only fighting when and where the conditions were most advantageous. This was the very quality that Loison lacked. He allowed events to dictate to him, instead of him dictating events.

Despite his blatant peculation of imperial taxes, he retained the favour of the Emperor. Despite Soult's own objections to his inclusion in the invasion force, he had been appointed to command in the field. Soult had not been able to confirm all the facts relating to the failure of Junot's expedition, but behind the military defeat lurked the shadow of Loison. The abject failure of his mission to subdue the north had dealt a fatal blow to Napoleonic supremacy, while his lack of despatch in coming to the aid of his commander contributed materially to the defeat at Vimeiro. Would Loison risk his neck to do battle to save Soult's campaign? Probably not. The best thing to do was to keep him out of sight so as not to compromise his attempts to establish better relations with the Portuguese.

He could send him north to maintain the supply line open as far as Valença. Of the total number of effectives, 5,000 were still in Spain, engaged in convoy duties, 5,000 in Tuy and almost as many in Braga. And then there were about 2,000 sick or wounded. He could garrison Oporto, but any advance on Lisbon would be impossible without the intervention of Victor along the Tejo valley. By a certain irony of fate, the balance of power in the country had been inverted. The French now held Oporto, formerly the main focus of resistance, although they had insufficient strength to move on Lisbon. The British now held Lisbon, formerly in French hands, but had insufficient strength to move against Oporto. Any change in the balance could only result from outside assistance. Would the English receive support by sea before the French received support by land? In either case, the highest strategic priority now was to open a line of communication to Spain via Vila Real and Bragança.

A smile spread over Soult's face. He knew what mission he would entrust to Loison. He would send him along the Douro valley. He bent over his map and traced a line with his finger: Oporto – Villa Real – Bragança. He studied the map closer. They would need to cross the River Tâmega at Amarante.

-33-

Grimpil had never knowingly sampled a wine with a roman profile, and was about to drink when interrupted by Flower.
'A roman profile,' he said, laying his hand on Grimpil's shoulder, 'is distinguished by its nose. To be appreciated, you must gently swill the liquor in the glass like a brandy, to release its full aroma.'
Taking the glass from Alfredo, he demonstrated the action and, inhaling over the glass, closed his eyes. When he opened them again, Alfredo noticed a look of doubt on the man's face. He had not counted on the presence of the more experienced man, who threatened to discover his secret.

Grimpil was sampling the wine, swirling it round in his mouth and feeling an agreeable sensation of warmth. He found it difficult to compare this sensation with the previous one, so he asked to repeat the first. Perhaps because his palette was now familiar with the taste, he was unable to make a comparison, and decided to press on to the third.

Sousa served the two men.

'With a truly great Port wine it is difficult to tell where the art of nature ends and the art of man begins. True harmony is when the two become inseparable.'

Handing one glass to Grimpil, he held the other up to the light. The liquid in the glass glowed with a richness of colour which perhaps could only be found in Damascene velvet.

'Observe, Mr Grimpil,' he said, 'how the light reawakens the dormant tones. What artist could reproduce the depths of these colours?'

Indeed Grimpil had not seen such chromatic majesty outside the stained glass windows of St Botolph's.

Alfredo detected a cloud pass over Flower's countenance. He nosed the glass, swirling the contents to release its full bouquet, and then shot an inquisitive glance first at Sousa, then at Alfredo, where it rested a little longer, and finally at Grimpil, who was sitting in his chair with a rapt expression.

'It sounds in the mouth like a chord issuing from the organ of New College, whose lingering chords reverberate in the buccal cavity,' he said, carried away by lyricism. Catching Flower's glance, he inquired, 'Tell me, Mr Flower, do you not agree that this is by far the best?'

'I would say that we are faced with three wines of such outstanding quality that it is barely possible to distinguish one from another,' he replied, with a slight hint of irony directed at Alfredo.

While Sousa was blissfully unaware of what was going on, Alfredo could tell that Flower had realised something was amiss. He did not know the man well, but he calculated that he would not do anything that would prejudice the cellar-master.

'Yes, quite right; perhaps we should try the first again,' continued Grimpil, oblivious to the exchange of glances. 'I do not seem able to fix it in my memory; no sooner do I taste another that I forget the former. I don't believe you have tried it yet, have you, Flower?'

'I'm not sure,' he said darkly.

Alfredo felt distinctly uncomfortable but at the same time could not forgo witnessing the scene.

'Let us have another glass, then.'

Silence reigned while the two sampled the first wine. After Grimpil had downed the glass, he noticed that Flower only sampled the wine in his mouth, after which he spat the wine into a porcelain bowl.

'Not to your taste, eh! Yes, this one is inferior to the others; it is quickly forgotten. Would you not agree?' Grimpil asked Flower.

'I would not be so ready to arrive at this conclusion.'

'Then how would you advise me?'

'I should say that you would be well advised to consider the age. When do you expect this Port will be drunk? If it is to be drunk in the next decade, then choose either the '42 or the '47. Ten years' ageing in the bottle will transform a Port in the same way that the passage of a decade will change the fresh-faced youngster into the bearded visage of the man. If your college has stocks sufficient so that this batch will go untouched for the next two decades then by that time this young man,' and he raised the glass to indicate the identity of the young man in question, 'will be an adult ready to reveal his accumulated maturity.'

-34-

Tibães cradled the piece of silverware in his hands, and had a faint notion how Abraham must have felt in contemplating the act that God had required of him. It was a fine piece of workmanship, not of this century certainly. His fingers traced the slightly raised burr of the engraving. How would he dismember the body? Would it cut with shears, or would he need to use a saw blade? He preferred the shears for the cleanliness of the cut and for their silence. He did not want to attract attention, even from his daughters. It was a sacrifice he was making in their interest, but it was unlikely they would understand his motives, even less agree to his action. It was important to melt the piece down without delay, for it was a witness threatening to denounce him as long as it remained intact.

He would need to fire the furnace, but he would wait until after nightfall, in case some neighbour noticed the smoke issuing from the chimney. At night it could be easily confused with the smoke from any other oven. He could at least lay the kindling and firewood. Working at night was strictly forbidden by the regulations governing goldsmiths. On the other hand the penalty was nothing compared to that reserved for counterfeiters: exile for life to some godforsaken corner of the Empire. Did Portugal still have an empire? Did Portugal still exist? He was navigating in waters of moral relativism for which no chart existed. He turned his mind to more practical considerations. Turning the metal into coins would be complicated. How long would it take him to make the dies? It was a process he was not very familiar with, but it could not be so different from making a cameo, except that it had two faces. Did he have all the tools and materials he would need in his workshop? He would surely need to start with either clay or wax. Which would be better? Wax would be more difficult to work with but would enable going directly to the metal stage. He halted abruptly. Of course, there was the question of exactly what coin he should make. A silver coin of sufficient value to justify the work but not too large to attract suspicion. It would be an advantage if it was a coin that was not too familiar; a Spanish coin, perhaps? But where would he get the model? Would he find anyone with a Spanish coin from the time of Balestá? It could take a long time and might attract attention to himself. Better if it were national or... Brazilian! A provincial coin minted in Rio de Janeiro or Minas Gerais. There were a lot of coins put into circulation in the time of Dom João V; some of them were even produced in Oporto. A coin from the crowned 'J' series would be fairly simple to execute. After all, someone might mistrust the composition or weight but would be unlikely to consider the possibility of the coin being counterfeit if the former had proven sound. Suddenly he remembered having mounted a similar coin on a pendant for his wife, as a token of good fortune. He had found it one day by chance while taking a stroll by the waterfront. He had looked down and there it was at his feet, waiting to be found. It must be in the box of keepsakes in which he kept various mementos of his deceased spouse. He couldn't recall the value, but it would be an excellent option. Suddenly he began to feel more positive about the task.

-35-

Having passed so far unmasked, even if not undetected, Alfredo felt sufficiently emboldened to enter the game.

'Mr Flower is clearly a gentleman of great discernment, whose many years in the trade permit him to appreciate qualities which other men might not notice,' began Alfredo, anxious to ingratiate himself with the connoisseur. 'The '51 is an interesting option in the long term, but meanwhile the '47 is ready to be bottled and the '42 to be drunk. Therefore I would suggest a different approach to the matter: it is not so much a question of which, but how much? There is no need to choose between them, only decide how much of each you intend to buy.'

Flower smiled inwardly. The lad was sharp, no doubt about it. He had to admire his skill in turning things to his advantage, not to mention to the profit of the company.

'Our young friend is not far from the truth,' he admitted. 'Indeed, I would go further. What matters here is not our opinion, but the taste of your fellows. You are more likely to please Greeks and Trojans by opting for a variety of wines, for it is unlikely that one alone would satisfy all tastes.'

'Quite so, quite so,' said Grimpil. Looking at the altar of Bacchus with greater perplexity than ever. 'But how am I to know?'

'Suppose you were to write a report to your superiors stating the facts, giving your opinion, and let them indicate their final decision in the matter?' he suggested, as the only way he could see of bringing the situation to a timely conclusion.

'Capital idea,' replied Grimpil, seizing on the proposal with relish. 'I can write my report and await their decision.' He appreciated the beauty of a solution that relieved him of any further responsibility in the matter.

'Excellent! Well, if you gentlemen will excuse me, I shall leave you to conclude your business,' said Flower, pressing home his advantage as rapidly as possible. 'Take the carriage back to Woodhouse's, Mr Grimpil; I shall walk home from here.' He would still have time to catch the late afternoon light. He wondered what west-facing scene he still wanted to capture. He would look at his notebooks as soon as he arrived; he might still be able to salvage something from the wreck of his afternoon. And then there was the question of Whatman's paper! How much '49 did he still have? With these thoughts in his mind he bade farewell to Sousa, shook Grimpil firmly by the hand, wishing him a good stay, and walked briskly out into the afternoon.

-36-

In Penafiel, Loison was neither in Oporto nor at the front in Amarante. Malingering in this halfway house, he continued to brood over the injustices he had suffered. He had not wanted to accept a command in this campaign. What advantage could there be in being here? Thanks to Junot, Portugal had already been milked dry. There was no gold and precious little silver left in the country. The Emperor had given him the choice between Portugal or Poland. He accepted a mission in Portugal, but his suggestion to be made field marshal went ignored. After the praise that Napoleon had bestowed on Soult after the battle of Austerlitz, there was no doubt who was the Emperor's blue-eyed boy. The fruit of victory had been the province of Dalmatia, annexed to the kingdom of Italy and given in title to Soult. High reward indeed for a general.

Why did good luck go arm in arm with good looks? Although he was no appreciator of masculine beauty, he recognised that Soult was a handsome man, a man whom women certainly found attractive. Regretfully he could not say the same for himself. What nature had not bestowed on him, he compensated for by the exercise of power. Where he could not inspire love, he would inspire fear, and when he could not impose either he would punish.

The memory of the Archbishop of Evora came to mind. The man who had sworn to bow down before no other than the Lord his God, had grovelled at his feet, begging pardon for the town's offences against the French; the very man who had preached rebellion from the pulpit, serving him hand and foot like the most abject servant. The Archbishop's palace had served as headquarters for himself and forty other officers, although in their zeal for slaughter his soldiers had killed the cook, the very man whose life should have been spared, given the general lack of victuals and provisions of all sorts. The Archbishop's cellar was, of course, generously stocked, although the wine from that region is rude and fierce like the noonday sun.

Despite all the protestations to the contrary, they had still been able to find money hidden away. These clerics had such a unique capacity to attract money to themselves! The Bishop had also had accumulated a large number of specimens, which he had organised into a sort of natural history museum – which the soldiery had taken great pleasure in reducing to dust. However, there is nothing quite like a library to trigger the destructive sentiments of a soldier. In no time, all the books in the Bishop's well-stocked library had been emptied onto the floor, and what couldn't be ripped into shreds for future use as bum-wipes was pissed on.

The only real spoil he had been able to carry off himself was the episcopal ring, a moderately large gem set in a gold mount, which he gave to his Lorena. This time he had not brought her with him. He did not want to expose her to the risks of life in the front line and consequently his flesh yearned for the voluptuousness of her caresses.

Evora would have made an excellent bonfire, but they had been obliged to leave the city before having the pleasure of setting it on fire. The stench from the corpses of the unburied dead decomposing in the streets was too much to bear. He hated it when he couldn't keep his promises, and it would have been a warning to all the Alentejo of the fate of those who dared affront the might of his Imperial Majesty. No doubt Amarante would burn, but who would notice? They would reduce everything to smoking ash, with the charred corpses of the dead roasted on the flames. Nobody could defy the will of Napoleon and prevail. For those who raised their arms against the Imperial Eagle, no quarter would be given.

-37-

Grimpil was less than enthusiastic at the prospect of returning across the suspension bridge on his own and welcomed Sousa's suggestion that Alfredo accompany him. Alfredo smiled warmly. Here was an opportunity that might only come once in his life.

'Will you be staying long in the city of Oporto?' he inquired urbanely. It was a simple question but one which caused Grimpil to knit his brows. The certainties that he had brought with him from England seemed to have dissipated. Until now, the question of the Port wine had been his horizon, and now he had overcome the obstacle he did not have a clear idea of what came next. His mind was further clouded by the effects of the Port wine itself. It would certainly be a better idea to review the matter the following morning.

'I'm not sure.' came the reply.

Alfredo would have to try a different avenue. He would make up for the deficiencies in hospitality that Grimpil's compatriots seemed to have shown. 'Do you wish to stop for refreshments?' This time the reply came with more alacrity, and in the negative. Alfredo tried a different tack. 'Is this your first visit to our city?'

'Quite so. Indeed it is my first visit to your country, and there is a great deal I wish to do.'

'Naturally, there is great deal to see and do in a city such as Oporto, and you must count on me for any assistance I can offer.'

'Most kind of you, I'm sure, but I doubt that is the case.'

Alfredo was not going to be easily deterred from his objective.

'Oh, you know, I was born here; no corner of the city is foreign to me. What, then, are you contemplating in which a native would not be a useful ally?' he inquired artfully, more anxious than ever to know Grimpil's business so that he might be able to interpose himself to his own benefit.

'I have some family affairs to settle,' came the rather dry reply.

It was a small fragment of knowledge that would have to

suffice for the time being, although Alfredo would not content himself with being thus excluded from Grimpil's affairs. He would know more, and if he could not draw more information from its source, then he would have to find it out for himself. Alfredo eyed his companion as they recrossed the river in silence. Grimpil may have only spoken one word, but that one word – family – was enough. From that acorn he would grow a mighty oak tree!

-38-

'Why should we not unite around him, and proclaim him our Father, our Liberator? Why delay in expressing our desire to see him at the head of the nation, whose affection he has so quickly been able to win?'

The pages of the newspaper concealed the sceptical expression of Quesnel as he read the lines from the *Diario do Porto*, although a more impartial listener would have detected a hint of disbelief in his voice. Propaganda was all very well and good, but the first rule was that it should be used to convince its public and not its author. Responsible for the policing of the city, he had received innumerable reports from Taboreau at the head of an extensive network of paid informers and knew better than anywhere the true affections of the inhabitants of the city lay.

Soult, however, was gazing at the painted ceiling and lost in the prospect of a future even more glorious than the past. He nodded approvingly. 'We really need some kind of mandate from the people; something along the lines of a signed petition addressed to the Emperor, requesting that he nominate a prince of his own choice to occupy the throne of Portugal.'

'Yes, sir, I understand your desires but the Senate claims that it does not have the necessary jurisdiction to decide such matters.'

'Well, assemble the town council!'

'The aldermen say that only an extraordinary assembly plenipotentiary can deliberate matters of such gravity. It would be necessary to summon the three estates: the clergy, the nobility and the people.'

'I know who the three estates are!' Soult replied with some acerbity. He felt that Quesnel was either being excessively pedantic or deliberately dilatory. 'Advise the governors of the city to be present at a meeting in the town hall on 21 April. My secretary will provide you with the text, in which the city requests of Napoleon Bonaparte that I be chosen to assume charge of national government as sovereign of the Portuguese.'

Quesnel limited himself to slightly arching an eyebrow and exchanged looks with Argenton. He had not thought that Soult would be so overt in his ambitions. Would the Emperor be disposed to bestow so high an honour on him? A dukedom was one thing but a principality! Surely Napoleon would be more disposed to see Portugal disappear into a united Iberian kingdom than perpetrate the memory on the country that had been a thorn in the imperial side, so richly exploited by the British.

'This is just the beginning,' continued Soult. 'Once we have the signatures of the most prominent members of society, the rest will follow suit. And no excuses this time; everyone must appear, unless they can justify their absence. In fact, anyone who fails to appear will have their property confiscated.'

Quesnel was very much in favour of confiscating property. It served both to increase his power and his revenue.

'Is that all?' asked Quesnel, with a slight note of irony in his voice.

'For the time being, but everyone must sign. You understand?

'Perfectly, sire.'

The first thing he did as soon as he was back in his office was to write a letter to Loison, apprising him of the latest developments.

-39-

From the high ground alongside the remains of the convent of Santa Clara, Flower looked down on the river that separated the steeply terraced slopes of the Tâmega valley. The impressive volume of the dome of the Church of São Gonçalo prevented him from seeing the bridge that spanned the fifty yards that separated the two banks. He worked his way round the perimeter wall and descended sharply to the chapel of Nosso Senhor dos Aflitos. He found himself standing on a parapet, slightly below the level of the roof of the church, some sixty feet above the square before the bridge. He could see the carved figures that decorated the flank of the church in great detail. The late afternoon sun was shining directly on them. It was an excellent spot on which to set up his tripod and photograph the sculptures that, by nothing short of a miracle, had survived the artillery exchanges intact. Higher up the belfry, the cratered stonework was witness to the intensity of the conflict that had made the surrounding hills tremble with the thunder of cannon.

Ahead of him, the narrow bridge rose from the river bed on two stone piers. On the far side, the river bank was generally flatter and broader. Whereas the town on the right bank was dominated by the convent and the monastery, the town on the left bank was filled with more modest dwellings, flanking the road as it curved away, following the bend in the river as far as Magdalena, where it split into two, one path continuing upstream, while the other climbed to a cleft in the flanks of the mountains, making its way south to Mesão Frio and Régua. The more substantial mansions on the far side were all ruined, testimony to the ferocity of French gunners. The owners had never troubled to rebuild their devastated residences, leaving them as silent witnesses to the intensity of the struggle for the mastery of the river crossing.

Flower descended the ramp that lead down to the square. He

could appreciate the skill of the stonemasons in raising the three arches that carried the deck above the waters of the River Tâmega. The recent rain had created a certain flux, but he could imagine that in full flood the water level must rise well above the massive buttresses on which the arches rested.

'Splendid, is it not?'

He turned round to a see a man of unquestionably eccentric character, judging by his style of dress. The stranger must in turn have recognised Flower as an English gentleman, for he continued in English. 'I hope I do not disturb your reflections.'

'Of course not. The name is Flower. And who might I have the pleasure of addressing?'

'Jules Pellerin, at your service. I saw you studying the view from the ramparts. One might even think you were contemplating painting the view.'

'You are a perceptive man, Mr Pellerin; that was indeed my intention but not through the medium of painting.'

'Ah, how so, then? By engraving?'

'No, by photography.'

'Ah! You are a follower of Daguerre?'

'No, of Fox Talbot. I use the calotype method.'

'Let us not get technical, Mr Flower. The result is the same, is it not?'

'The methods are similar, but the results are quite different. However, I shall not tax you with technicalities. What brings you to these parts?'

'This,' he replied, pointing to the bridge. 'It is in itself a great work of art. I wished to dedicate an even greater work of art to it, but, alas, I have not had any success.' He looked around him. 'Everything is here, but I have not been able to bring the elements together: the parallel horizontal lines of the water and bridge, the vertical of the tower, the arc of the masonry, the dome...' He appeared to be moulding it with his hands. 'Like a giant breast,' Pellerin sighed heavily. 'What more could you ask for?'

'Quite so. But tell me: if all the elements are here, then what is missing?'

Pellerin studied the ground while he tried to put his ideas into words, like someone trying to explain a complicated concept to a child.

'By means of photography, it is possible to register what is visible, but painting can render both what is visible and invisible. In these geometric forms I see the heroic struggle of freedom against oppression. The masonry expresses the will of the people to achieve their destiny; with the help of art they can take massive strides overcoming seemingly insurmountable obstacles. While the cupola of São Gonçalo is the attempt by obscurantist hierarchies to prevent them from reaching their historical goal.'

It was an aspect of the landscape that Flower had not fully appreciated.

'I'm afraid I cannot fully agree with you. I admit the limitations of photography over artistic creation, but it is science that will enable mankind to overcome physical obstacles, not art. Art, unfortunately, has always served the interests of the governing classes and ruling elite.'

'That is precisely what I strive to change. I wish to depict the whole landscape as a criticism of Bonapartism.'

'Well! I wish you luck in your endeavours,' said Flower, in the soothing tones usually used on fractious children.

'Luck is for gypsy fortune tellers,' came the uncompromising response. 'To achieve anything great, one must suffer; only through suffering can great works of art be created.'

Flower could see that the two would never agree on basic principles. In his philosophical economy, sacrifice was equal to wasted effort. Work on the other hand, produced results commensurate with the time and energy invested in producing them. He would have liked to explain the difference between the daguerreotype and calotype. The supremacy of the latter lay exactly in its capacity to multiply the same result indefinitely, thereby creating the economy of effort that justified the original investment. However, he knew he would be preaching to deaf ears. Instead, he drew the conversation to a conclusion.

'In that case, fortitude, my friend, and perseverance!'

Flower left Pellerin listening to the silent siren song of the river weed and made his way back along the narrow road that ran alongside the river meadows, following the rise and fall of the terrain in the direction of the Misericordia and the wine merchant's house.

-40-

While the trade in wine was largely in the control of foreigners, the instruments by which they conducted their business was all native, creating a community among those whose livelihood depended on shipping Port. Alfredo communed with a large number of messengers and clerks, bookkeepers and cellar men, coopers and chandlers, carters and haulers. He was not given to complex thought. If Grimpil was here to settle some family affairs, then he must have family in Oporto, although he personally could never recall having heard the name before. Therefore he began to make inquiries among his many cousins, one of whom suggested looking in the British cemetery for any headstone with the same name. It was a good idea, but it produced nothing. At the same time he began to ask around the colleagues who worked for other houses – but the name continued to produce nothing. Alfredo was not to be deterred by lack of any immediate result. He would persist, although he was beginning to doubt if he would discover anything while Grimpil was still in the city.

Then he remembered the old sailor, whose reminiscences of the French invasions he had listened to. Alfredo eventually found him mending nets on the strand at Cabidela.

'Grimpil, you say!' The old man pondered as the mists of time slowly cleared. 'Would that be Captain Grimpil? Captain Alexander Grimpil?'

'So you knew him?'

'Aye, I knew him by sight. He was a frequent visitor to the bar of the Douro, especially during the reign of Dom Miguel. When I was a younger man and not away from home, I used to work as a lighterman. I must have put him ashore often enough when he first started visiting regular. That would be around the time of the departure of Dom João. He was sweet on one of the daughters of a silversmith. If I recall rightly, he lived behind the Assizes, because he always asked the cab driver to take him to São Bento. Whether he was courting the daughter, who was a fine-looking woman, or the old man's money, which must have been a pretty penny, I can't rightly say, but either way the business must have gone well because he came back to marry her.'

'And they married here?'

'They must have done, for he carried her back to England with him before the French took Oporto.'

'But I thought you said the French went back to France?'

Aye, that they did. That's the problem of making a gentleman's agreement with someone who isn't a gentleman. Napolião didn't keep his word, for in the spring of the following year the French army was back again.'

'The scoundrels!'

'In a war, there's some people who get dead, others who get famous and a few who get rich. Our seafaring gentleman belonged to the latter category, already captain and master of his own vessel by the age of thirty. There can't be many marriages whose legitimate issue is a three-masted brig.'

'In any case, he married the daughter of a silversmith from São Bento.'

'Aye. More than that I can not say, but certainly the parish priest can tell you more.'

-41-

The Woodhouse residence lay beyond the city walls, in an area already given over to fields, kitchen gardens and orchards. Located on a steep rise, it commanded a fine view of the river and of the hills of Gaia on the other side. Further down the hill, nestling on the river bank, was the more populous suburb of Massarelos, but from his bedroom window Grimpil could see none of this. The house had a most pleasant garden where oriental camellias basked in the sun and Andean fuchsias sought out the shade. Walking in the early morning sun after breakfast, he could see that the day would be fine and decided that the best way to restore his sense of purpose was to familiarise himself with the city, on his own and on foot. Having taken the decision, he lost no time in preparing his satchel with his block of watercolour paper, colours and brushes, and, advising his hostess that he should not be returning for luncheon, made his way down the lane towards the river.

Halfway down the hill, the lane was intersected by a major thoroughfare, on the far side of which stood a very substantial house bearing the plaque *João de Rocha e Sousa*. Following the metalled road for the rest of the way down to the river, Grimpil arrived at Massarelos and, turning left, walked along the edge of the river, past the Cais de Pedra where the *Flora* was still moored. Although there was no sign of captain or crew, there was much activity on the river, with vessels of all sizes and shapes plying their trade of provisioning the city with food, fuel, raw materials, luxuries; all manner of goods to be consumed by a large city.

Everywhere lumbered the ox carts that Grimpil had seen the day before, the powerful, yet docile, beasts hauling their loads stoically up the steep gradients that could be found at every turn. The turmoil of movement reached its peak by the time he arrived at Ribeira, the main fish market. Here, each fishwife sang her wares as loudly as possible. If Grimpil had been interested he could have compared the quality of sardines caught off the rocks of Leixões to those caught off the shallows of Cabidela, but he was a stranger to all fish unless he saw them on a plate, accompanied by potatoes and peas. Here, too, the *broeiras* of Avintes plied their trade, clustered alongside the waterfront, standing upright in their boats, selling their round brown loaves that looked more like stones than bread. From mature women to young girls, they managed their skiffs with a dexterity that a Thames boatman would have envied.

He made his way through the vociferous throng, ignoring the solicitations he received from the anxious vendors and traders, leaving behind him the confusion for the calm of the riverside beyond the chain-link bridge.

-42-

Francisco Silveira was polishing his top boots when his brother entered the room. His uniform was one of the things that set him apart from most of the men under his command. They were mainly volunteers without battlefield experience, who had come from the surrounding areas of Cabeceiras and Mondim to stand beside the local forces to resist the invaders, while others had arrived from further afield, Barcelos, Braga, even Viana do Minho. He knew that the prestige of his own person and the force of his own example would be crucial in sustaining the morale and determination of his men. They were woefully few in number; they could never face the enemy head-on. They were poorly armed and inadequately provisioned, carrying little in way of supplies and ammunition. They would stand, fight and then retreat in order to be able to fight another day, but he had enormous respect for them. Although relatively few, his men had inflicted on the French the only defeat they had experienced so far on Portuguese soil; the garrison of Chaves had surrendered to him and 1,400 French soldiers had been taken prisoner. If he had not received orders to the contrary, he would have marched on Braga and retaken it, isolating Soult in Oporto. However, orders had come from Lisbon to hold Vila Real and block the French line of retreat through Trás-os-Montes.

Silveira preferred to characterise High Command as 'Lisbon', the traditional seat of government, rather than consider that the orders emanated from the person of Beresford. He was well aware of the critical state of the nation, and appreciated the need for the British to cover for the lack of Portuguese officers. Beresford was undoubtedly doing an excellent job in reorganising the country's armed forces, but it smacked of colonialism to have a foreigner as the titular head of the chiefs of staff. The British were sending an army to rid their country of the invader, and they would have to accept some sacrifices in the defence of their own interests.

'Brother,' said António Silveira, 'the men are ready.'

Francisco was well aware of their limitations. They had done infinitely more than could ever be reasonably expected of an irregular force. Attack was the best means of defence. They would advance across the Tâmega and take up positions on the heights of Vila Meã, from where they could try to prevent the French from gaining access to Amarante. Since the end of the first invasion, the inhabitants of the town had shown much readiness in preparing to resist a second invasion. Now both the men and the positions they had prepared would be put to the test.

-43-

Beyond the chain-link bridge, the scene immediately became more tranquil. On the other side rose the Serra do Pilar, crowned by the ruined monastery with its strange circular church, still bearing the scars from artillery fire from the days of the siege. On the far side, the mood of the river suddenly softened compared to the rocky severity of its lower course. It was wider and the currents slower, the landscape more verdant. It would be an excellent place to stop and do some painting. On the far side, there were marshes, thick with reeds and bamboo; in the distance a village could be seen, with a whitewashed church, and in the interval farmhouses and some larger mansions. There were farms on this side of the river, too, rich river meadows for pasture, enclosed by stone walls and overhung by vines. As Grimpil sought a vantage point on which to sit, he plucked a low-hanging bunch of grapes from the vine, for it was now some time since breakfast and he had already walked several miles to get here. He shoved them in his pocket and, from time to time, pulled one from the stem. They were still under-ripe, but the downpours of the previous days had left them bloated.

He considered the landscape before him. What he needed was a vertical element to counterbalance the horizontal of the landscape. Possibly the tide was low, for the water here was so shallow that sandy islands showed their backs between the slow-moving water. One of these close to the shore had been colonized by a band of urchins. The attraction of the water on a sunny day was too great to resist. They had stripped off their clothes and were playing naked, diving in and out of the water from a wooden jetty. It was a sport which gave occasion for much shouting and screaming; oaths and insults filled the silent air. Amid the rumpus and general confusion, one lad was noticeably older. He was clearly the chieftain of this band of savages. They hauled themselves out of the river, water running in rivulets down their bony spines and disappearing between the clefts of their buttocks. Only moments later their incredibly slender, underfed bodies would fall back into the water. Their silhouettes were almost without hips, their rumps so lean that even green fruit seemed over-ripe by comparison. Horace slipped a grape into his mouth, pressing it between his teeth. The skin was taut and bitter. The older boy was now shouting orders to those below. The sunlight illuminated the drops of water that had collected at the tip of his penis. At any moment the force of gravity would make them fall. Suddenly the grape skin yielded under the pressure of his teeth, bursting in his mouth in an acid explosion of pulp and pips. He turned his head and spat the leathery skin from his mouth. Turning back to the river, the boys had vanished as suddenly as they had appeared. Their appearance had been an intrusion; their disappearance now left the scene lifeless and inanimate. It no longer appealed to him. He decided instead to head towards the turrets and balustrades of Freixo Palace.

-44-

Now that Alfredo had a name, a date, a wedding and a parish, he set off for São Bento at the first opportunity. Although there was no silversmith practising currently in the street, he made inquiries in the commercial establishments until he was directed to an elderly ledgerman, who lived in a large house at the end of the road overlooking the river. The old man lived alone in an attic apartment. He listened to Alfredo's description.

'You must mean Porfirio Tibães, a widower, with three daughters. That was well-nigh fifty years ago; troubled times they were, and the mother and grandmother of troubled times. It was back in '08 or '09. All was in great turmoil because of the French. Tibães had convinced himself that Bonaparte had sent an army to Portugal especially to despoil him of his livelihood and abduct his daughters. Poor man was in a great state of anxiety because of them. The eldest was Maria das Dores, but her father always called her Doroteia. The youngest was Maria dos Prazeres, who was known as Zéze. But the most beautiful of them all was Quitéria. They say she inherited all her mother's beauty, as well as her name. There was not a man below the age of forty who would not have traded his soul to take her as his wife. She ended up marrying an English sea captain and, much to our disappointment, left immediately for England; for had she married the Captain and stayed in Oporto, us local lads could have still tried our luck at comforting her in her loneliness while her husband was away at sea.' The old man broke out into laughter, which Alfredo shared before drawing a sheet of paper from his pocket.

'Do you have a writing implement, sir, so that we may make a note of these facts?'

The old man had a dry cake of ink, which he spat upon and worked until it produced a writable mixture. Dipping a quill in the ink, he began to write.

'Let us see… we have Porfirio Tibães, native of—'

'Vila de Conde,' said the old bookkeeper, writing as he spoke. 'We were neighbours for some time here, until he moved on. Went to Póvoa de Lanhoso, by all accounts.'

Alfredo stored the information for future reference, while the old man continued scratching the paper with his nib.

'Married to Dona Quitéria.'

'Excellent,' said Alfredo, more than pleased at the progress.

'Daughter – Quitéria Tibães, resident of Rua do São Bento, number... The number I cannot recall. You'll have to see for yourself. It's the house with the pillars at the front, next to the tavern... married to Captain Alexander Grimpil' He paused in his writing. 'It was in the year of the French occupation. What would that be? 1807? 1808? Such a long time ago. It was the beginning of our disgrace; so much has happened since then and so little of it has been good!'

-45-

Colonel Patrick was crouching in the shadow of the narrow bridge that crossed a minor tributary of the Tâmega at São Lazaro, less than half a league from the entrance to the town of Amarante. Since he had volunteered to command the rear guard of Silveira's retreating forces early the same morning, he had harassed the French advance. Unable to halt the advance of De Laborde's division, he sought to delay them as much as possible in order for the defenders to make an orderly withdrawal of their troops and citizens from the right bank of the River Tâmega. Another division under the command of La Hussaye was on its way south from Guimarães and had already reached Lixa. They did not have sufficient forces to meet the combined weight of the enemy head on.

Patrick had already laid one ambush that morning. Seeing the Portuguese retreat, Loison had immediately ordered his cavalry to advance, but as it descended from the high ground of Burgada it found itself under unexpectedly intense musket fire from the rear guard, causing much injury and confusion among the enemy ranks. Patrick immediately retreated to his second line of defence, the bridge of São Lazaro, which the French would have to cross to enter the town.

De Laborde reacted to this first setback by despatching a larger number of troops and, meeting no further resistance, ordered the column to advance, believing he had flushed out the last of the resistance. Meanwhile, the 12th Regiment under Patrick's command, lying in wait in São Lazaro, had been reinforced by the 24th and other groups of peasants and militias, who, having heard the previous engagement, were anxious to come to grips with the enemy. They strained their ears to catch the first telltale sounds of the advancing cavalry, until the thud of hooves and jingle of metal accoutrements denounced the approach of the enemy. Each man readied himself to deliver his fatal blow. They would have to wait until the column was a stone's throw away before discharging their lethal volley. The change in the sound of the horses' footfalls announced the fact that the first riders had passed from the dirt road to the flagstones of the bridge. It was the moment for the men to stand, aim and fire.

The advance column of De Laborde's division, already on the narrow bridge, was caught in a withering crossfire that left twelve of their number dead on the road, while the others rode back as fast as they could for the cover of the pine woods. Patrick knew that as soon as the French brought up their artillery they could no longer hold their position and was already instructing his men to fall back and adopt new positions.

-46-

'You mean to tell me he walked to Freixo by the river and then returned via Campanhã and Santo Oviedo for no purpose whatsoever?'

The *Comendador* looked incredulously at his nephew, who replied, 'I swear by the Bible, that was exactly what he did. He left early in the morning and returned late at night.'

The *Comendador* had to doubt the word of his nephew. The information was either wrong or incomplete; unless, of course, Grimpil knew he was being watched and deliberately sought to confuse his guardian angels with apparently inexplicable movements. If the equation didn't add up, there had to be something missing.

He could only conclude that his nephew was at fault. The lad was willing, but this was a task for someone with more persistence and insight. There was only one person he knew he could trust implicitly, and he rang a small bell on his desk to summon his manservant. Xavier had entered his service during his years of exile in Galicia. In a minor barbarity that had been eclipsed by the major atrocities of war, Xavier had had his tongue ripped out. The *Comendador* quickly discovered this was a quality that made him a perfect agent. Xavier always prevailed because it was impossible to argue with a man who was unable to speak. Xavier was also his only companion, and he would feel his absence keenly, but he saw no alternative. When he was gone, he would feel a cordon of solitude close around his heart. He would fast, he would pray, he would read, but he would not forget the name that was graven on his heart, for there would be no peace in this world nor in the next until he had settled the score with his nemesis.

–47–

Amarante was only a small town, conditioned by the uneven topography of the banks of the Tâmega. The Rua da Ordem, beginning alongside the residence of the Magalhães at the entrance to the town, wound its way towards the river-crossing. Patrick distributed his men in the cover provided by the houses and waited once again to surprise the oncoming enemy. When they finally succeeded in crossing the bridge of São Lazaro, the French troops marched at double time as far as the town. Once again, convinced they had overcome the last of the resistance, the advancing troops were surprised by the concentration of fire that awaited them as soon as they tried to penetrate the confines of the street. The attackers were obliged to fall back, and only at four o'clock in the afternoon did Patrick order his men to the relative safety of the left bank and report to his superior officer.

'We owe you a great debt of gratitude,' said Silveira to Patrick. 'You have given us time to make an orderly withdrawal and prepare our final positions in the finest military style. Be assured that your actions will be mentioned in my despatches to Lisbon.'

'How long do you think we can hold our positions?' Patrick inquired.

Silveira smiled. 'As long as the French don't break through! Fortunately the river is high, or else we should not be able to prevent them from crossing the fords. Now get yourself a little well-deserved rest; our work here is still not finished.'

Patrick was not one for resting while there was still work to be done and the next time Silveira was to see him he was being carried on a stretcher with his head swathed in blood-stained bandages.

French soldiers had entered the houses overlooking the river and were firing on the bridge and its defenders. Having spent all day arranging problems for the French advance, he was less than content at seeing the enemy at such close quarters. He rallied his troops once more and ran back across the bridge to plunge into hand to hand combat with the enemy. The other soldiers on the bridge followed him up the Rua São Gonçalo in a counterattack that took the enemy by surprise. The division under La Hussaye, meanwhile, had arrived at the Campo da Feira, and, hearing the action around the bridgehead, began making their way down the steeply inclined streets towards the river in order to join forces with their colleagues. Not expecting to meet any resistance in the narrow streets, they were confronted by Patrick and his men, fighting hand to hand like crazed demons. In the confines of the narrow street, the soldiers barely had space to fix their bayonets and tried to turn back, slipping on the bloody cobble stones. In the mayhem of cold steel, Patrick received a blow to the head that laid him low.

-48-

Alfredo calculated the best moment to approach the parish priest was after morning mass, and, while the priest was arranging his vestments in the sacristy, he politely inquired if it was possible to consult the parish register. He thought it best to feign that it was at his master's bidding, for there was little prospect of the Anglican Woodhouse coming into contact with the Catholic priest of São Bento parish.

The priest complained that such requests should be made in writing, and Alfredo proudly presented the paper that the old bookkeeper had written for him.

The priest looked at the dog-eared request critically. 'I usually receive something a little more formal. Nevertheless... the year of the occupation, you say?' And he retrieved a tome from a locked cupboard and began to finger the pages. '1807.'

'Quite so, Reverend.'

'Grimpil,' he enunciated carefully, 'a foreign gentleman.'

'Exactly. British.'

'Here we are: 5 October 1807. Alexander Grimpil and Quitéria Tibães. He gives his place of birth as Kyle, Scotland, and place of residence as Bristol.'

'I would be grateful if you would add these details to the paper that my master sent,' Alfredo requested, and so the priest set about copying afresh the entry from the register onto the sheet of paper.

It was at this point that Alfredo realised that he would have to pay for the favour. He pulled the only coin he possessed from his waistcoat pocket, which the priest looked at askance but accepted nonetheless. At the time it seemed like an excessively high outlay merely for the acquisition of lines of text, but it would turn out to be the best investment that Alfredo would ever make.

-49-

Standing at the portal of the parish church of Vila de Conde, Horace Grimpil could see the giant arches of the self-same aqueduct that he had seen from the sea, arriving at their destination – the Monastery of Santa Clara. Its colossal mass rose above the River Ave, dominating the surrounding marshland. He followed a street uphill until he was standing below the aqueduct where it ran parallel to the old Franciscan monastery. The aqueduct made a sharp angle to pass behind the church and enter the rear of the convent. Looking west, he could see the river as it snaked towards the sea, the ribs of ships under construction looking like the skeletons of an extinct species. Further along, where the waters of the river emptied into the sea, stood the squat outline of the Fort São João. Grimpil looked down at the town. Somewhere down there his grandfather had had his workshop, and his mother had played as a child. But he knew not where. He had never considered the possibility that he would not be able to find the house; that he had no street name or number by which to identify it; that he would not be able to find anyone who knew his grandparents; that he would find himself alone in a strange place without any idea of how to conclude his mission. It did not seem possible that such a long journey could simply end so inconclusively.

He took the small silver urn from its velvet pouch and set it on the churchyard wall. It contained the mortal remains of his mother. Ashes to ashes, dust to dust. It scarcely seemed possible that all those years of existence, all the joys and tribulations, the hopes and fears, all the tenderness and affection had been reduced to a few ounces of powder. Would it be possible for God to collect up this dust and reconstitute the person on the day of the final judgement? Such an idea was certainly faulty science and even less accurate theology. The immortal soul had returned to its maker, leaving behind its mortal remains.

He took the urn in his hands and unscrewed its conical cover. His mother had spoken of returning her ashes to her native soil, not specifically to any one place. This, after all, was hallowed ground, as much a part of her native soil as anywhere else. He raised the ciborium to the heavens, as if offering a remembrance to the gods, and slowly rotated the vessel to empty the contents onto the ground. It was at that moment that a sudden gust of wind swept the falling ashes into his eyes, provoking burning tears that he had not cried at his mother's funeral and filling his mouth with the bitter taste of mortality.

-50-

The evening air around Campo da Feira was filled with sound of pickaxes striking stone as the French sappers opened breaches in the convent walls. The transcendent calm of the monastic retreat had been disturbed in order for the artillery men to set up their cannons on the crown of the hill overlooking the river. The wrath of the Imperial Army would soon fall on the few hundred houses and a few thousand defenders on the opposite river bank; the 12-pound cannon balls would soon start raining down, pounding the puny habitations into mounds of rubble. The soldiers went about their work unhurriedly, with well-versed skill. By this time tomorrow they would have flushed out the defenders and could continue on their way across the mountains to the Douro Valley.

On the high ground around Burgada and Fregim, where the 4,000 men of de Laborde's division, and the 2,000 men of Sarrut's division, the 1,900 dragoons under La Hussaye were bivouacked in the cover of the pine woods, the air was filled with the accents of Gallic speech, and the smell of resin blended with that of the cooking from the regimental cooking pots. Each column of smoke rising from the open fires imitated, on a smaller scale, the pillars of smoke that rose from the burning town below, joining together to form a turbid mantle filling the sky and obscuring the sunset of the evening of 19th of April.

The only major building to escape the flames was the monastery and church of São Gonçalo, still held by the defenders. Across the Tâmega, Silveira was organising his forces on the river bank and fords above and below the bridge. However, the bridge itself would be the key to the whole action, and he placed one corps at the end of the bridge under the overall command of his brother, António, with their headquarters in the house of Manuel Pinto de Miranda, at the top of the Rua do Covello. These would have to bear the brunt of any concerted effort to force a passage.

Immediately behind their position was an outcrop of rock

which created a natural platform overlooking the entire bridge. Under the command of Vieira, the Portuguese gunners were setting up their battery. Further upstream, at the Terreiro de Magdalena and Santo António de Boavista, a second battery was being mounted. They were of smaller calibre than the opposing French cannons, and therefore would not be able to challenge them directly, but their range was sufficient to hold at bay any attempt to cross the river upstream of the bridge.

They would have to expect a major offensive on the following day, and Francisco Silveira needed to take all necessary measures to ensure the safety of the military hospitals, the munitions and, if the worst came to the worst, a safe line of retreat for his men. Although he was tired and had not eaten since breakfast, he could still get to Mesão Frio and return by the following morning, even though it would mean riding all night. At least he would be able to get news of Captain Patrick. He hoped to find him at least partly recovered and suffering from no more than loss of blood. He was unquestionably one of the most valiant officers on his staff, who had single-handedly delayed the French advance for the whole afternoon, valuable hours that enabled Silveira to complete his retreat to the left bank and prepare their positions for the forthcoming battle. He couldn't afford to lose an officer, let alone one of such outstanding courage. As he spurred his horse up the long climb to Padronelo, he looked back over the smoking ruins of the town and thought, this, my friend, is only the beginning.

-51-

'Vila do Conde!'

'Quite so – Vila do Conde.'

The *Comendador* looked suspiciously at his nephew. 'Where did he go?'

'Nowhere. He wandered around town for a while and eventually went to the church, but didn't speak to the priest.'

'He didn't meet anyone else?'

'No one. But he was carrying a package that he brought with him. He still had the object when he left.'

'Strange. Maybe for some reason his contact wasn't able to make the rendezvous. But who?'

'I think we can safely presume that it was no one from Vila do Conde, otherwise we would know about their existence. Someone from Oporto, perhaps?'

'But it would be much easier to meet in Oporto and less conspicuous. There must be some other explanation. Someone not from Oporto yet sufficiently well known so as not to want to appear in Oporto; someone possibly living to the north or east of the city?' 'We need to look further afield,' said the *Comendador*, rising from his seat. He walked to an India Company *bargueño* that stood against the wall, and, running his finger down the herringbone moulding, activated a hidden mechanism, causing a secret drawer to spring open where only panelling appeared to exist. He withdrew a ledger book from the secret recess, which he took to the desk and opened it. Each double-page spread had the heading of a town and the left-hand page the title '*Infiés*' and the right-hand '*Fiéis*'. Some of the names of both sides had been ruled out.

'It dates from the time of the accession of our sovereign king,' he explained to his nephew, 'when it was necessary to know on whom we could rely to support the legitimate monarchy, and those who could be counted as an enemy of throne and altar. Only the names of those who have gone to the other kingdom have been erased.'

'A useful instrument,' commented Rodrigo, with a raised eyebrow.

'It has served its purpose on many occasions,' the *Comendador* replied. 'Now let us see, Braga, Guimarães, Prado, Vila Verde, Ponte da Barca, Viana do Minho...' He paused for a moment. An idea was forming in his mind. Viana do Minho – conveniently close to the Spanish border to be able to slip across at the first sign of trouble.

'Monção,' said Rodrigo. 'Better still!'

'Maybe or maybe not,' pondered the older man. 'Something tells me our fox would go to ground somewhere with good maritime connections; maybe somewhere where he could even have his own craft lying in harbour in case of necessity, rapid flight or perhaps a little extra business to top up the coffers.'

The quiet of his aged blood was stirred by the excitement of renewed action.

Yes, vengeance was a dish to be eaten cold. He could feel a calm determination unsullied by passion. Time was on his side. He would lay a trap and wait for his prey to rise to the bait.

-52-

The long ride back gave Francisco Silveira plenty of time to reflect on the troubled times in which he lived. As a man of deep religious principles he had an unshakeable faith in God and the righteousness of his cause. He was not concerned for his own physical well-being, for he knew that at any moment an exploding grenade or well-aimed shot could take his life. To a certain degree he was anxious to meet his maker so that he might demand from the Almighty an explanation for the things he found difficult to comprehend. He found it easy to accept that the Son did not embody all the wisdom of the Father and therefore that some of his teachings might be incomplete. For example, according to the Son, he should turn the other cheek to those who offended him. In his understanding it was the French who had come to disturb his peace and tranquillity and therefore deserved the punishment of the wrong-doer. Then again, the Son had preached to render unto Caesar what belonged to Caesar. All well and good, but what if Caesar demanded what did not belong to him? Should he stand by and not oppose the invader who sought to despoil him and his country of what was rightfully theirs? These things left him perplexed, and he was certain that, united in the three persons of the Holy Trinity, God would be able to reconcile these anomalies in such a way as to enable him to resist the invader and preserve his honour without infringing the Divine will expressed by the Fifth Commandment. Possibly like the masons of old, who had left inscriptions carved in the stones of the churches, God, in transmitting his instructions by tablets of stones, had abbreviated his message, leaving out some important sub-clauses.

His ponderings were disturbed by the artillery exchange, which could be heard several leagues away. By the time Silveira finally arrived at his headquarters on the outskirts of Amarante, he was eager to meet his brother and take full measure of the situation.

'How is Patrick?' was António Silveira's first question.

His brother shook his head. 'I fear he shall not recover.'

'A sad loss.'

'Indeed. With a company of men like that we would have nothing to fear from the French.'

'So how goes our enterprise?' he continued.

'We have reinforced our position, but so has the enemy. The morning was hard fought. They mounted a cannon in a commanding position alongside *Senhor dos Aflictos*, which neutralised our pieces on the bridge. In fact, at the end of the morning, the exchange of fire was so intense that you could not see the river nor the bridge, so thick was the smoke. The major in command of the batteries in the *Terreiro da Magdalena* was convinced that the enemy had succeeded in taking the bridge, spiked his guns and took himself off to Lamego.'

'The militia show more mettle than the regular army.'

'Quite so. When Lieutenant Vieira de Sá noticed that there was no more firing coming from that quarter, he left his command at the Chapel of Calvário and came running down to put them back in action.'

'Excellent man!'

'Indeed! His service today alone earns him a promotion. His fire has been so intense that he has silenced the French on several occasions and on some so accurate as to dismount the enemy guns from their carriages.'

'I shall thank him myself in the name of His Majesty, and he shall be promoted to captain forthwith. And losses? How are we bearing up?'

'Our losses are slight compared to those of the enemy. I can't say how many, but definitely high. Nevertheless, we have mined the bridge in case the enemy force should overpower our positions, but until now they have held.'

While the two men had been talking, Silveira had been attentive to the artillery duel which still raged across the river.

'One more thing, brother.'

'What's that?'

'Judging by the amount of shells and grenades falling on the Miranda's house, I'd say you're going to have a different headquarters.'

-53-

The Woodhouse residence was renowned for the opulence of its social gatherings and this was no exception; except that on this occasion, instead of being restricted to the British community, the house was open to all of Oporto society and its many foreign enclaves. An endless stream of elegant carriages delivered the guests to the canopied portico at the entrance to the whitewashed villa. The men were distinguished by the severity of their dress and the magnificence of their whiskers, while the women dazzled in their sumptuous gowns of velvet, organdie and lace, bedecked in splendid jewellery, the precious stones catching the myriad of lights from the chandelier that hung from the centre of the ballroom.

Woodhouse was in what he described as his inner sanctum, with his more intimate circle, which included some of the most influential figures in the British community in Oporto. The room was filled with an aromatic fog derived from some of the finest Havana cigars to be had in the city.

'I trust you are aware, sir,' said an elderly gentleman with bushy red side-whiskers and a strong Scottish accent, 'that the orchestra is playing a waltz!'

'My dear McEwan, the younger generation will have nothing else. We must cede to their wishes, for were it not for them, who would animate the ball?'

'Indulgence!' replied McEwan vehemently. 'The youth of today is spoilt rotten and pampered like French Poodles. How would Britain have withstood the Great Tyrant if our generation had been so mollycoddled?'

'The waltz is no more than a fashion, and like all fashions shall pass,' replied Woodhouse mildly. 'I don't think we should attribute the collapse of civilization to a little light music.'

'We are putting the younger generation on the path of perdition. Would you say it is decent, Mr Woodhouse, for lads and unmarried lassies to be cavorting so!'

'I would say it is a shame that I cannot shed the weight of several decades so that I might, too, be as light of foot as they, and thereby also benefit from the opportunity to cavort with a lass, be she wed or not.'

'Ach!' exclaimed McEwan, with the rich guttural expletive so expressive of the highland tongue, and left the assembled company, disgusted at such complicity with decadence.

-54-

'Pray tell me, monsieur, what is this?' asked Taboreau, placing a coin on the table between himself and Tibães.

'It is a silver *cruzado*,' Tibães replied. The proverbial bad penny had returned sooner then he ever expected.

'Indeed it is. One of the silver *cruzados* that you used in payment of your taxes.'

'Yes, sir. To meet Your Excellency's demands, it was necessary to have recourse to every last brass farthing, even if it is a collector's item.'

'Ah so! Is that why it appears so new?'

Taboreau lifted it up to his eyes, the better to examine it. 'Hardly a brass farthing! Very interesting, one would say, that it had never been handled, so pristine, so immaculate. It's almost as if it had been made... yesterday!'

He put the coin back on the table and fixed Porfirio with a steely eye.

'It belonged to my father. He was a collector.'

'What a coincidence, Monsieur Tibães, so am I!'

Taboreau set the coin spinning on its edge, the motion drumming on the desk top.

'Heads or tails?'

'*Coroa*,' replied Porfirio, almost automatically.

Taboreau's hand came down on the spinning coin, bringing its pirouette to an abrupt end.

'*Coroa*, Monsieur Tibães? Did you mention crowns?'

'Nothing more than force of habit, I assure you.'

Taboreau lifted his hand. 'Well, heads it is. You are in luck.'

His smile was like the ornamental brasswork on a coffin.

'They tell me you are a highly respected man in your neighbourhood.' After a short pause Taboreau continued. 'This city is in need of good men who will cooperate in the task of restoring good governance to the people.'

Porfirio made no comment.

'I think that the anarchy that reigned in the city before our arrival has been suppressed. However, we continue to rely on the good offices of the town's most eminent citizens to assist in the maintenance of good order. For example, the position of Overseer of Weights and Measures is vacant.'

Again he fixed Porfirio with his steely gaze.

'I don't think I would be the person most indicated to fill a post of such responsibility.'

'I'm afraid I don't agree with you. I think you would be an excellent overseer of such an important post for the regulation of commerce.'

'But I know so little about—'

'That is no matter, for we are to introduce a new set of standards according to the French model. It is very rational and, as soon as you are acquainted with the system, you will immediately perceive its benefits.'

'I'm afraid you overestimate my capacities.'

'I don't think so. The responsibilities include those of assayer for all articles of gold and silver in the city of Oporto.'

Porfirio remained silent. Could he accept? Could he refuse?

'I shall expect you to report to my office on Monday at midday so that I can explain your duties in more detail. I can rely on you, can I not?' he said, picking up the *cruzado* from the table. 'If you prefer, I can send my men to fetch you.'

'I don't think that will be necessary.'

'Excellent, then; Monday at midday.' And as the slipped the *cruzado* into his waistcoat pocket, added, 'Fine specimen!'

-55-

Grimpil was pleased to see some familiar faces. Inevitably, Forrester and Flower were side by side. Graham, however, was returning from the dance floor with a young lady on his arm.

'Allow me to introduce you to Miss Flávia Leite e Rocha,' he said, presenting the gentleman one by one. 'Miss Flávia is the daughter of Senhor Leite e Rocha of the Massarelos china factory, not to mention a great friend of Melissa Parker, and also a most accomplished dancer,' he added gallantly.

Amongst the older generation there was little social exchange between the British and the native community, reinforcing the idea that the British were unsociable. The younger generation communed more freely, however.

'Quite frankly,' remarked Flávia, flourishing her fan vigorously, 'I fail to understand why you men come to balls! If it is to stand around conversing you can do that at any time, but balls were made for dancing, and if there is not a gentleman here who will invite me to dance then I have no option to make the invitation myself. Will you dance with me, sir,' she said, resting her hand on Grimpil's arm.

'I'm afraid I must decline, for I am a very poor dancer,' Grimpil replied.

'In that case, I shall teach you; all you need is some practice. Come,' she said, imperiously leading Grimpil to the dance floor.

'I must protest,' he said feebly.

'Nonsense! You must dance and talk to me. Tell me, what is your profession?'

'I'm a Fellow of St Botolph's.'

'And what is a Fellow of St Botolph's doing in Portugal, dancing with the prettiest girl at the St John's Ball?

'I see that false modesty is not part of your nature.'

'If you will not compliment me, as a gentleman should, then I must do so myself. Perhaps you could find something about my person worthy of your praise,' she said, distancing herself from him as they danced for him to better appreciate her.

She was wearing what he supposed was the latest Paris fashion, with a white camellia in her corsage. Grimpil searched his memory of the poets for something suitable to say, but he found it difficult to recall anything appropriate while concentrating on the movement of his feet so as not to tread on her own rapidly moving ones.'

'Evidently I don't inspire you to great raptures, Mr Grimpil,' she said, somewhat severely.

'On the contrary, your beauty leaves me speechless,' he replied, taking himself by surprise at his answer.

Flávia threw back her head to release a laugh. 'Why, Mr Grimpil! Are you flattering me or making fun of me? Please don't reply,' she added dramatically. 'Let the truth remain unspoken so I may maintain my illusions.'

She shot a wicked smile at him that brought a malicious sparkle to her eyes. 'For if the truth be said, I could add that I find myself without words to describe your dancing.'

Grimpil felt injured by these words, for if he was dancing it was to please her and not himself. She quickly detected his change of mood. 'You never did tell me your reason for being here. Are you here on boring business, or have you come to lose your heart to a dark-eyed Lusitanian?'

'If I should lose my heart, I could not imagine a more seductive temptress. However, my business here is almost concluded, and my time is my own to decide how best to profit from the opportunities that present themselves.'

'Your answer pleases me more than any of the previous. I should be happy to present you with some opportunities, if you would accept my company.'

'My dear young lady, do all Portuguese women have such measure of liberty?'

'Suitably accompanied, of course. You know my friend, Melissa?'

'Indeed we are acquainted.'

'And what of Rodrigo Junqueira? His family is terribly stuffy, but he is quite modern. I think he's a bit keen on Melissa, but that is a confidence and you mustn't say that I told. Will you keep my secret, Mr Grimpil?' she said, in a conspiratorial manner.

'To the grave,' he replied earnestly, which made her throw back her head in laughter once again.

-56-

On the morning of April the 24th, Captain Bouchard of the Engineers climbed the stairs to the top of the bell tower of the Monastery of São Gonçalo. The stones were stained with the blood of the shattered gun crew as they staggered down, bleeding profusely after taking a direct hit. Although the top of the bell tower rose nearly a hundred feet above the Largo de São Gonçalo, it was only a dozen feet above the level of the Largo das Freiras. The engineers had succeeded in building a ramp on the sheltered northeast side and managed to haul a 9-pounder into position. The platform gave a direct line of fire over the bridge and on to the enemy gun emplacements on the far bank of the river. Because the angle of the tower only presented a narrow aperture to the facing enemy, the gun crew believed they could work, relatively immune from enemy fire.

Unfortunately, hardly had they readied the piece for action when Vieira, with unerring accuracy, fired a ball which sliced through the great bell like a knife through an apple, showering the gun crew with a deadly rain of fragmented brass. Those who had not been killed outright, abandoned the position. The platform was littered with the smashed remnants of the gun carriage. For this reason, Bouchard did not want to show himself, lest he suffer the same fate.

With his back against the stonework, he could see by naked eye the full extent of the bridge, its defences and the defenders. He could clearly see that the far end of the bridge had been mined. A cord ran from the house beside the mouth of the bridge and disappeared into the masonry of the last arch. As the final act, the enemy would cut the bridge to prevent them crossing. So far, all attempts to break through the palisade in the centre of the bridge had proved fruitless. It was impossible to put enough men to work on it to make any real headway. To make matters worse, the enemy was in the process of raising a wall at the far end, sealing it off definitively. Obviously they had been working at night. They must act within the next few days or else they would be confronted with this second, more permanent, obstruction. If the enemy worked at night, then so would they. Bouchard calculated how many barrels of gunpowder he would need. Better to err on the side of excess. The bigger the explosion, the better; not only would it stun the enemy, but it might just dislodge the mine.

-57-

'I had not suspected your Mr Grimpil to be a ladies' man,' observed Forrester to Flower.

'In the first place, I refute the assertion he is mine to any degree whatsoever. As for the rest, one swallow does not make a summer!'

They were joined by the Piedmontese Consul, who was accompanied by Jules Pellerin. He greeted Flower, who introduced him to Forrester.

'I understand that you gentleman are both advocates of the art of photography,' inquired the Frenchman.

'Speaking for myself I would rather say I am an acolyte of the science of photography,' replied Flower. 'What would your reply be, Forrester?' he inquired.

'Neither one nor the other. Photography is an instrument, a useful addition to the available means, saving time and effort in certain measure to achieve more mechanical ends.'

'It is interesting that you should use the word mechanical, for I believe that the camera is to art what the steam engine is to industry – once the machine supplants the hand of man, then human skill is replaced by the endless repetition of the same object, or, in this case, image. We artists are the last generation of artisans defending their dying art from extinction.'

'I cannot agree with you,' objected Flower. 'Art is the highest aspiration of humanity. There will always be art as long as man seeks to perfect himself through the expression of his search for the absolute, the ultimate.'

Pellerin smiled. 'And you call yourself a man of science? These are the words of a poet.'

'A wheel has many spokes, but they are all joined at the hub.'

'I should not aspire to such universal truths. I am but a humble painter, who tries in vain to recreate the three-dimensional universe in a two-dimensional world of coloured daubs.'

'Who, then, would you elect as the greatest painter of all time?'

'This is a parlour game for children. There have been many great painters of many great eras. Ask me rather who is the greatest painter of *our* time '

'And tell us, what would be your reply?' It was Flávia, who had rejoined the group in time to hear the last statement.

'I should say, mademoiselle,' he replied, bowing deeply, 'that it is I.'

Flávia was delighted by the boldness of his answer.

'Then allow me the honour of saying that I have danced with the greatest artist of our times,' she said, sweeping him towards the dance floor.

'High-spirited lass,' commented Forrester.

'Youth is the season for high spirits, for responsibility will come with time. But tell me,' Flower said, turning to the Consul, 'is there any foundation to his claims?'

'I would not consider myself competent to make such an evaluation. I know he was highly regarded by his master, but since then – alas – I fear he has not lived up to expectations. Pellerin is most excited about his latest ideas, but in my opinion his canvasses are not only bereft of content but also artistic quality. For all his concern at the demise of painting, it seems that he is the one to have delivered the coup de grâce!'

'A damning opinion for one who felt himself unqualified to make an evaluation,' commented Forrester in a whispered aside to Flower.

-58-

'Welcome, monsieur.' Taboreau motioned Porfirio to a chair. 'Do sit down. May I offer you a glass of wine to celebrate our partnership?'

'It is not my habit to drink at this hour.'

'Maybe not, but this is a special occasion, and this,' he held up a decanter of wine, 'is probably the finest Port to be had in the city at the moment – a present from the Bishop.' He poured two glasses of the liquor.

'To the success of our collaboration.' He raised his glass so that the translucent liquid reflected golden fragments in the sun light that filtered through the half-closed shutters.

'*Saúde*,' said Porfirio. The Intendant was not mistaken. It was an exceptionally fine white Port, light and dry, with a faint aftertaste of almonds.

'*Lágrimas do Cristo*,' he uttered.

'Quite so, my friend; the Tears of Christ.'

The two men sat down. Neither of them was religious, but both of them respected the sublime.

'Do you know what this is?' asked Taboreau, pushing a wooden box in Porfirio's direction. The rosewood casket was about as long as his forearm and as wide as his hand but shallow, no more than two fingers deep.

'I have no idea,' confessed Porfirio.

'Then open it; it is not locked.'

Apart from two keyholes, the box was secured by three brass catches, which Porfirio flipped open. Inside its red velvet lining nestled a series of circular dies in diminishing sizes. Porfirio instinctively recognised their function but said nothing, only drawing a pair of white cotton gloves from one waistcoat pocket and an eyeglass from the other. With a gloved hand he took the largest die, and putting the glass to his eye, examined the inner surface. Embossed in reverse relief were the unmistakable features of Napoleon Bonaparte, crowned with the victor's laurels. He looked at Taboreau, who was sipping his Port. He replaced the die in the case containing the masters for minting coins of the various values in use throughout the Emperor's territories. He closed the box, but, before he could withdraw his hand, Taboreau, in a lightning reflex, grasped his wrist.

'I have chosen you because I believe I can rely on your discretion. I trust that I am not mistaken?'

'Your Excellency can rely on my silence, but what is it that I must not say?'

Without replying, Taboreau took a bunch of keys from his pocket and proceeded to unlock the door to an antechamber. Even in the relative obscurity, it was possible to discern through the open doorway the contours of many objects piled high in the centre of the room. The sheen which reflected from their contours identified them as being made from gold and silver. It was a treasure trove from a whole looted city. It seemed that he recognised some items, but as he stepped forward Taboreau barred his passage.

'That's enough,' he said, closing and locking the door.

Porfirio sat down. He understood the Intendant's purpose, but the realisation made him feel slightly ill.

'But it would take…'

'Yes, monsieur. What would it take?'

'I would need a team of—'

'My men will give you all the assistance you need.'

'But they have no experience.'

'No buts, Monsieur Teibães. No half-buts nor quarter-buts. This operation needs to be completed within a week!'

'A week! That's impossible.'

'Everything is possible given the right conditions.'

'Where would this take place?'

'Right here. A furnace has already been built and fuel set by.'

'All of that,' said Porfirio, gesturing towards what lay behind the locked door, 'needs to be broken down.'

'My men can see to that.'

'It will be necessary to make copies of the masters.'

'What do you need?'

'I would need my instruments.'

'They shall be fetched here today.'

'But even working day and night, such a major undertaking could never be completed in a week. It would take at least three.'

'Two weeks, then.'

'Your Excellency does not appreciate the scale of the task.'

'And Monsieur Tibães does not appreciate the urgency of the need.'

'I need three days just to make the moulds.'

'Then you had better get started immediately. I will have my men take you home. You can return with everything you need. And one more thing: until the operation is finished, you will stay here. I have prepared a room which I hope you will find comfortable. The bed used to belong to the Governor.'

The last time Porfirio had seen d'Oliveira, he was being dragged through the streets by horses, until the furious mob had thrown his senseless body into the Douro. He distinctly felt he was running the risk of the same fate being reserved for him.

-59-

'If you were to go to Amarante,' suggested Forrester, 'Grimpil could travel with you as far as Guimarães. Have you set a date for your trip?' he asked, turning to Flower, who shot him an exasperated look in return.

'In fact I've already been to Amarante, the most charming town in the whole of the North.'

'And was the trip successful?'

'Yes, I am now sufficiently skilled to prepare the chemicals in the field, as it were. It is a delicate task, but I am happy with the results I have obtained so far.'

'And your trip to Guimarães: do you still intend to go?'

'I do, but my plans have not yet been fully finalised,' he said vaguely. 'I think I shall partake of some refreshments,' he added, taking his leave of the group.

'I shall join you, if you don't mind?' Grimpil said.

'No, not at all,' replied Flower in a resigned voice.

They went to a side table that was laid with a large silverware mazzarin, full of punch, where they met Pellerin, who was also filling two glasses.

'What a splendid creature,' he said to Grimpil, referring to Flávia. 'All fire and spirit. I must rejoin her at once.'

But Flávia was already at his side, taking the cup from his hand and drinking its contents in one swift draught.

'The spirit all seems to be acquired from the punch,' Grimpil replied.

'My word,' she said, 'so many handsome men to dance with; I don't know who to choose next.' She ignored Flower, being married and, apart from that fact, conspicuously uninterested in flirting. 'Come, my dear Botolph,' she said, tugging at Grimpil's sleeve. 'Let's see if you have remembered my dancing lesson. Let us see who will win the battle of chivalry: Arts or Letters.'

-60-

At ten in the morning of April the 26th, the square in front of the Senate House began to fill with the citizens, dressed in ceremonial finery. Soult had summoned by order all property owners to affix their signatures to the petition to the Emperor. Neighbours stood in nervous groups, discussing the morning's business in hushed tones, not only from aversion to the act they were about to perform but also for fear of there being spies infiltrated in their midst. There was no man there who would not have preferred to have been in any other part of the city on any other business than that they were compelled to discharge.

'I cannot believe the British have let it come to this,' lamented Porfirio to his neighbour, Domingos Freitas. 'How could they allow the French to take their principal stronghold on the peninsula and fail to react?'

'Because the Brits are losing the war, that's why. There's not much chance of them returning now,' replied the bookkeeper, who did not share his neighbour's faith in Albion. 'They're being shut out of Europe. How much longer do you think they will be able to hold on to Lisbon? Before long the French armies will close in on the capital, forcing the British back into the sea, just as they had forced out the House of Bragança.'

'Do you really think it's over?'

'Look around you, my friend. What do you see?'

The square was filling with French soldiery. The officers were giving orders for the civilians to arrange themselves in double file, the burghers flanked on either side by armed soldiers.

'My friend,' said the book keeper, 'old Portugal has been banished across the seas. If you want Dom Joao then that is where you must seek him. In the meantime, learn to say "Viva Napoleon" and sound as if you mean it.'

With the sun high in the sky, the cortège began to file out of the square in the direction of the Palácio dos Carrancas, accompanied by military escort, marching to the beat of drums.

When the company finally drew up along the Rua dos Quarteis, a deputation entered the ample atrium of the palace, climbed the great staircase and appeared at the balcony on the first floor above the entrance. The County Sheriff gave a speech in the presence of Marshal Soult, who had insisted in being addressed throughout by no other title other than that of Duke of Dalmatia.

Standing bareheaded in the noonday sun, the citizens were obliged to listen to the endless compliments paid to the Duke as saviour and liberator of the fatherland, and to proclamations of the gratitude and devotion of the thankful nation. He concluded with the words, 'It is our intention and heartfelt desire that our gracious lord and emperor Napoleon deign to name a prince of his house, or,' and here the speaker paused to direct his eyes at the figure of Soult in full dress uniform, 'any other of his choice, to succeed to the throne, formerly occupied by the House of Bragança.'

The speech ended with the street filled by a profound silence. The men listening in the square shuffled with the brims of their hats and pulled at their high collars.

The Duke of Dalmatia now began to speak in French, which few would admit to understanding. The words fell like autumn leaves on the cobbles of the street. Silence reigned, until a voice could be heard declaiming, 'Long live the Duke of Dalmatia, King of Portugal!' A few half-hearted hurrahs arose from the assembled multitude, probably by agents paid for the purpose, since Quesnel had an ample budget to pay his extensive network of spies.

The citizens now filed in to pay homage to their new sovereign by signing the petition and returning to their daily lives as rapidly as possible, hoping that the moment would be expunged from public memory for ever.

-61-

Flower found himself with Pellerin again, but at least he had been relieved of Grimpil. The Frenchman was chastened by being so rapidly abandoned by his dancing partner. Flower had the opportunity to observe his broad, even faun-like features, a sensuous mouth and hands of a woodcutter. Hardly the image of an Academy artist, but he remembered the self-portrait of Goya or even the Gnome Booth, neither of which equated to the romantic aesthetic.

'Will your work detain you long in these parts?' enquired Flower.

'I fear my work here is to no avail, I have not found the glory I seek, nor, for that matter, an accommodating patron. I have not finished a canvas since I am come here, and I must soon do society portraits or return to France. I'm not sure which is more odious.'

'Have you been to Lisbon, monsieur? It is called the City of Light, and light, after all, is the midwife of artistic creation.' Flower felt a certain empathy for the artist and was pleased to help an opponent of the Third Empire. 'Let me present you to Thompson. He has many connections in the capital, where I'm sure you would find better possibilities for advancement, both materially and professionally. The last I saw him he was playing cards with the ladies.' And the two proceeded to the green room, where, after making the necessary introductions, Flower left him with the assembled company, thus freeing himself to enter the inner sanctum.

Woodhouse greeted him with his usual joviality, although he could not deny his genuine affection for the young man. Flower, however, was more interested in making the secret sign in such a discreetly simulated way that none of the other persons present should detect it.

'I have received a paper on the application of Dobreiner's

Triads to metallic salts and was wondering if I might consult your copy of Dalton's *New System of Chemical Philosophy*.'

'I possess such a work?' enquired Woodhouse, whose interest in the physical sciences did not extend beyond specific gravity.

'Yes, sir, it's in your library.'

'Well, if it favours your alchemy, I should not deny such a simple request.'

Flower was not pleased by the reference to alchemy, but knew that Woodhouse meant no harm. It was a mere association of ideas.

'In that case, I shall not trouble you further than asking permission to go to the library.'

'Permission granted, dear boy. May God bless your studies.'

Without further ado, Flower withdrew and, making sure there were no stray guests in the corridor, directed his steps to the library. From an open door he could hear a rendition of a sentimental German song in a shaky male voice, accompanied by a no less uncertain pianist. The guests were all entertained. He gave the special knock on the door, which opened from the inside, admitting him silently into the library.

-62-

Soult decided to make the alderman wait in the ballroom of the *Palácio dos Carrancas* while he dealt with urgent military business. He was anxious to hear some good news, but the latest information from the front against Silveira was unpromising. The tenacity of the defence of the Amarante bridge was an encouragement to all those who defied, openly or not, his attempt to impose his rule over the country. Cartloads of wounded soldiers were arriving everyday, and there was always a large gathering of populace to witness their passage as they made their way to the steadily filling military hospitals. This was not to speak of those killed outright. Much as he might deny the gravity of the situation publicly, it was evident to French and Portuguese alike that the French war machine had ground to a halt at the River Tâmega, and for the time being there appeared little prospect of forcing a passage across the bridge. He had read Boucher's report, but the latest despatches informed him that the unanimous opinion of the generals, on the recommendation of La Foy, was that the plan was unworkable.

He called his first Aide de Camp.

'I want you to go to Amarante and make a personal appraisal of the situation there. If you consider Bouchard's plan viable, then do everything necessary to expedite matters as fast as possible. I'm sending the five barrels of powder that Bouchard reckoned would be necessary, along with two more 12-pounders. We must put an end to the Portuguese resistance and we must open the road to Vila Real. Not only do we need a supply line, we must secure an eventual line of retreat, in case our enterprise here falters. Not a word to the other officers, mind you. Tell Loison that it is of the highest strategic importance to take and hold the bridge. And one more thing: a *Légion de Honneur* to the first man who crosses the bridge, and another ten for whoever follows the first. The passage must be forced.'

-63-

The Feast of São João, the patron saint of the city, is the major festival of Oporto, where the religious and profane mix in time-honoured popular custom. The twenty-fourth is a public holiday, and on the eve all the city is in the streets. For the older guests at the house of Mr Woodhouse, the evening was observed in festivities of a more limited nature. For the youngsters, however, it was the night of bacchanalia *par excellence*. Flávia, however, with the impetuosity of youth, had already partaken amply of Woodhouse's hospitality and was feeling indisposed. She called upon her knights errant to escort her home.

The more populous neighbourhoods were thronging with festive crowds. The whole town had taken to the street, and an endless procession of merrymakers flowed up and down the streets in a steady flux of seemingly inexhaustible motion. With carefree abandon, men, women and children thronged the streets, heavy with the redolence of grilled sardines and illuminated at regular intervals by votive lights in wayside shrines. In a carnival atmosphere of collective delirium, friends, acquaintances and strangers alike were greeted with an irreverent tap on the head from the bulb of a long-stemmed garlic plant, which many people carried. Wherever the narrow streets opened into a small square, there were people dancing to the sound of accordion and violin, the women's clogs sounding a percussion accompaniment to the pounding of the bass drum. Swirling with upraised arms the skirts of the women ballooned, a blur of vivid colours against the black costumes of the men, only the backs of their waistcoats providing a splash of colour. Onlookers clapped enthusiastically to the rhythm, until the dancing was replaced by singing the *desafio*, a spontaneous lyrical duel in which couples took it in turn to improvise verses. Judging by the gales of raucous laughter which each stanza provoked, the subject matter could only be of the most lewd nature.

It was impossible for the three of them to walk abreast in the crowded streets, and much as Grimpil tried to remain at Flávia's side he continuously found himself being forced behind, while somehow Pellerin miraculously stayed beside her. Even when the three of them could continue in unison, the confusion was such that it was difficult to engage in conversation, a problem which Pellerin did not seem to be experiencing. They could often be seen with their heads close together, exchanges which frequently ended in outbreaks of mirth.

With such a crowd in the streets it was difficult to be certain but Grimpil had the distinct impression that they were being followed. The same three characters remained a short distance behind them, their less than festive appearance distinguishing them from the rest of the merrymakers.

-64-

'Good to see you again,' said Tibães, clapping Pellerin on the back. 'How goes the war?'

Pellerin looked round to make sure no one was within ear shot. 'Not good,' he replied. 'We are held up in Amarante and cannot cross the Tâmega.'

'Everyday I see cartloads of wounded soldiers returning from the front. Silveira is doing a good job.'

'It is the French infantryman who pays the price of their generals' impatience. They have wasted the lives of so many men in their desperation to force a passage. It is impossible to approach without coming into the range of the Portuguese cannon and musket fire. We tried to construct a wooden cantilever bridge to provide an alternative river crossing, but we could not get a footing. The river is still too high. The enterprise goes from bad to worse.'

'But surely you will prevail.'

Pellerin lowered his voice even further and drew close to impart his secret. 'You know that Silveira has retaken Chaves.'

There was a moment's silence.

Pellerin continued. 'This war is all wrong. Why are we here destroying cities? All because of the ambition, the pride, the intransigence of one man! Thousands of lives are being wasted, thousands of livelihoods destroyed, thousands of families uprooted. We should be spending our time, energy and resources building France, not destroying our neighbours. If there is a reason for us being here at all, it should be to build roads – which this country so badly needs – bridges, factories, institutions for technical training.'

'Patience, my friend. The world is as we find it not as we would wish it. Let us limit ourselves to what is in our power to do. Explain to me how your system works.'

'This is where the coins are struck,' said Pellerin, walking towards a contraption with a solid olive-wood base, above which was poised a massive beam with a wooden mallet at the end.

'I've done everything to make this as rapid and as accurate as possible. You don't want to waste time with spoilt coins. You see this pedal here?' he said, pointing to the right. 'Pressing here lifts the die assembly.' As he pressed, the top die rose from the hole bored into the wood. 'To reduce the amount of physical effort you need to secure the dies, both of them are recessed into this hole. You just lift out the top die – it doesn't enter very far; just enough to prevent any lateral motion when it's struck – then out comes your coin, in goes your blank, release the pedal, drop in your top die, and the assembly is ready.'

He readjusted his position to put his foot on a much larger pedal connected to the overhead beam.

'This operates the hammer. I've also arranged this so that you don't have to exert too much effort. Foot on the board takes up the slack. There's a pin here on the right, which locks the beam into the upright position to avoid any accidents. So, take out the pin, and the hammer falls under its own weight. It's counter-balanced so as not to fall too fast, but it delivers quite a punch, quite enough to get a perfect impression on the first strike. It would be a good idea to strike the blanks still hot, or at least not cold – the metal is more malleable and gives a better result with less effort. Less force means less wear and tear on the machine and a longer life for the dies. I've got no idea how long you can go on minting, but you'll have to see how it works in practice. I reckon you can strike about 350 coins an hour, which is not bad for one person working on their own, and, what's more important, they should all be good, so no wasted time or blanks.'

'Congratulations, young man! A most ingenious device. With your help I see my task being slightly more feasible than it at first appeared.'

'Well, the problem really is the production of the blanks.'

Tibães interrupted. 'No! The real problem is that Taboreau will not let me leave until the job is done. I must ask you one thing more. As you will be returning to my house, let me ask you a favour, man to man. Look after my daughters' in my absence.'

'I will defend your honour as if it were my own,' replied the Frenchman.

'I am much relieved; I cannot think of anyone else I can trust.'

'Let your mind rest easy on the matter, for you have much work ahead of you. I just couldn't find material to make a roller mill, so the only solution was this.' He took Tibães to the side of an even more exotic contraption. 'I got the idea from my mother, making pancakes. If the results are as good as hers, we're in luck!'

−65−

When they finally reached Flávia's house, she declared that it would be a shame to retire at such an early hour when the festival was still so animated.

'Let me propose that we go to the public gardens, where we will certainly be able to dance,' Pellerin said, a suggestion which Flávia received with approval.

'But for that we must return to the upper city,' objected Grimpil, who did not relish the prospect of battling uphill through the crowded streets, only to return from whence they had come.

'Come,' said Flávia gaily, laying a gloved hand on his sleeve, 'it will be such fun.'

'May I escort, Mademoiselle?' asked Pellerin gallantly.

'Certainly, my darling chevalier,' she replied, sliding her arm under that of the Frenchman.

'Will you come, too, Mr Grimpil?' she inquired.

'It appears that the young lady has already arranged a dancing partner.'

'Nonsense, Grimpil. Don't be contrary. I'm sure I could out-dance both of you; I feel I could dance all night.'

Grimpil could see no real alternative except for conceding. Although they had left Woodhouse's as a group of three, it was painfully apparent to him that he was now the third person.

As they sauntered back along the streets arm in arm, Grimpil struggled to keep pace. They passed amidst the tide of humanity that flowed down to the waterfront without resistance, while he was constantly finding his path blocked.

Whenever he fell behind, he would cast a glance behind him. The same three characters were still there, even though they were now retracing their steps. Pellerin would turn around to bid him not to tarry, which only annoyed him further, so that by the time they reached Rua das Hortas he was most irritated.

'Do try and keep up,' said Flávia, when they stopped at the corner of Rua São João.

'Perhaps it would be better for you to go on without me,' said Grimpil bitterly.

'Don't be ridiculous,' she insisted.

'I think I shall return to Woodhouse's,' he replied.

'It would be most ungentlemanly of you to abandon me so.'

'I'm sure your escort will accompany you wherever you wish to go.'

'And you would leave me to my fate in the hands of an unscrupulous Frenchman' she said, in a slightly mocking tone.

'I must protest,' rejoined the Frenchman in question, 'to the epithet – "unscrupulous." '

'Very well, a highly principled Gallic gentleman.'

'I fear that it is I who is now being mocked, mademoiselle.'

'Enough of this talk. Let us go! Grimpil, will you come?' she added in a more imperious tone.

'Pray forgive me my boorish ways, but I shall leave you here. I believe my evening has ended.'

'As you wish,' she said, rather archly, and set off on Pellerin's arm. In a matter of seconds, the two figures were absorbed into the mass of people who swirled around the Largo das Carvalhas.

-66-

Antonio Silveira and his officers were sitting down to lunch on the tenth day of their confrontation with the French across the bridge of Amarante. They had inflicted considerable losses in killed or wounded on the enemy, who had only managed to advance as far as the mouth of the bridge. As soon as they had taken the monastery of São Gonçalo, they set up an artillery piece in the Prior's cell, which had a window that commanded a view of the bridge. However a well-aimed shot from Captain Vieira destroyed it after it had only been able to fire two rounds with little effect. There was still hope that reinforcements would come. There was much talk of Beresford leading an army north from Lisbon. If it strengthened the will to resist, all well and good, but Silveira had little faith in anything but their own resolve.

When a concerted artillery barrage erupted from all points along the French positions, he knew that a major offensive had begun. Given the uncertainty concerning the viability of Bouchard's plan, the French generals had decided to make one last concentrated effort at conquering the passage over the Tâmega. They had reunited 10,000 men on the right bank and strengthened their artillery to a total of fourteen cannon plus two mortars. At 2 o'clock on April the 29th the attack was launched over three fronts, one on the bridge itself and the other two on the fords above and below it.

By the time Silveira had arrived alongside the battery commanded by Captain Vieira, fourteen sappers were already halfway across the bridge, hacking at the palisade with their axes. The defence of the bridge was in the hands of the 12th Regiment, but their number had been increased by militiamen drawn from the surrounding areas. Although they had never received any military training, they were skilled in the handling of arms. All of them were skilled huntsmen, used to tracking down and killing wild boars and wolves when these threatened their crops or livestock.

When they had a target in their sights they were not used to missing their objective. Before long, the fourteen sappers were all dead, bar one, who took refuge in one of the semi-circular bays in the parapet. There he stayed for the rest of the day while the battle raged around him, and only in the dead of night did he risk emerging from the sheltering parapet to return to his comrades, like Lazarus raised from the dead.

The first wave was repulsed, but the enemy was determined to break the resistance of the defenders. They united a column in closed rank to advance on the bridge, but, as the *Terreiro de São Gonçalo* was in the sights of the Portuguese artillery, the infantry was decimated even before they could come under the musket fire that covered the bridge. Not once, but three times, did their commanders attempt the same manoeuvre, until the small square was filled with piles of slaughtered soldiery. Those who had been killed outright were the lucky ones. Those who had only been injured or maimed lay groaning in pain, without hope of being rescued or treated, their life force leaking away from their bleeding wounds, running in red rivulets to join the waters of the Tâmega, where the corpses of the comrades killed on the fords floated face down.

The battle raged all afternoon until early evening, when the sun began to sink behind the crest of the high ground of Fregim and Burgada. The heavy artillery persisted in the barrage from the convent grounds on the right bank, while on the left the smaller, but more accurate, cannons of the Portuguese continued their deadly work, filling the air with smoke until neither could see the other across the narrow stretch of water that separated the two sides. Vieira, on the rocky platform that overlooked the bridge, did not have the benefit of any sheltering parapet. Stepping forward to be better able to judge the effect of his rounds, he took an enemy bullet and fell dead at Silveira's feet.

-67-

Grimpil turned into a narrow lane which would take him onto Rua Dom Manuel.

Unlike the other streets, it was almost completely deserted, and Grimpil set off at a determined pace up the steep incline. It was then that he heard the echoing footfall of several feet and, turning round, saw the now familiar sight of the three figures. A sudden truth dawned on him. The three men had not been following them: they had been following him – and now he was alone. He quickened his pace, but from behind came the sound of hobnail boots striking cobbled steps. His pursuers were now running. He, too, began to run, fearful for the first time. The road climbed steeply, and, if at first he managed to gain some ground, he soon began to tire, his breath rasping in his lungs. His pace began to slacken, his legs feeling weak at the unaccustomed effort. He dared not turn around but could sense the presence of his hunters closing in on him. The sound of iron striking stone echoed ever louder in his head as the counterpoint to the pounding of blood in his ears. He could almost feel the hot breath of his pursuers, panting on his neck. If only he could reach the avenue ahead before they caught up with him, he might yet save himself. But the remaining distance seemed unconquerable. It was at that moment that he saw a familiar figure alongside him, holding open a carriage door, as the horses strained up the hill.

'I say, old boy, hop aboard,' invited Rodrigo with a smile. 'It's a bit late in the day for athletics.'

Grimpil gratefully received the helping hand and jumped aboard the slow-moving carriage. Falling in the seat beside Rodrigo he looked back to see the three men doubled over, recovering their breath. It was in that moment that Grimpil decided he would seek Flower's permission to go with him to Guimarães.

-68-

At nightfall on 2 May, Bouchard put his plan into action. The battalion of grenadiers that would rush the bridge immediately after the explosion were installed in the monastery where they would remain out of sight until the appropriate moment. Meanwhile, Bouchard prepared his sappers. The five of them were wrapped in sackcloth to be as undetectable as possible, and the barrels had also been treated in the same way so as not to make any noise as they rolled over the flagstones. Under the cover of the shadow of the parapet, each man would have to crawl forward gently, pushing the barrel ahead of him with his head as far as the palisade. Once the barrel was in place, he would have to turn round and make his way back in the same way before the next man could do the same. The army really does march on its stomach, thought Bouchard with irony.

When the sound of firing could be heard from the weir upstream, Bouchard knew that the diversionary manoeuvre had begun and sent the first man forward. Painstakingly, the sapper slowly nudged his barrel across the bridge, turned around and returned with equal stealth. The second and third followed suit. As the night wore on, a mist began to rise over the river. Bouchard was pleased. It was as if the weather was favourable to the successful realisation of their scheme. The last sapper set off at a snail's pace towards the enemy trenches. Perhaps being the last, or possibly because he believed himself to be hidden by the mist, having put his barrel in place, he stood up to run back. He was immediately spotted by the guard on the far side, who opened fire on him, wounding him in the leg. Bouchard, therefore, considered it best to wait before laying the fuse, lest any more activity arose the suspicions of the Portuguese. In fact, the wall they had started to build at the far end also favoured Bouchard's plan, for it reduced the guard's line of sight across the bridge. Only at two in the morning did he consider it safe to send in the last sapper with the fuse.

With all the preparations made, the assault force took their positions. At their head were the sappers, some with buckets of water to douse the Portuguese mines if they attempted to blow the last arc of the bridge, the rest with axes to break down any remaining barricades that might prevent the movement of troops to the far side of the river. Behind them, the first wave of troops would be the four regiments of grenadiers, waiting to emerge from the safe confines of the monastery. Finally the batteries in the monastery were also in readiness to open fire on the left bank as soon as the action started. The river was wrapped in a heavy mist when without warning, at four in the morning, an enormous explosion rocked the silence of the night.

-69-

The *Comendador* stroked his whiskers with the back of his hand. It was a gesture which Rodrigo recognised as meaning perplexity. He leaned back in his chair and eyed the immobile features of Xavier, who stood behind his master. Rodrigo also knew how to interpret his posture. By frustrating the execution of the *Comendador's* direct orders, he had simultaneously put the servant's loyalty and competence in check. The *Comendador* was seeking an explanation that would satisfy Xavier. He was too valuable to have his service compromised by a grudge against his nephew.

'Xavier,' said the *Comendador*, 'I thank for your display of loyalty, which I have never had occasion to doubt. You must understand that I felt it necessary to give fresh instructions to my nephew, while I was unable to inform you of the fact, for which I apologise. You have once again carried out your mission with great credit. However, as my nephew must travel again on the morrow, I would be grateful if you would take care of the horses.' He directed his words towards his nephew in a chiding tone. 'You must find yourself a decent groom; your horses really are in a deplorable state.' And then, in warmer tones, 'Make sure that you give them a good brushing, will you, Xavier?' the *Comendador* said with a smile. 'There is no one who knows how to treat an animal as well as you.'

Once Xavier had left them alone, the *Comendador* continued.

'Don't worry about him; he is excessively zealous in carrying out my orders. I must confess I had not expected such perspicacity from you; it was indeed a master stroke. So the pup went running directly to the Mason's lodge to seek shelter. No better place for the whelp's cry to reach the ears of his progenitor!'

'If indeed he is still in Portugal, as you suspect.'

'No, I don't suspect it: I feel it my bones, like I feel the onset of rain. He's here somewhere.'

'Whether you are right, Uncle, I cannot say. However, I can affirm that the pup now believes me to be his salvation. He will confide to me all we shall need to know to take this matter to a favourable conclusion.'

'So Flower is taking him to Guimarães! It could not be better. It is a place where our friends are legion and sufficiently small to be able to monitor his every move. Excellent strategy. I can but repeat my admiration for the subtlety and efficiency of your scheme. I have to admit you oblige me to reassess my opinion of your qualities. If you continue like this, I see a fine career in politics ahead of you.'

Rodrigo smiled with satisfaction at the *Comendador's* praise.

'I shall draft a directive at once for you to deliver to the Count in person. Then we shall dine, for tomorrow you shall have to set out for Guimarães to ensure our preparations are made in good order and in good time.'

Rodrigo was pleased to see the animation in his uncle's being, something he had not witnessed for many a long year.

-70-

After a fortnight of virtually uninterrupted artillery barrages, the hills were strangely silent. The defenders of the bridge had retreated south, leaving the French to lick their wounds. Loison was calculating the number of effectives he could count on when word arrived from Oporto via Argenton. Wellesley had disembarked in Lisbon and was leading a combined Luso-British army of 250,000 men north. It would be the kind of military parade he had always dreamed of, making steady progress at a leisurely pace, no skirmishes, no ambushes, friendly natives.

Since his great map had been stolen the year before, along with other personal possessions, he had to make do with a much smaller, less complete map. Studying it, he calculated Wellesley's movements. From Lisbon to Oporto was about a week's march; the line of march would take him first to Leiria, then Coimbra. And from there on? Would Wellesley continue due north to Aveiro and Oporto? If he did, how would he cross the Douro? Or would he turn inland at Coimbra to follow the route through Viseu to Lamego?

It was the same route he had taken himself the year before: first northward with pomp and ceremony, then southward in an undignified retreat, pursued by a furious enemy that seemed to spring from the very rocks themselves, appearing from every quadrant without warning, fighting with anything that came to hand, from ancient muskets to agricultural implements.

If Wellesley were to follow this route, the march would take slightly longer, but by crossing the River Douro at Peso e Régua, as he had done, and continuing north to Mesao Fio and Amarante, Wellesley could outflank Soult in Oporto, cutting off his retreat. It was the kind of strategic sweep which would certainly appeal to Wellesley. It meant that in about two weeks Loison could find himself facing old Nosey across the Tamega with a force over five times superior to his own and counting on the full cooperation of the peasantry. The bridge would become redundant. They could cross wherever they wished and leave him completely cut off and surrounded. From Amarante they could either make for Oporto, if Soult decided to stand fast, or to Braga to cut off his retreat. There could be no doubt about it: without reinforcements from Lapisse to the east or Victor from the south, the game was up.

'Bring me a pen and paper' he called.

While he was waiting, he toyed nervously with the signet ring on his finger. At the Convention of Sintra, the British had shown great magnanimity towards the French army. In a strange way it served as a kind of dress rehearsal for the evacuation from Corunna. There was nothing which demonstrated British genius better than a really good evacuation, thought Loison, as he felt his own bowels move. Having shat away his remaining scruples, he dipped the quill in the little silver ink pot and began to write.

> *Henri Louis Loison, Comte de Abbeville and Commander of the Second Infantry division, salutes His Excellency Artur Wellesleigh, Commander-in-the-field of the Combined Luso-British Army, and offers his respectful greetings.*

He reread the lines and was satisfied that they conveyed the appropriate tone. Now for a little flattery, he thought.

> *Knowing that Your Excellency is moved by the highest principles of honour, I feel sure that you will receive my emissary with due regard to his person and his mission.*

So far so good. Now for the difficult part: how was he going to insinuate what he intended without stating it baldly?

> *Your many virtues are well known to those who have had the pleasure of serving under you as well as against you. Apart from your clemency in victory, your concern to spare the life of your men is a laudable example from which other less naturally gifted generals may learn an invaluable lesson. It is in this spirit that I approach you and trust that, in the interest of not*

committing the imprudence of unnecessarily wasting the lives of the men under our command, it may be possible to devise an alternative to armed confrontation.

Certain of your adherence to the highest military ethics, I am at your entire disposition to advance these matters towards a mutually beneficial conclusion, and with this objective in mind I hope that you will avail of my emissary to serve as a means of conveying a favourable reply.

Permit me to express the highest regard in which I hold Your Excellency.

Your humble servant,

Henri Louis Loison, Comte de Abbeville.

He sealed it with his signet ring and immediately set about writing to Colonels Lafitte and Donadieu. Once he had finished, the three letters went into a pouch, which he instructed Oboussier to deliver to Major Argenton.

-71-

One hot July afternoon, Severino was pulling clouds of blue smoke from his clay churchwarden's pipe, sitting, as was his habit, in the shade of the spreading branches of the chestnut trees that grow close to the Chapel of São Miguel do Castelo. Behind him rose the imposing stone walls of Guimarães Castle, its central keep rising above the towers and crenellations of its walls. It was here that eight centuries previously the Countess Mumadona had erected defensive works to protect the fledgling township against the incursions of the 'barbarians'. It had been turned into the stronghold of Afonso Henriques when he dreamed of founding an independent kingdom. It had been the refuge of him and his followers when his cousin laid siege in his attempt to frustrate his plans for independence from León. Three centuries later, after it had been strengthened by Dom Dinis and adopted an appearance similar to that which it bears today, it resisted the efforts of conquest by Henry Trastamara. At the time of the *Mestre de Avis*, it had been taken by subterfuge after open assault had failed.

Severino, however, knew none of this. Just about all he knew was encompassed by the barracks and parade ground of infantry regiment that was installed in the still-serviceable part of the ruined Dukes' Palace. He derived a certain grim satisfaction in seeing the ruins of so grandiose a royal dwelling serving as shelter for the humble foot soldier. Moreover, it afforded him a vantage point from which he could observe all the movement that took place around him as far down the Rua do Poço as the Terreiro do Carmo.

He drew on his pipe, the smoke flavouring his lugubrious contemplations. Years of pipe smoking had enriched his bronchia with viscous phlegm. Years of passing time in idleness had perfected his ability to propel it with the accuracy of a trained archer in a well-defined arc into the confines of a spittoon. In the course of time he developed this prowess into a fine art, a rich vocabulary of expectorations that more eloquently expressed his sentiments than the finest rhetoric.

On that day, as he sat watching the movement in the street, he noticed something that made his chest contract. At the bottom of the Terreiro do Carmo, two men he had never seen before were standing in front of the Doctor's house. Not only were they visitors, but also outsiders. He screwed up his eyes, the better to survey them. One of them was tall and thin with sandy-coloured hair. The other was dressed in a most untypical fashion that immediately suggested foreign tailoring. Severino withdrew the stem of his pipe from between his compressed lips and, from the depths of his larynx, brought forth a gob of phlegm which he projected with force against the dusty earth at his feet – 'Foreigners!'

-72-

No sooner had they settled in the Doctor's house than Flower had pressed him to participate in what he described as a 'reconnaissance mission', in which he was ascribed the role of 'cartographer'. Unpacking a sketchbook for the purpose, they had set off up the hill to the top of the street, where it joined Rua da Infesta and opened into an irregular square before the parade ground in front of the ruined Ducal Palace.

Flower consulted his compass. 'Northwest aspect. It will only catch the setting sun at an acute angle, and we would certainly need permission to get within a reasonable distance. Not very promising! Let's work our way around to the east,' he said, going left in the direction of the gateway. 'Look, this path will take us up to the castle.' And he turned right, striding purposefully up the incline leading towards a simple chapel. 'Make a note, good fellow: "Romanesque chapel – morning shot/southeast side, northeast face of Palace – very degraded." We can continue up here.' And he continued his march, scarcely leaving Grimpil time to write.

They drew closer to the castle. It was clearly a defensive structure without any concessions to anything other than its military function. Flower suddenly stopped and pulled a lens from his waistcoat pocket, peering at the scene through this monocle.

'Yes, that's fine. About this time of day, approximately 6.30/7.00 should do fine. Make a note, dear boy.'

They passed close by one of the faces where the severity of the garrison gave way to signs of living quarters, with large windows opening high in the stone face of the walls. Flower was already descending the other side. 'Do keep up, Grimpil!' he shouted good-naturedly, their path leading them away from the Castle walls and towards some terraced fields.

'Midday shot!' he called out.

'I'll make a note,' Grimpil called back, before being instructed to do so.

'We shall have to cut across these fields to get to the east side,' said Flower, pressing forward, Grimpil following dutifully behind. The passage was more problematic than originally foreseen, since the fields backed on to some vegetable gardens belonging to the houses that fringed the road on the other side. An elderly native was surprised in the task of tending his beans by the unexpected appearance of two English gentlemen, who emerged between the vines from the direction of the castle. Raising their hats with a cheery '*Boa tarde*,' Flower and Grimpil passed the peasant, who stood looking suspiciously as he watched them pass. Once again on the road, they found the view was to a large degree impeded by these houses.

'Morning shot, partly obscured by houses. I'll make a note of it,' said Grimpil, anticipating Flower's directions.

'Yes,' he replied pensively. 'Shame that.' Indeed, behind the roofs of the humble abodes rose a most impressive facade, containing a double gothic window and some extremely tall, cylindrical chimneys, which projected high into the evening sky above the level of the missing second floor of the building.

'Do come on, Grimpil! I still have to talk with the Doctor about setting up a darkened room, and there is still much to see!'

So they set off at a brisk pace down the hill, passing by the rear of the barracks and finally emerging onto Rua Santa Maria, well below the Terreiro do Carmo, so that they had to return uphill as far as the Viela do Campo Santo, which marked the corner on which the Doctor's house stood.

-73-

Severino's thoughts were filled with the apparition of the foreigners who had erupted so unexpectedly in the midst of his bean plants. It was an augury, and not a good one. No good had ever come from outside, and now the two foreign devils were not just in town: they were loose in his own back yard. It was an invasion! He would have to be very watchful.

He was old by his own admission, many more years than he could count. Even though he was no longer active, it was hard to separate himself from the regiment that had been his family for all his adult life. He had begun when he was little more than a lad, shouldering a weapon for the first time and marching with the rest of the column out of Guimarães, to confront O Maneta. All the citizenry had taken part: priests and friars, apprentices and masters, squires and noblemen, stable lads and pot boys, even a few soldiers and some officers, their hats decked with a branch of the miraculous olive tree, singing hymns mixed with patriotic songs, along the seven leagues to Amarante.

From there they descended on Mesão Frio and had surprised the French in the process of looting Régua, chasing them as far as Lamego. It was his first taste of action. That night they had surprised four French soldiers in a vineyard, dividing their spoils. There was an exchange of musket fire, but, even wounded, the officer in charge would have escaped the ambush if Severino had not chased him with a flail and brought him to the ground with a cracked skull. By the time of the second invasion, he was a trained soldier, and, by the third, a veteran. That was a good war. It felt good to kill the invader, who had desecrated churches, looted them for their gold and silver, burnt farms and shot peasants. Before long the novelty wore off, and by the end of the campaign he could no longer recall the number of victims he had accounted for; the important thing was that he had survived, when he had seen so many others die.

-74-

As his carriage bumped over the poorly metalled highway to Mesão Frio, Loison cursed the state of Portuguese roads. At best they were narrow and full of bends; it was difficult to proceed a few yards in a straight line. This time he travelled simply. He had dispensed with the twenty-four piece marching band and the gold-embroidered silken drapes for his carriage, but retained the mounted escort for fear of ambush.

This terrain was totally inadequate for an army. The men had to march virtually in single file, stretching out in a thin line for miles on end. It was full of hills and dales, thickly clad with forests and dense undergrowth, where ruthless militias could ambush at will, seizing wagon trains, killing escorts, plundering arms, provisions, even despatches. The last time his own baggage had been stolen. In an attack on his rear guard while it was crossing the Douro, he had lost three of his finest dress uniforms, garnished with gold braid, and his best Morocco leather wallet. Now he understood why Napoleon always kept his left hand inside his jacket. Not even a French general could travel in safety without fear of being robbed.

To add insult to injury, they had captured his two boys, who, by all accounts, had been taken into the custody of monks of Vila Real. He remembered his own days in the seminary and cursed again. He hated this river valley where the heat of the summer lay trapped between the mountain ranges to the north and to the south. He hated the blanketing silence that suffocated any sound. Worse still, he cursed the fate, which, scarcely a year later, led him to face the same enemy in the same place. The only difference now was that he was approaching from the opposite direction. Soult had ordered him to press home the advantage gained in Amarante and advance as far as Régua on the banks of the Douro; the same place where he had crossed the river a year before, that he had abandoned hurriedly, with attacks from partisans on all sides, the town in flames but the sack still incomplete.

How was it possible for the Portuguese to mount a systematic armed resistance after having dismantled the national army a year ago? Beresford and Forjaz might be capable administrators, but where had the men come from? Not to mention the arms and munitions. And in the field? Was Beresford a desk general or could he command in the field? In either case he had superiority in numbers and the full support of the local population. Loison was on his own and his lines overextended. Nor had he received any response to his overtures to Wellesley. It meant one of two things: either Wellesley was so confidant of success that he was not interested in compromise, or that the despatches or the reply had fallen into the wrong hands. In either case, the prospects were not good. At the first sign of concentrated resistance he would fall back on Amarante. He had no intention of being a dead hero, and even less a live prisoner.

The Doctor had been waiting for them on their return, and Flower was immediately deep in an exposition of his requirements. Already fatigued by the briskness of their campaign, Grimpil left the men to their business and retired to the calm of the garden to make the following entry into his diary before dinner.

Friday, July 7th, 1854

By early afternoon our carriage passed by a large extent of marshland, and, crossing over a humpback bridge, proceeded along the right-hand margin of a small river. The presence of women washing clothes on its banks suggested that we were drawing closer to the city and, leaning from the window, I glimpsed the battlements of a castle silhouetted against the horizon. So great was my curiosity to see more, that when our carriage was drawn to a halt by the congestion of vehicles and people that thronged the narrow street leading up to the town, I could brook no further delay and alighted at once, suggesting to Mr Flower that we continue unencumbered on foot.

Almost immediately we came upon a most magnificent specimen of market cross, crowned by a stone canopy. The natives of that place passed by completely indifferent to this monument and, as I stood to appreciate it better, I was delivered of such blows and insults from the passers-by that I had to abandon the prospect. The street was narrow and gloomy, overhung by the wooden balconies that hemmed in from both sides. Further ahead we came to the cause of such congestion, there being an especially large cart stopped in the street, from which a group of men were heaving and straining to manoeuvre an enormous barrel on to a ramp made from two timbers in order to deliver it to a nearby tavern. The already narrow street was further constricted by this impediment, allowing but a trickle of persons to pass. The manufacture of these vehicles appears to have remained unchanged since time immemorial, and, much as I would have wished to study its design in more detail, the press of the populace who made their way with difficulty to and from the town, amidst much swearing and cursing on the part of both the users of the thoroughfare as well as those responsible for the congestion, obliged me to continue.

Having passed this obstacle and climbed the rest of the street, we arrived at a wide open space, which the inhabitants of the town call the 'Toural', for once having been the marketplace for trading cattle. Apart from the row of commercial establishments of obviously more recent construction that stood facing us, the appearance of the town was very much more antique, from the imposing tower, to a most elegant three tiered fountain, which occupied the far end. Almost directly ahead of us stood one of the principal gates to the town within the walls. Having passed through this narrow constriction, another square opened up, surrounded by some stately mansions but many more humble abodes, with wooden verandas crammed in to every available space. On a hilltop overlooking the town could be seen the outline of the castle, while the ruins of the Duke's Palace peered above the rooftops. The town went about its business in the narrow streets, oblivious to their presence.

Having confirmed that the large building to the right was the Misericordia, Flower enquired after Dr Joaquim and we were ushered into a cool courtyard where a fountain played. He arrived within a few moments, lamenting the delay in attending us and, unable at that moment to leave the hospital, summoned a young fellow to escort us to his house, which lay in the upper part of town. We were most handsomely received by Dona Eugenia, the Doctor's wife, the very soul of hospitality, in a house of generous proportions, which none the less retained the intimacy of a family abode. Our rooms, at the rear of the house, overlooked a large garden with an orchard of fruit trees, although I would have preferred a view on to the street, for the Duke's Palace and the castle were tantalisingly close.

-76-

Upstream from the city of Oporto, where the river described a wide arc and the slow-moving waters formed sandbanks, Colonel Waters, at the head of an advance party, was exploring the reeds in the hope of still finding some hidden craft that the French had not already withdrawn to the far side of the river. In an explosion that had awoken the sleeping city, Soult had ordered the pontoon bridge destroyed, cutting the only link between the two banks of the river. The ferry at Avintes had been sunk, although it had been recovered and hurried repairs were being made. Even so, it would be hours, if not days, before it would be serviceable again. It was still in the early hours of the morning, but without some form of transport the army would be unable to proceed further, allowing the enemy to regroup. Waters had set out on his mission to find anything that floated with Wellesley's final words ringing in his ears: 'Either we can get across the water or we can return to Lisbon.'

As he skirted the strand, scanning the undergrowth on the far side of the river for any hidden craft, his soldiers escorted a rather frightened-looking individual into the presence of the Colonel.

'Have pity on me, Your Excellency,' said the man in Portuguese. 'I am but a humble barber going about my business.'

Civilian life continued despite the presence of two foreign armies.

Waters, who was fluent in Portuguese, quickly interpolated in the man's own language.

'And what would a barber be doing here at this hour of the morning – shaving bulrushes?'

'Oh no, Your Excellency! As there are no French patrols here, I slipped across the river to attend to a client last night, but by the time I had finished it was too late to return. I have but returned at this very moment.'

'Returned? Returned how?'

'In my little skiff,' he said, pointing in the direction of the river bank.

'You say there are no French patrols?'

'No, sir. The French believe an attack will come from the sea, so all their forces are concentrated to the west of the city. They believe that the Douro cannot be crossed so there are no pickets to the east.'

'And do you know of any boats on the other side of the river?'

'Indeed, I do. There are three barges waiting for the taking, just o'er yonder.'

'Will you take me to them?'

'It shall be a great honour, my lord.'

At this moment, the Prior of Amarante, who was attached to the party as a liaison officer, spoke.

'If you intend to bring back the three barges, you need a third person. Allow me to accompany you gentleman on this mission.'

'No, Prior, I should not want you to risk your life; I shall take one of my men.'

'Colonel, let me remind you that my town and my church have been destroyed by the invader. This was my battle, long before it was yours. I would not allow you to risk the life of one of your men in my place. Come, gentleman, let us go; time is too precious for us to tarry here.'

And, so saying, he led the group of three men to where the barber had moored his skiff.

Before leaving, Waters turned to his adjutant and ordered him to inform Wellesley that within half an hour he would have the transport he had requested and to ask him to be good enough to send up a division of men to cross the Douro.

-77-

The billowing clouds of blue smoke that Severino was drawing from his churchwarden's pipe matched the fervour of his thoughts. What were the foreign devils up to and was the Doctor aware of their plans? What infernal scheme were they perpetrating? Sooner than he expected he was confronted with the resolution to the mystery. He was presented by a singular sight which surpassed anything he had ever seen before. Of the three figures who laboured up the Rua do Poço, he recognised Dr Joaquim from the Hospital of the Misericordia. The others were the two foreigners. They had come equipped with the strangest of artillery pieces, which they proceeded to assemble in the centre of the square: a three-legged contraption on which they placed a stout box with a very squat brass muzzle. Should he run and sound the alarm, rouse the captain of the guard, warn the commander of the castle? Severino narrowed his eyes against such an improbable cannon and felt the vapours in his chest condensing in suspicion.

The youngest of the men was talking loudly, and by the tones of his voice, he was able to identify him as a compatriot of MacDonnel. The second of the strangers, a sleek individual with sandy-coloured hair, paid scant heed but was giving instructions to the Doctor, who was carrying what appeared to be two medical bags. He spoke in Portuguese, but the unmistakable accent also betrayed him as a son of Albion.

The performance now became more intriguing, for the sandy-haired one pulled a cloak about his head and, covering the machine as well as himself, embraced it, carefully adjusting the brass protuberances. He emerged from the cover to take a large envelope from one of the bags and disappeared once again under the cloak. Finally he stood upright and drew his watch from his pocket. The device was now armed and ready to fire, but there was no flash of fire. Seconds passed in the profoundest silence until the sandy-haired one withdrew his hand from the mechanism and returned the watch to his pocket.

'Very Good, Doctor. Now, if you don't mind...'

The Doctor opened the second of the bags, which he passed to the sandy-haired one, once more under the protection of the cloak. What strange art were they practising that could not be done in the open light of day? Why such furtive secrecy amidst such a public deed? Severino was no policeman, but the whole scene reeked of an act of theft. But why would the Doctor openly collaborate in thievery and what could they be stealing?

The party shouldered the equipment to move on.

'But tell me: why do you prefer calotype over daguerreotype, when the latter has already been perfected?'

'A good question, Doctor! Daguerreotype is an excellent medium, producing extremely sharp images, especially in the studio. However, I have chosen to work in the field, building a visual memory of the places around me. It would be problematic on these journeys to carry the glass plates on which the daguerreotype is registered, not to mention hazardous, for the risk of breakage is always present, and, being the only record, once the glass is broken, the image is lost.'

Grimpil continued to grumble at the volume of the equipment.

'Watercolour may not be as accurate in rendering a faithful impression of the subject, but it has to be admitted that the process is much more pleasurable. This appears to be more of a military manoeuvre than an artistic exercise.'

Flower ignored him, attentive to the angle and intensity of the light. 'In addition, as I am not a professional photographer, the storage of the glass plates would also present a fresh problem.'

'Interesting,' relied the Doctor, keen to know more. 'So once the latent image has been retained on light-sensitive paper, how is it reproduced?'

Severino felt the decisive moment had arrived. He narrowed his throat and tilted his head back like a blackbird about to break into song. From the depths of his being shot forth a gobbet of mucous, which shone like green-veined amber as it arched through the morning sunlight. 'Foreigners' he muttered under his breath.

-78-

Wellesley had brought his troops up behind the cover of the Serra do Pilar, hidden from the sight of the French, who had withdrawn into the city, confident that the Douro would protect them from any attack from the south. Climbing up to the convent, he made a reconnaissance of the situation. Upstream, to the left, the river wound sharply around the Serra in a meander that was not visible from the city. On the other side, he could see a building under construction.

The seminary stood on an elevation, commanding its surroundings, and was large enough to house two divisions. It was surrounded by a high wall that extended as far as the river, the only breach in it being a large iron gate facing the Valongo road. Would he be able to invest the position without the French noticing? It was a calculated risk, but one which would pay high dividends if successful. If Murray could get his cavalry across further upstream, they could cut off Soult's retreat in the direction of Amarante, forcing him to go north to Braga.

Wellesley immediately gave orders to position the artillery around the convent, which afforded them a commanding field of fire both in the direction of the city as well as the seminary compound. All that lacked now was the transport. As if to answer his thoughts, at that very moment Water's adjutant arrived, bearing the good news about the three barges, and he immediately gave orders for Paget to take the Buffs across the water. Everything was going most favourably, but the next hour would be critical. He calculated that he could only get about 300 men across in an hour, men who could hold the farmhouse unless the French counterattacked in force. Time was of the essence. The important thing was that the French remained unaware of their presence for long enough to strengthen their position. The men on the other side were still few and very vulnerable. On the terrace in front of the convent, eighteen artillery pieces were being set up, the men toiling up the slope, carrying kegs of powder and shot. He would need to prepare a diversionary manoeuvre, a frontal attack on Oporto from the Gaia side of the river to draw attention away from the vulnerable bridgehead.

He turned to his aide de camp.

'Send for Sherbrooke, would you?'

Apart from Flower and himself, the Doctor and his wife had invited a number of close friends including Canon António de Freitas Costa of the Colegiada de Nossa Senhora da Oliveira. Dressed in a black soutain, the scarlet cummerbund that circled the area where his waist had once been only called greater attention to his impressive girth. Mr Flower was seated between the hostess and Constância, the wife of Senhor Jaime Gominhães, who appeared to be frequent visitors to the house. Grimpil sat next to his friend, with Senhor Gominhães's daughter, Isaura, to his right. Between Isaura and her father lay an as yet unoccupied place. Against the black garments of the men, the pastel hues of the ladies' dresses appeared like tropical blooms. The elegance of the matriarchs was nothing compared to the radiant beauty of Isaura, who sat in the midst like a diamond set in stones of lesser quality. She wore the latest fashion, which set off the whiteness of her unflawed complexion and the elegance of her neck. She wore her hair piled upon her head and held in place by tortoiseshell combs. For most of the time she kept her eyes downcast and hardly spoke, beyond answering questions that were directly addressed to her. Grimpil had never been so perturbed by a female presence, nor could he remain indifferent to her beauty. Much as he tried hard to find ingratiating words, he seemed unable to engage her attention.

At this stage, a young gentleman entered the dining room, apologising for his late arrival. The Doctor rose to greet him, saying, 'Senhor Martins Sarmento. I'm so pleased you could tear yourself away from your books long enough to grace our table with your erudition.'

Turning to his two foreign guests, he said, 'Allow me to present Martins Sarmento, who, despite having read law at Coimbra, even graduating early, has never practised advocacy. Instead he spends his time lost in reading the most obscure texts, which may mean that you may find some common ground of interest with Mr Grimpil here.'

'What is your field of interest then, Mr Grimpil? Do you share an interest in our past?'

'I am interested in the career of Wellington.'

'In that case, you may yet find those about with a direct experience of the subject. Will you be staying here long? If so, I could make enquiries.'

'Thank you, but our stay will not exceed a few days at the most.' He turned to Flower for confirmation.

'No, indeed I must be back in Oporto by Tuesday at the latest.'

Martins now turned his attention to Isaura. A whispered gallantry brought a smile to her lips.

'Mr Sarmento, leave the ladies alone for a second. Mr Flower has been explaining the prodigies of the photographic process. Did you know it was capable of producing a virtually unlimited number of copies of the same image?'

'Then it is to art what the printing press was to literature.'

'I believe so. While many are impressed by the ease and accuracy by which photography may record images, it is their successive reproduction which will ultimately weigh in its favour. It suggests applications far beyond its potential as an artistic medium.'

'In what sense do you mean?'

'Well, as you may know, much of the pioneering work upon which Fox Talbot based his developments was originally undertaken by Wedgwood, who was interested in its potential for applying designs to ceramic. Take that dish for example,' he said, pointing to a large serving dish hung on the wall. 'At the moment, to arrive at this design it requires the intervention of various artists to reproduce it manually. Using the photographic process, it would be possible to reproduce it exactly, quickly, and mechanically.'

Grimpil sprang to the defence of the endangered artist. 'Surely it is the hand of the artist that imparts the grace that makes us consider it beautiful. Whereas the same potter may repeat the same decoration on all his pieces, no two will ever be exactly the same; each one is unique, and occasionally, by a fortuitous conjunction of circumstances everything is exactly as it should be, producing a flawless example, not just perfect, but perfectly inspired and inspiring, the thought made flesh, the spirit incarnate.'

'I should not have thought my wife's faience could provoke such philosophy.'

'Philosophy? Sounds more like theology to me!' replied the Canon.

-80-

Scarcely had the third boat touched shore when the furious beating of drums sounded the alarm, announcing the fact that the French were aware of the British presence at the seminary. Wellesley surveyed the scene. Two craft were on the return journey to their side of the river; the other was beached in a sheltered position. At least there were no troops exposed on the water.

A column of soldiers was marching towards the seminary compound. He could see Paget on the roof, taking stock of the number and disposition of the attackers. Indeed, their numbers were such that it seemed likely they would eventually overrun the defenders, if support did not come from some quarter. The enemy was taking up position in front of the compound, sweeping the defenders with an intense volley of musket fire. Wellesley scanned the seminary. Hill was now on the rooftop, coordinating the action despite the evident danger. He had taken command from Paget, who had been knocked down by an enemy bullet only seconds previously.

Wellesley turned to the nearest artillery officer. 'I think now would be a good time to open fire.'

From the top of the Serra do Pilar, the British cannons roared into action, the heavy artillery pounding into the defences of the Oporto river front, while those pointing towards the seminary fired the new canisters developed by Colonel Shrapnel. They had timed fuses, which exploded the projectiles in a hail of metal fragments above the heads of the enemy. The devil's own invention, Wellesley thought, as he observed the scene through his eyeglass. He was not entirely in harmony with modern warfare, but had to admit its efficacy. He much preferred to see the enemy fall than his own men.

The concerted volley on the area before the seminary had sewn havoc in the French ranks, relieving some of the pressure from the attack. The attackers were now crouched in the cover of the wall, yet a hail of musket fire continued to pour into the seminary enclosure from the gateway. If they were to bring up light artillery, the farmhouse, bridgehead and position on the river bank would quickly become untenable. There was still no sign of Murray and his dragoons. If the situation did not improve, he would have to go and take command of the engagement himself. The action could not result in failure.

-81-

Gominhães was eager to know what news Flower might have of the wine trade. 'How is it, sir? Will we have another year of Comet wine?'

Flower smiled. 'Even if it is true that the vintage of 1823, the year of the Great Comet, was exceptional, in my point of view this is mere coincidence. Although the study of weather patterns is called meteorology, I believe that alterations in climate due to the passage of a comet is not proven; even less is there sufficient evidence to make an equation between comets and vintages. This year the comet was visible in March and April and has since disappeared from sight; if it has had any influence then I am not aware of it.'

It was Gominhães's turn to smile. 'Spoken like a true scientist, but a very poor salesman. If you were a better businessman, you would tell me that it will be a year to remember for the rest of eternity and advise me to buy immediately, ahead of the market, for later it will be both scarce and expensive.'

'I would not deceive you in such a fashion.'

'Admirable quality, admirable.'

'The passage of comets has always portended great events,' observed Grimpil. 'It is enough to look at the Bayeux Tapestry to realise how a comet announced the Norman invasion.'

'Quite so, and here the comet of 1807 heralded the French invasion, a comet not with one but two tails,' nodded the Canon in agreement.

> From his huge vapouring train perhaps to shake
> Reviving moisture on the numerous orbs,
> Thro' which his long ellipsis winds; perhaps
> To lend new fuel to declining suns,
> To light up worlds, and feed th' ethereal fire,

declaimed Grimpil in a stentorian voice, adding by way of explanation, '*The Seasons* by James Thomson, an English poet from the last century.'

'Not just public calamities but plagues as well,' added the Canon. 'Our wine merchant denies a connection between comets and vintage wines. What do you say, Doctor? Is there a connection between comets and contagion? Look you, following the passage of the comet comes an outbreak of cholera, fit to reach epidemic proportions.'

'That I can dismiss on the authority of John Snow, whose study of cholera outbreaks in London proves conclusively its connection with contaminated water supplies,' asserted Dr Joaquim with firmness. 'Indeed it is a matter that the town council should address with serious concern. The state of affairs in the poorer neighbourhoods of the city is a matter of public scandal.'

'I can assure you that the town council has already given serious consideration to the problem of the public water system on several occasions,' said Gominhães, defending the record of the public authority. 'But how are we to finance a new water supply network when we scarcely have resources to maintain the old system.'

The Canon sensed a certain political confrontation and turned the conversation aside, asking Flower why he had brought his photography to Guimarães.

'Up till now, I have limited myself to my immediate surroundings. However, I wished to undertake a special study of a subject of symbolic importance. Here are the monuments to the foundation of the kingdom and the nation. But how long will they survive?'

'Good question,' interjected the Canon. 'Not long, if the *Associação Patriotica Vimaranense* had prevailed! You remember, don't you, Gominhães?'

'Remember? Remember what?'

'The *Associação Patriótica Vimaranense*, back in '35; they wanted to demolish the castle and use the stone to pave the streets. The archdeacon was a member and voted against the proposal, as, I am pleased to say, did the majority.'

'Is that a fact, Canon?' commented Flower, nodding his head. 'Then it only proves my point.'

'Just look at the ruined Palace of the Dukes,' the Canon added.

'And perhaps it would still be standing today if the friars had not carried off the stones to build their monastery,' observed Gominhães.

'Times were other; they did not give the same symbolic value to these buildings as some of us do today,' Sarmento replied and, directing himself to Flower, asked, 'So what else would you photograph apart from the castle?'

'Let me suggest the Church of Our Lady of Oliveira,' ventured the Canon. 'Indeed, if you gentlemen were to visit, I should have great pleasure in conducting you personally, and showing you Our Lady's Treasures.'

-82-

Tholozé bounded up the steps of the grandiose staircase of the Palácio das Carrancas, two and three at a time. He brushed asides the guards outside the ballroom and, entering, found the Commander-in-Chief poring over a map with some other generals.

Soult turned towards him, and with his laconic smile and ironic tone of voice, asked him if he was the bearer of good tidings.

'I'm afraid, Monsieur Marechal,' Tholozé replied, 'that news comes from our picket in Campanhã that Wellesley has an army at Freixo and already holds the right bank.'

The generals looked at each other in consternation.

'How the devil did they manage to get across the Douro?' asked Soult.

Tholozé shrugged his shoulders. How no longer mattered. What mattered now was how many!

'By all accounts, the advance party runs to several hundred already. The latest reports talk of a company of horse, but our column was repelled with loss of life.'

The generals eyed each other in silence.

'What reinforcements are available to strengthen our western flank?'

'Only the detachments defending Ribeira.'

'Then send them at once.'

'But that will weaken the defences at the river gate,' objected Donadieu.

'That is not the main focus of the enemy attack. We must delay their advance as much as we can, if we are to save ourselves.'

He did not relish the prospect of being trapped inside the city, without hope of receiving support by land or even less by sea. Before Tholozé's arrival they had been studying the possibility of a British landing and had decided that Mindelo, off Vila do

Conde, only a league and a half north of the city, was the most probable location for putting a force ashore. It would cut off the possibility of retreating to Spain by the shortest route, due north.

'And what of the British squadron?'

'There have been no sightings, Your Excellency.'

'Thank God for small mercies. Well, gentleman, I consider our position no longer tenable. I believe we should evacuate the city forthwith.'

'Quite so. We must abandon it and make for Braga,' urged Lafitte. 'It would—'

'No!' interrupted Soult. Apart from being unnerved by the memory of the silent city, there were good strategic reasons against the choice.

'We know that exit via Chaves is out of the question, and Monção is far from guaranteed. In any case, going north we would have to cross the Ave, Cavado and Lima, not to mention the Minho. Furthermore, Braga is exactly the direction that the enemy would expect us to take. Gentlemen, we must derive what profit we can from our victory at Amarante and rejoin Loison at once. We can reunite our forces and follow the king's highway to Vila Real and Bragança. Silveira's forces are defeated and dispersed. Even if Beresford can bring an army up in time to face us, they will be tired after the long march. I would much rather face a tired Beresford than a Wellesley fresh from victory.'

Saturday, July 8*th*, 1854

Our party followed the Rua dos Fornos into the lower town, where it opened into an irregular square, flanked by balconies, at the centre of which was a decayed chapel dedicated to St James. The atmosphere of the square was dilapidated; however, proceeding under the arcade of massive stone arches that support the council chambers, we arrived at the Praça Maior, dominated by the Church of St Mary of the Olive Tree.

A public fountain stood at the foot of the bell tower, a fine piece of work with three water-spouts and two sets of coats of arms sculpted in stone – those of the town and those of the king. Immediately in front of the church is a venerable market cross, housed within a stone canopy, which they say is dedicated to Santa Maria da Victoria, and beside it the miraculous olive tree. The spectacle pleased Flower enormously, who was anxious to set about the business of taking his calotypes, but we felt obliged out of respect to the Prior to first make the promised visit to see the treasures of Oliveira.

The Sacristan led us through the church into the sacristy, which smelt faintly of incense and strongly of wax. He lamented that much of what had belonged to the Chapter had been confiscated by order of Junot in 1808. Over 2,540 ounces of religious artefacts in gold and silver had been surrendered, although his predecessors had taken measures to preserve some of the major pieces.

He produced a copious bunch of keys with which he unlocked one of the darkened wood cabinets. Residing in the shadows was the most ornately decorated processional cross. The rich detail of its decoration was nothing in comparison to the elaborately constructed base on which it stood, rising in architectonic splendour like a gothic cathedral, tier upon tier of richly ornamented buttresses, niches, corbels and crockets, replete with tiny statuettes and bas-relief scenes.

Flower was most appreciative, and the cleric explained that it had been left to the Chapter House by one of its most famous canons, Gonçalo Anes, although he never lived to see it finished. He was also the donor of a monstrance which exceeded all expectation. It was a piece of the most exquisite craftsmanship. The ghostly luminescence of the white silver cross was totally eclipsed by the golden majesty of the monstrance, crafted with great delicacy. An ethereal radiance highlighted its finely balanced proportions. Slim buttresses and elegant tracery framed and surmounted the glazed void where the host would be displayed. Two angel musicians silently serenaded the ensemble with bass and descant shawms, while little bells hung from below the platform on which they stood, pregnant with unsounded tintinnabulations.

We were lost in contemplation of this piece until the Sacristan presented a statue of the Virgin and Child – Our Lady of Oliveria – bequeathed by another canon, the famous jurist João das Regras, whose coat of arms it bore on the base. What the other pieces could boast in terms of delicacy, the statue possessed in terms of solidity. Standing on a buttressed plinth of tracery windows, the Virgin Mary seemed to turn towards the viewer, the folds of her gown frozen in an uncompleted movement that had already lasted centuries. The immobile expression of their enamelled gaze stared out from the darkness as if surprised by the intrusion to their intimacy.

-84-

Tibães was exhausted. The floor of the workshop was littered with scrap metal. He really should collect it up for reworking, but he was too tired. The furnace was virtually extinct, and he surveyed the piles of shiny coins lying in profusion in the shallow wooden casks which he had used to assemble them. It was the last batch. Thanks to Pellerin's system, he had fulfilled the task required of him. He should go and inform Taboreau that the last batch of coins was ready for collection. He banged on the door for the guard outside to open up, but nothing happened. He sat on a stool and rested his forehead against the cold stone. He was too old for this kind of forced labour.

He awoke with a start. Such was his weariness that he had fallen asleep with his head resting against the wall. Everything was the same. How much time had passed? No guard had come. He banged on the door again. Beyond the room he could hear only silence. He clambered onto the workbench to peer over the dividing wall. He could see nothing. With difficulty he finally managed to haul himself over and drop to the other side. There was no sign of any living soul whatsoever. He saw the ring of keys hanging on a nail in the wall, and he tried them until he found the right one to unlock the workshop. With the caution of a man used to safeguarding precious objects, he relocked the door and slipped the key into his pocket. The courtyard was equally deserted: no sound of marching boots or shouted orders. He walked the abandoned corridor that led to Taboreau's office. It, too, was empty. The papers were still piled on the desk and the door to the antechamber was ajar, but it was empty.

What could have happened? he wondered. He wandered the empty hall until he reached the stables. There was not a single horse; everything was totally abandoned. He would have to return home on foot. Then he spied something with wheels leaning up against a wall. It was a pushcart, so he took it with him back to the workshop. He remembered seeing a trunk in Taboreau's office, so he stopped on the way past and checked. Indeed there was a sturdy leather-covered chest, studded with brass nails. He put the trunk on the cart and proceeded to the workshop, where he began to fill it with as many Napoleons as he thought he could manage. He manoeuvred the handcart to leave. It was extremely heavy. He was not certain if he would be able to reach home with such a load. He transferred some of the coins to his pockets, although the difference was negligible.

Suddenly he felt extremely anxious to get as far away as possible. Taking a deep breath, he heaved against the inertia of the cart and it moved forwards, its axle complaining bitterly against the weight. Having cleared the main gates, he had barely arrived at the avenue leading to Cedofeita when he stopped in his tracks. It was a party of soldiers, marching briskly towards the city; except that their uniforms were not blue but red, and the tongue they spoke was not French but English.

Tibães stopped in his tracks. 'The devil incarnate! How had the British taken back Oporto? How could they have expelled the French?' He had heard no sounds of fighting. The French had simply vanished from the map. The soldiers had noticed him. They stopped their singing and slowed their pace.

'*Viva Inglaterra!*' he shouted, with as much emotion as he could summon. '*Viva Portugal! Morte aos Franceses! Viva a Aliança!*'

One of their number approached him. It was a fellow countryman wearing the new infantry man's uniform.

'What do you have there?' he asked, pointing to the trunk. From his accent it was possible to tell he was from the capital.

'These are the tools of my trade.'

'And what trade is that?'

'I'm a gunsmith, I've just come from the arsenal. We've been working day and night to make a stock of old muskets serviceable again. With a bit of luck we'll be getting some new weapons soon, but until then we have to make do with what we have.' His unshaven face, covered with grime and sweat, only served to confirm the veracity of his story.

'Well, we've got the French on the run now,' boasted the soldier.

'Great,' replied Tibães. 'So now make sure they don't stop till they reach Paris.'

The soldier looked at his load. 'Here, that looks pretty heavy for an old man.' He called over two of his fellows, who took the handles of the cart between them.

'Gorblimey!' they complained, 'What you got in 'ere? It's as 'eavy as lead.'

'Oh yes, that's right, lead. I'm taking it home so I can carry on making shot.'

The soldiers accepted the extra burden with the good spirit that only soldiers in adversity can find and renewed their song, Tibães walking in their midst.

> When will you pay me?
> said the Bells of Old Bailey,

sang the tenor voices, and the baritones replied:

> When I grow rich,
> said the Bells of Shoreditch.
>
> When will that be,
> said the Bells of Stepney.
>
> When I grow old,
> said the Great bell of Bow.

-85-

Flower expressed his thanks for the Sacristan's courtesy in receiving them, but stressed that his time was limited and he must soon return to Oporto. Grimpil, however, knew that Flower was more anxious to return to his calotypes than concerned with his business interests. As they walked back up the nave, the Sacristan was reflecting on the nature of treasure.

'Treasure cannot always be measured in earthly terms. Sometimes the symbolic value of an object far outstrips its material value. I can remember my father telling me of the sermon by the orator, Friar António Pacheco, in which he displayed the captured uniform of General Loison. During the oration, he struck the uniform with such vehemence that you would have thought its owner was still wearing it, a dramatic effect which greatly pleased his audience. However, I digress; the sacred relics of the Holy Cross, for example, would be no more than worthless fragments of wood if they were not transformed into priceless vestiges of Christ's presence on Earth.' As he spoke, he unwrapped an object, proudly presenting a sacred vessel. 'This is the Chalice of São Torcato.'

'St Torcato,' repeated Grimpil. 'I don't believe I know any saint by that name.'

'St Torcato, sacred martyr, had the distinction of being both the Bishop of Oporto and the Archbishop of Braga; the only person to do so. At the time of the Muslim invasions, he went forth to parley with the Arab chieftain Muça, whose army was close to Guimarães. Torcato hoped to assuage the fury of the infidel, but the unpitying Moor was not to be deterred from his savage intent and instead slaughtered him where he stood, along with his twenty followers.'

'A tragic fate,' lamented Grimpil.

'But the ways of the Lord are unknowable, for the death of those who repeat the supreme sacrifice of Our Saviour may yet bestow the grace of God on others,' said the Sacristan reverently. 'Nevertheless, the centuries passed and God maintained the body of the saint hidden from the eyes of the unbelievers, until the Christian kingdom of Portugal was established. Then one day God decided to reveal the presence of the fallen prelate; he made tongues of flame appear, just as he had done to Moses. When the local populace went to examine the phenomenon, they found a heap of stones from which the sweetest scent arose, but, as no one dared to approach the site, they sent for the monks of the nearby monastery. When the monks removed the stones, they uncovered the body of the holy bishop, incorrupt and still wearing his mitre. They carried his body to the monastery and placed it in a stone tomb, and from the place where they removed him, sprang forth a miraculous spring of healing waters.'

While the Sacristan spoke, Grimpil's eyes examined the cup. It rested on a wide splayed foot, worked in the shape of a six-pointed star, a small enamelled saint resting in each intersection. The cup itself was smaller and completely plain, contrasting with the heavily decorated knop, divided into bulbous segments, giving every indication of not being coeval.

'So when you say the chalice of St Torcato, you mean of the monastery of St Torcato?'

'No! Of the saint himself.'

'But did you not say he lived in the seventh century?'

'Quite so,' affirmed the Sacristan.

'But this chalice is of much later date, It would be an anachronism to consider it coeval with St Torcato.'

The Sacristan withdrew the sacred cup from the disbelieving eyes of the foreigner. Typical, he thought to himself. They always think they know better than us.

-86-

The unit that had been detached to turn back the spearhead of the British advance was now fighting a rear guard action, as the city emptied of French troops, fleeing from the city in a disorganised retreat along the road past the seminary towards Valongo.
Pellerin had managed to keep his unit intact, but, as they marched past the French position, he saw a gun crew in difficulties. The officer had been killed outright, but the men were struggling to keep their piece in action if they were not to be overrun by the redcoats. British soldiers seemed to be emerging from all quarters.

'Goddammit!', complained the artillery man as he wrestled with the jammed breach. 'They call us frogs, but it seems to be them that are the amphibians. How the hell did they get across the Douro? By swimming?'

Although not in the artillery, Pellerin recognised the nature of the problem as once. Seizing an iron bar from a shattered railing, he used it as a lever to free the cannon from where it had become lodged against the mounting.

'That should do the trick. Reload and try again,' he said.

The gun crew went into operation. From behind, his own men were calling to him. 'Let 'em get on with the job. Let's get going while we still can.'

'Go on ahead; I'll follow right behind,' he replied.

If there was one thing he could not tolerate, it was a malfunctioning machine. His engineering spirit would not let him pass by without intervening.

The cannon fired its shot and immediately became stuck again.

The gunner swore vehemently. 'It's no good! It's fucked to buggery!'

'Nonsense! Now I see what the problem is.' insisted Pellerin. It was a case of excessive wear; the mounting had worn down until the recoil finally sheared off the top bracket completely.

Under normal circumstances it would be a routine operation to make a substitute, but in the field, under fire, it would not be an easy matter to resolve. Perhaps the gunner was right after all. Looking up to speak to the artillerymen from where he knelt beside the crippled weapon, he realised he and his companions had disappeared from sight. Before Pellerin could fully take stock of the situation, the air erupted in an explosion as a shell burst over the emplacement. The words 'fucked to buggery' crossed his mind as the sky drained of colour and he fell face down in the dirt.

–87–

Tuesday, 11ᵗʰ July, 1854

I felt somewhat relieved by the departure of Flower. I did not feel entirely comfortable in his company nor, it seemed, did he in mine. On the other hand, he obtained permission from Woodhouse for Alfredo to accompany me, as I had now grown used to his company. Therefore we took the first opportunity to make the journey to the village of São Torcato with its shrine to the saint of the same name. Leaving the town by the north, we put the castle behind us and descended into the valley of the River Selho.

We eventually came to a small settlement on one bank of the river where the road crossed over a humpback bridge. A sudden drop in the river bed was fully taken advantage of by a pair of corn mills, which, even at that relatively advanced period of the summer, still had head of water sufficient to work two pairs of stones. Captivated by its picturesque qualities, that I bade the carriage stop so that I might paint the scene, believing that here I would be able to work peacefully, without interruption, while Alfredo prepared a modest lunch.

Needless to say, I attracted a small group of wide-eyed children, who accompanied my every movement, until, summoned by their mothers, they disappeared into the humble dwellings that cluttered the banks of the stream. The presence of the adults was more difficult to bear. They informed me that close to this village lay the place where Dom Afonso Henriques gave battle with his mother – a place evocatively called Campo de Ataca. To my eyes, the terrain did not seem propitious for such an engagement, but, according to popular memory, so fierce was the combat that the river ran red with the blood of fallen warriors. I replied that I wished to conclude my painting of the bridge, which they insisted was Roman. I tried to disabuse them of this notion by explaining the difference between Roman and Romanesque; however, the more I sought to elucidate, the more obstinate they became in their insistence. In the face of such stubbornness, I eventually desisted, for what I most desired to do was paint and not debate architectural styles. In the end, however, I had to leave my painting unfinished and continue our journey, lest we should find ourselves without time to complete our trip.

-88-

There is nothing to compare with the feelings of a soldier after a victory. Prior to a battle, there is a certain state of anxiety that can not be found in any other experience. But when the battle is over and crowned with victory, he finds himself with a feeling of elation not easily defined. When the victory has been obtained over an enemy of slightly superior numbers from a well-defended position without significant loss of life, then the jubilation of victory is elevated onto an even higher plane. When this jubilation is shared by a grateful populace, singing the praises of their liberators and strewing flowers in their path, then a soldier may sense something akin to absolute bliss!

Wellesley was unquestionably the hero of the hour, having attained his second victory over the French; this time, a clear unequivocal triumph. Installed with his officers in the dining room in the Palácio das Carrancas, the shades of foreign occupation were banished. Theirs was a self-righteous enjoyment of someone enjoying the pleasure of one's own house after expelling a troublesome tenant. The tenant in question had not only provided vacant possession, but also a banquet waiting to be served. There is nothing so gratifying as a good dinner when most wanted, especially when it is provided at the cost of a defeated enemy. So they sat down to enjoy the meal that had been prepared for Soult and his officers.

'Gentlemen, I propose a toast.'

The company fell silent.

'His majesty, King George.'

'God save the King.'

Cranfield rose.

'I wish to propose another.'

'Propose away,' chorused the assembled company.

'To the French!' A moment's silence filled the room. 'For not only have they served us a resounding victory, they have also served us a damn fine dinner!'

The room broke into hearty laughter.

'Here, here! May their generals always taste defeat, so that we may always taste their sauces.'

It was at that moment that Argenton first sensed what life would have in store for him as a defector. Although he had saved his own skin, it had been at the price of severing all ties of patriotism, language and fellowship with his comrades-in-arms. He would never be able to return to his native soil. He would probably never see his family again. Curse you, Loison, he thought bitterly, as he reached to fill his glass again.

'So how did we manage to dislodge the French?' enquired a Lieutenant who had been in the rear guard.

'When Soult discovered we had crossed the river at Campanhã, he reinforced his flank by taking the guard away from Ribeira. As soon as the towns' people saw the French leave, they rushed to bring boats to ferry us across the river and open the Watergate to us. We followed hot on their heels as they fled, and if Murray had arrived sooner with his dragoons we could have had them,' he related, crushing a walnut in a nutcracker to add emphasis to his words. 'As it was, we didn't so much as get a whiff of garlic to tell us they'd been here.'

'And what next?' enquired the Lieutenant.

'What next? Well, first some pudding and then some more wine, and finally a good night's sleep,' came the reply.

At high table, the Commander-in-Chief was also sampling the sweet taste of victory. Such a feat of arms could only be celebrated with the finest libation, and the Palácio dos Carrancas had been stocked with the best that the city had to offer.

'Damn fine drop of wine,' commented Wellesley. 'What name does it go by?'

'It is Port wine, sir.'

'It is produced here?'

'No, it is only shipped from here. It is produced up in the interior, along the upper Douro valley.'

'Well, I must take some back with me to offer the Duke of York. He is very appreciative of a good drop of wine.'

–89–

Tuesday, 11ᵗʰ July, 1854

The village of São Torcato is quite unexceptional, overlooked by the old monastery. There were still a number of tents remaining from the festival, and groups of pilgrims stood in groups or sat in the surrounding fields, resting after their exertions or recovering from the effects of a hearty meal. From a sense of obligation, I visited the incomplete sanctuary where the body of São Torcato lay in a glass-sided sarcophagus. The sight of the wizened mummy left me uncomfortable and with the sensation that the dead were better left buried than on display, however saintly their martyrdom.

When I stepped back out into the late afternoon sunlight, there was no sight of Alfredo. A band of musicians had struck up, a big bass drum hammered out the rhythm, while viola and mandolin played a crude melody. However, worse was still to come, for when the female vocalist joined the musical accompaniment, she sang in such a high-pitched, strident voice that my ears had never before been assaulted by such a caterwauling, which seemed to endlessly repeat the same refrain.

To escape the banshee wailing, I took refuge in a tent that served as a wine cellar. Sitting around a barrel, the men drew wine, which frothed purple in the plain white ceramic bowl that passed from hand to hand. They gestured to me to join them, extending the bowl in my direction, but I declined the offer. At once, one of the members of the group fetched a fresh bowl and filled it, taking my reticence as being based upon an aversion to sharing the same cup with them. Perhaps this hygienic measure was not ill founded; however, not wishing to give offence by refusing the proffered cup, I accepted the libation. It proved to be an exceptionally thin young wine, almost entirely lacking in body, slightly effervescent to the tongue, little more than pressed grape juice, and apparently quite devoid of graduation. I drained the bowl in order to fulfil my obligation and returned it, expecting thereby to end the matter. However, my dispatch was interpreted as a sign of appreciation, and the cup immediately refilled and proffered anew. With vigorous nodding of heads and approving words, my objections were in vain, and I found myself confronted with another bowl of this dubious distillation. I took a sip and tried to relieve myself of it, but this time it was they who adamantly refused to accept the bowl without my having imbibed it all. By this time, I was feeling slightly vexed by this social entanglement, and my ears ever more injured by the caterwauling of the singer, which had reached the limits of tolerance. I therefore finished the draught with haste, and bidding the gentleman farewell, removed myself from the vicinity for fear of further embarrassment.

-90-

Soult began to gather his scattered thoughts at the same time as he regrouped his scattered regiments. In a lightning change of fortunes, they had been transformed from victors into vanquished. Only a year previously he had been the hunter, pursuing Moore in full retreat to Corunna until he had expelled the enemy from Spanish territory. Now the boot was on the other foot; he was no longer the hunter but the hunted.

The situation was desperate by any measure. They needed to put as much distance between themselves and the enemy as fast as they could. Ahead of them lay the fertile plains of the Sousa valley and, beyond those, a mountain range. They would have to travel as best they could in the absence of any roads worthy of the name. To do so they would have to relieve themselves of all but the essentials. Even the artillery would have to be dispensed with. He ordered a huge pile to be made of the baggage train and all the remaining artillery dismounted from its carriages. To lighten their load and quicken their pace, everything would have to be destroyed. Speed alone would now save his army from complete humiliation.

Wellesley would certainly rest his troops a day or two, allowing them to savour the sweet flavour of victory in the embrace of a gratefully liberated city, a two-day head start in which to salvage what he could from the wreckage of their enterprise. Only one part of his plan remained valid: to reunite the army along its line of retreat through Amarante.

'Tholozé,' he called out. 'Urgent despatch for General Loison.' He wasn't sure if in the confusion of their hasty withdrawal he still had his writing implements. In their flight, the able-bodied had only had time to save their own skins, leaving the sick and wounded behind to their fate.

It was imperative to get to Vila Real ahead of Beresford. And then there was the question of Silveira. Where was he? He would have to leave these questions unanswered until the time arose to confront them. For the time being he needed to solve more immediate problems; finding his way to Penafiel. At that moment, Lefevre appeared before him.

'I believe I bring good tidings.'

'Then you are welcome; good news is what we most need.'

'My scouts have brought in an itinerant merchant from Navarra who knows the roads to Spain like the back of his hand.'

'Then he is the answer to our prayers. Bring him forth at once, so that we can put this army on the march as rapidly as possible.'

'It is inevitable that receiving guests in one's home is likely to disturb one's usual routine, even more so when they are foreigners, but I hardly expected to be awoken in the small hours of the morning with one's guest returning home shivering, clad in nothing but his small clothes. Such was his state of affliction that I felt it impolitic to enquire as to the motives, but attended to his physical needs, which passed for nothing but a slight fever, but also it would require a better man than me to resolve his spiritual crisis.'

When the Doctor had finished speaking, the *Comendador* drew a silver snuffbox from his pocket and, taking a pinch, extended it to the doctor, who refused.

'And pray tell me, for what reason does an English gentleman come home in the early hours of the morning in a state of complete undress? Surely not for the motive that I have in mind,' asked the *Comendador* raising the snuff to his nostrils.

'According to the explanation given to Mr Alfredo, he was set upon by bandits, who stripped him of his belongings and cast him into the river.'

'Hardly surprising. I could not recommend that rich foreigners parade about the countryside in the dead of night. What with the strife of recent years and the continuous upheavals which have troubled our nation, the countryside is full of malcontents and malefactors. So we must look for a well-dressed brigand, wearing Northampton boots;' said the *Comendador* with heavy irony, 'What exactly was stolen – apart from the man's apparel?'

'His watch, his pocket book, containing a sum of money in cash, a *laissez passer*, a banker's draft of considerable value.'

'Hmm... Well, he almost certainly will never see his watch or his money again, the *laissez passer* he shall have to replace – he shall have to make representations to the Consul in Oporto – and the banker's draft shall have to be cancelled, but that is his affair, although there is little prospect of the bandits being able to present it. As for his clothes... who knows? Let it be a lesson to him,' said the *Comendador* finally, with little sympathy. 'In any case, what brings him here? He is lodged with you?'

'Unfortunately, yes. He came with Mr Flower, wine merchant of Oporto, although he was not travelling on business, but for a private interest.'

'And what might that be?'

'He is making records with an instrument which he refers to as a camera obscura.'

'What might that be, pray tell me?'

'It is an exceedingly curious instrument, equipped with a lens, able to capture light and fix the image received on a sheet of paper impregnated with chemicals. It needs only to be exposed for a short time to produce a most faithful register of whatever subject is placed before it.'

'Really! And what purpose does it serve?'

'Whatever purpose one desires, I suppose.'

'And the other subject, our nocturnal wanderer?'

'A client of Flower's, who accepted the invitation of visiting our city.'

'Well, by all accounts he shall be staying here longer than he thought.

The prospect of having Horace extend his stay did not fill the doctor's heart with joy, but he suppressed his disquiet.

'And tell me, Doctor, does this fellow have any family or other relatives in the country?

'Not as far as I know; however I can ask him.'

'Yes, do that, Doctor,' said the *Comendador*, with his most disarming smile. 'After all, were it to be the case, I am sure they would wish to be informed of his circumstances, and, one would expect, come to his aid.'

'Quite so,' replied the Doctor, pleased at the prospect of a relative coming to succour his unwanted guest. 'I shall inform myself and let you know the outcome.'

'Excellent, my dear doctor, and my best wishes to your lady wife.'

-92-

Dona Eugenia looked into the pier glass and studied her reflection in the mirror. She had maintained the elegance of her figure despite the years of child bearing, and her face all the radiance with which it had shone at her coming out, when the hem of her gown swept the Lisbon ballrooms. The only changes she could perceive in relation to her immature features was the dignity conveyed by acquiring and maintaining her station in society, even if it was of a rather limited provincial nature. If she had remained in Lisbon, she would have made a very striking figure at court, perhaps even a lady-in-waiting to the Queen herself.

If she could not serve the monarch, however, she could at least serve God. Since God, being engaged in matters of more universal importance, was a busy man, it was her duty, as his collaborator here on Earth, to intervene in affairs of lesser importance. This distraction on the part of the Eternal Father was best manifested by the manner in which He neglected to guide the hearts of men towards their natural partners. As an archer, Cupid was notoriously inaccurate in his aim and it behoved to her to deflect the arrows of love so that they might fall where most socially convenient. If Dona Eugenia had known anything of agriculture, she would have known that there are many seeds, cultivated under ideal conditions and with the most assiduous care, which fail to flourish, while the same seed may fall accidentally on the most unpromising ground and thrive vigorously, producing flower and fruit not only without any attention but against the severest hardships.

Grimpil was a comet that had entered her skies unexpectedly, and whether he was a favourable or unfavourable omen she had not yet decided. His was, in any case, a phenomenon to be taken advantage of. Grimpil's reaction to Isaura had not gone unnoticed and, although Englishmen generally had strange habits, she would put the two young people together and await the consequences.

So, with this in mind, she sent an invitation to Dona Constância to take tea with her so that she might develop her plan further. Her husband's business was evidently highly profitable, and other people's generosity was the dynamo for her charitable deeds. After all, money was another of God's misdirected arrows. It inevitably went to those who least deserved it, or those who least knew how best to dispose of it. If she could encourage some of it to fall in the direction of the needy, the credit would go to her, while the debit would go elsewhere. Of course Dona Constância had other ideas about how to dispose of her husband's money. As they were both of humble, though respectable, backgrounds it was important that they now assume the social trappings by which the older families distinguished themselves. In this introduction to the ways and manners of the social elite, Dona Eugenia was an important ally, and any invitation to go to her house well received.

-93-

Tuesday, 11th July, 1854

As I descended the terraced olive groves, the cacophony gradually diminished, until, out of earshot I came upon a larger field open to the skies, which enabled me to appreciate the full glory of the heavens. I know not if it is a characteristic of these latitudes, or whether it was merely an exceptionally clear night, but the sky seemed to be invested with a plenitude of stars, such that I cannot recall having witnessed elsewhere. At the same time, the whole scene was bathed in moonlight with such clarity that one could easily have read by it. While I was savouring the immensity of the firmament, my attention was drawn ground ward by some movement, which I presumed to be emanate from some beast of the field, but as I began to focus on the source of this disturbance, so did my mind begin to discern the import of the scene I was witnessing.

In a corner of the field lay two human figures locked in an amorous embrace, who, being oblivious to my presence, began to increase both in intimacy and ardour. Incapable of movement for fear of being detected, I could not divert my gaze from the spectacle which presented itself before my very eyes. Indeed, the generous luminescence of the moon illuminated the participants in such way that no detail of their intercourse was veiled from my sight. I could not *help but observe the hirsute nature of the individual's back and nether regions, which rose and fell to a rhythm reminiscent of the beam of a pumping engine. Like an eager jockey riding a mount, his paramour folded her legs across his buttocks and dug in with her heels, as one would encourage a horse into a gallop. Her partner responded by quickening his pace so that the motion resembled more that of a factory machine plying its industrious toil. The labours of love began to demand an ever increasing effort from her, causing them to utter groans and moans, at times in unison and at others alternately. Indeed, I began to wonder at the passing of time, for I had no notion of how long I had been thus transfixed, without any sign of their passion being spent.*

It was then, however, that this concert reached its crescendo and, with a final chord, subsided into silence. I therefore took advantage of the moment to slip away, at once relieved, yet at the same time strangely congested. Proceeding downhill I became aware of the sound of a burbling brook and, reaching the lowest part of the decline, found myself at a low stone wall which dammed the stream, forming a shallow reservoir. The river bed was carpeted with watercress, which did not cease to dance in the current, and the banks were thick with reeds. I resolved, therefore, to lay my outer garments aside in order neither to soil nor moisten them, and waded in the intoxicating freshness of the cool water. So agreeable was the invigorating sensation, which drove the turpitude from my limbs that I divested myself completely and, reaching the deepest part of the reservoir, submerged totally into its refreshing embrace.

-94-

Captain Tholozé saluted General Loison and presented him with Soult's despatch. Loison took it and turned his back to the Captain. A few moments passed while both men waited.

'You may leave,' said Loison.

'I have instructions to take your reply back to the Duke of Dalmatia.'

Duke of Dalmatia! No one addressed Soult as Marshal any more. Why not go ahead and call him Prince of Lusitania – for what it was worth. Everywhere there were southerners in places of power. The men from the north had been passed over by the Corsican lieutenant.

'The Duke was very firm that his orders must be carried out. All of our lives depend on the army uniting under one command.'

Loison gave a sarcastic smile. Under his command, he thought to himself.

'Subject to operational considerations,' Loison added.

'Irrespective of any other consideration. The line of retreat passes through Amarante to Vila Real. Vila Real is our immediate objective. Once there, we will have the luxury of deciding how we head for Spain. The crossing of the Tâmega is crucial and must be maintained at all costs. In fact, there is no resistance nearby.'

'What do you know of the disposition of the enemy troops,' rejoined Loison angrily.

'Very little,' replied Tholozé, with more assurance than a captain usually speaks to a general, in full knowledge that he was transmitting his commanding officer's orders. 'Especially since you have not filed a despatch since you left for Mesão Frio.'

'I do not have reliable intelligence of the enemy's whereabouts,' replied Loison caustically, 'although it is widely rumoured that Beresford is in Lamego.'

'Rumoured,' echoed Tholozé, leaving the word hanging in the air.

'His objective is certainly Peso e Régua,' said Loison, stating the obvious. 'Do we have the forces to impede him?'

'That is not part of the plan. Soult wants us to advance as rapidly as possibly, so as to put the enemy behind us. He has ordered all the artillery and baggage destroyed, for the army to march as fast as possible. He counts on being in Vila Real within two days.'

Loison adopted a more haughty air. 'He appears to be drawing his strategy from Sir John Moore, with the exception that Moore kept his cannon to defend his rear guard, which saved the lives of his men, even if not his own.'

The irony of the situation was not lost on Tholozé.

'The enemy does not know where we are. They have gone galloping off in the direction of Braga. No one knows for sure where Beresford is. Our first priority now is to preserve the integrity of the army and reach Spain. That is why it is imperative that Amarante be held.'

An idea passed through Loison's mind in a flash. Of course, that was the plan. Soult had destroyed his artillery to move all the faster, while he still had his. He would be required to constitute the rear guard, to hold off Beresford with his cannons, while Soult hotfooted it out of the country!

'Remaining in Amarante is not a militarily viable option,' Loison stated baldly.

'What! Not militarily viable? Why on earth not?'

'We don't have the munitions to resist an attack.'

'The orders from your superior officer and Commander-in-Chief are explicit: hold the crossing.'

'Yes I know, at all costs. You've already told me.'

'Loison!' The tone of Tholozé was suddenly different. 'You know that Argenton has been arrested, don't you?'

'Argenton?' he replied vaguely.

'He was arrested in the possession of a communication from the commander of Anglo-Portuguese forces, addressed to certain French generals.'

'When the English cannot win by force of arms, they will always try and make their gold prevail.'

'That is not the version of events that Argenton is telling.'

'The man is obviously lying to try and save his own skin.'

'According to Argenton, the initiative came from our side,' said Tholozé pointedly.

Loison furrowed his brows. Surely Tholozé didn't have any evidence; he must be just fishing.

'A case such as this, which clearly smacks of treason, will certainly be referred to the Emperor,' he added.

Perhaps it would not be a bad idea for him to moderate his position a little.

'What does Soult want of me?' he asked.

'Hold the town for one more day. One more day will be enough to bring up the advance party.'

'One more day,' Loison repeated, calculating the odds of the enemy appearing within the next twenty-four hours. 'One day more?'

'Just one day. You promise?'

'Captain, I regard your last remark as impertinent. If I give my word, I do not expect you to question it.'

'You give me your word, then.'

'You may convey my reply to your master.'

-95-

Dona Constância sipped tea from Dona Eugenia's best porcelain, while the latter lay the groundwork for her scheme.

'You met Mr Grimpil, did you not? He's staying on some time longer, you know,' she said carefully, failing to mention the reasons for the extension to his sojourn. 'What do you make of him?'

Dona Constância cast her mind back to the dinner. She could distinctly remember the older of the two men, but, as for the younger, she couldn't remember him saying anything. 'A charming young man,' she replied.

'My opinion exactly.'

Dona Constância flattered herself at having correctly guessed the mind of her hostess, who continued, 'One thing I consider very important for young people is that they fill their time in profitable pursuits. Those who do not yet have the burdens of family and social position, as we do, must make full use of the unencumbered hours to develop themselves. Don't you agree?'

'Oh, absolutely.' Dona Constância was relieved to hear that she was excluded from this programme of self-improvement.

'In my opinion, there is no greater social grace than the ability to speak languages. With the gift of tongues we can commune with our fellow man across the barriers of nationality.' Mention of the gift of tongues brought Pentecostal scenes to the mind of Dona Constância, who had never quite decided if she should interpret the words of the liturgical passage which spoke of tongues of fire literally or figuratively. It always brought to mind the painting in the chapel of the Senate House.

'I agree completely; my Isaura speaks beautiful French.'

'And English?'

'English' echoed Dona Constância, faintly.

'Quite so. French may be the language of diplomacy, but English is the language of commerce. At the moment, your husband's business is doing well in the local market. But what of the future? If he wishes to acquire machinery, where would he go?'

There was a short pause for Constância to contemplate her husband setting off for distant parts to buy machines. She was about to ask why he needed machines while his workers worked so well, when Eugênia continued.

'England, of course. He would have to go to England. And to do good business there, he would have to speak English.'

'But I can't see my Jaime learning English,' Dona Constância admitted with great honesty.

'Not your husband: your daughter!'

'Isaura?'

'Of course.'

'But how is she to learn English?'

'Why, with Mr Grimpil, of course!'

'Oh, and is he willing?'

'Leave that to me.'

-96-

After Tholozé had left, Loison could reflect on the situation at leisure. So Soult had abandoned Oporto. The dream of princedom was ended. In fact, the campaign was over. Not only that, but Soult had destroyed his guns and baggage train, leaving himself virtually defenceless. He had reduced the army to an infantry column running for its life. At best they could flee through the mountains; at worst they would be surrounded and captured like a gang of outlaws on the run from justice.

Justice! British justice he was not afraid of, but Portuguese justice? If he fell into their hands there was little doubt in his mind what type of justice would be reserved for him. Humiliation would only be the beginning. The lynch mob would certainly follow, and no number of British officers would be able to restrain the fury of the people, no doubt fully shared by the Portuguese element in the allied army.

Meanwhile Argenton had been arrested with incriminating evidence of the treasonable communication with Wellesley. On the part of whom? Donadieu? Lafitte? Himself? In order to protect himself, Argenton would have denounced his own mother. Tholozé was right. The matter would certainly be referred to the Emperor. Who would Soult send? Who had Soult already sent? What he needed was to reframe events so as to appear in the right and Soult in the wrong. After all, he was in the field, fighting the Emperor's battles, while Soult had abandoned effective command of the campaign in favour of pursuing political ambitions. It was a good start. Then he had abandoned Oporto without a fight, fleeing like a common criminal before the parish bailiff. He had not only put the life of his men in jeopardy, but dishonoured the standards of the Imperial Army. The action was thoroughly un-Napoleonic!

What else had he learned from his conversation with Tholozé? Wellesley was heading for Braga. Braga lay two days march away.

Soult was heading for Penafiel. If he left immediately he could anticipate events, get to Braga ahead of Soult, make honourable terms for a French surrender, and leave Soult to be captured and brought in under enemy escort.

He would be transformed from traitor to saviour in one fell blow. It would be the greatest piece of generalship in his whole military career.

-97-

Grimpil had just finished drafting his letter to the Consul when Jorge informed him that the lady of the house wished to speak to him. In her presence Grimpil felt an intellectual torpor which invaded his mind, a pervading miasma as dense and impenetrable as any Thames fog.

'Do sit down, Mr Grimpil. I trust your indisposition has fully passed?' she asked.

'On the road to recovery, madam,' he replied, although it was not a topic of conversation he was keen to pursue. It had not been an easy matter to contrive a version of events to account for the loss of his possessions which would withstand the scrutiny of Her Majesty's representative. 'I'm afraid, however, it may be some time before I can replace my documents.'

'In that case, your stay with us may extend over a certain period of time?' she enquired artfully.'

'I believe that may be the case, madam.'

'And how had you planned to make use of your enforced leisure?'

'I confess that as yet I have not made any definite plans.'

'But you would certainly wish to spend the time in fruitful pursuits of an intellectually stimulating nature.'

'Quite so. I should like to spend some time with Mr Martins, who is most knowledgeable on an impressive range of subjects.'

Dona Eugenia was not interested in Mr Martins. Apart from being a young man of independent means, he also possessed an independent mind. Although attractive to ladies, she considered him totally unmarriageable, for his attention to books virtually excluded any other state than bachelorhood.

'I was thinking of something that might revert to the general good of the community.'

Grimpil had been speculating on the size of Senhor Martins's library and failed to accompany this twist in the conversation.

'I beg your pardon?'

'Mr Grimpil is a man of considerable gifts. Would you not want to share a few of them with us?'

Dona Eugenia observed the puzzled look on Grimpil's face. Obviously she was being too subtle in her approach; she would have to try something more direct.

'I have always considered the speaking of tongues to be the greatest of social arts. Would you not agree with me? It enables us to transpose the artificial barriers of nationality and communicate with our fellow man, irrespective of race.'

'Indeed, I would be in favour of the introduction of Latin as a universal tongue. It has been used by the Curia, and has proved most effective in maintaining the unity of the Catholic church, despite its widespread distribution over different territories and peoples. When we think that it has spread its faith to…'

This was not what Dona Eugenia had had in mind, and she sought to interrupt the progress of the heterodox idea before it went too far.

'But Latin is a dead language; a living language is much richer, as well as more useful.'

'Indeed, the ability to speak French is a necessary accomplishment of any educated person.'

'Mr Grimpil, I was referring to the English language.'

'Indeed, English literature contains many works of inestimable value. Who could fail to appreciate the verse of Spencer, the prose of…'

Grimpil was off at a tangent and Dona Eugenia needed to correct his course again.

'While there are those who teach the French language in our city, there is not, at the moment, anyone to teach English.'

'Teach English?' echoed Grimpil.

'Yes, quite so. How would you wish for those to learn without someone to teach them?'

'And there are those who wish to learn?'

'Only the other day I was speaking to the Dona Constância, and she mentioned that her husband's business necessitated contacts with England.'

'I should be more than pleased to draft a letter on Mr Gominhães's behalf, if it will facilitate matters.'

'Dona Constância spoke of the possibility of giving English lessons.'

'English lessons?'

'To her daughter.'

'To her daughter?'

'To her daughter, Isaura. She was present at the dinner last week, you remember.'

'Of course, most clearly.' This certainly put a different light on the matter. 'A most charming creature.'

'I would suggest an hour a day in the afternoon, between lunch and tea. It is a difficult time to fill during the summer months, as there is little that can be done at this time. They may come here and the lessons can take place in the library. She will be so pleased.'

'But what shall I teach her?'

'I don't know; that's up to you. After all, you're the teacher!'

-98-

Since the arrival of the foreign gentleman, Amélia had done even less than usual, spending every available moment doting on Alfredo, who only seemed too happy to receive her attention in such generous measure. When he was absent she did even less, claiming she was pining for him. This left Francisca with work redoubled, but she was quite relieved by Amélia's idleness, because left alone she could work twice as fast as when she had Amélia helping her. Amélia's contribution usually came in the form of criticism, when it did not come in the form of idle chatter.

The elder of the two gentlemen had departed on the Monday morning, leaving the younger to prolong his stay. She had served him at table and had immediately sensed a great solitude in him, an emptiness that before long she was filling with fond imaginings. She wondered what his life could be like in his homeland. It could not be that very different from this. As one travelled north, it grew colder; therefore, if he lived a sea journey north, then perhaps the sun never shone, for his skin was exceedingly pale. She imagined him alone in a big cold mansion, something like the *Paço dos Duques*, something that she could transform into a more homely environment.

Her notion of married life did not differ very much from that of service. She knew all the domestic arts, and they would need no other servants with her to manage the household. Even though she presumed he lived in a world beyond purely monetary problems, her skilful management of his affairs would result in economies that would revert in their favour. She would rise early to light the fires so that the house would be warm when he awoke. And when he descended, breakfast would be on the table. While he was at work she would clean and shop. Almost certainly the tradesmen took advantage of his distraction to overcharge him or to charge him top prices for low quality. With her in charge they would save a lot of money.

The only family she had ever known was that of the Doctor's household. Having entered at a tender age, she had no memory of another, and was, in fact, a foundling, being discovered as a baby on the steps of the Franciscan church. The Doctor had taken her in when she was five, and she had always demonstrated dexterity in her chores, as well as the will to do well, a quality that was difficult to find in the lower orders. Francisca knew that she had to rely on her own resources if she was to overcome her disadvantages in life, and would have to create her own opportunities for self-advancement. She also knew that the mistress of the house did not like her. She was too forthright. Amélia was lazy and disobedient, but knew exactly the flattering tones to use so as to achieve her ends, generally in passing the more irksome work in Francisca's direction. Occasionally she had had to appeal to the sense of justice of her master against the partiality of his wife, but she never begrudged the extra duties, because they widened her experience of life and provided further opportunities for excellence.

She couldn't understand why an intelligent man like the Doctor should marry such an ineffectual woman as Dona Eugenia. Her interventions in the household only served to disturb the good order that she and Jorge created. She had no useful occupation except for her charity work, which she did, as far as Francisca could tell, not from any love of her fellow being but in order to bask in the praise she received from her peers. Her position in society enabled her to interact with all the notables of the town, contacts she was now using to further a scheme to create an orphanage – a project that would enable her to extend the range of her incompetence further over the most innocent of victims, and provide her with a platform on which to perform greater works of charity. Despite this, the Doctor, in all his goodness, seemed oblivious to her failings and genuinely happy in her company.

–99–

'So, what was your impression?' asked Soult.

'He claims to have given his word,' Tholozé replied, 'but…'

'You didn't believe him.'

'No. I don't think we can trust him.'

'I suspect you are right. Well, thank you. In any case, you have done as much as anyone could have done. Better get some sleep. We may have to move on at short notice.'

To a certain extent, Soult was relieved to be back in the field. The months spent politicking in Oporto, cloistered in the *Palácio dos Carrancas*, had not been entirely to his taste. He now appreciated even more the outstanding qualities of the Emperor, able to handle the affairs of the Empire, edit legislation and take to the battlefield with equal ease, and with equal success in all of them.

So the question now was simple: would Loison keep his word, and what would he do if he didn't?

He turned to study the map. If he didn't stay in Amarante, there was only one direction for him to go: the road that led to Alto da Lixa. And what then? The road to Oporto via Penafiel. No, that didn't make sense. Lixa–Felgueiras, Felgueiras–Guimarães, Guimarães–Braga. Wellesley would soon be in Braga. The road led in both directions. One day would make the difference between success and failure.

Soult studied the map closer. He followed the line of the river Sousa up the valley as far as its headwaters. There was a short interval before descending on the River Vizela, a ridge separating the two valleys. More or less halfway between Felgueiras and Guimarães, there was a point with a bridge – Vila Fria. Above it, the Vizela divided into various tributaries. If one kept to the right bank of the Sousa until its source and then headed due north, one would inevitably fall directly onto Vila Fria, without needing to pass through Felgueiras itself.

A fine state of affairs, he thought to himself. I'm now planning a campaign against my own army, trying to outsmart the generals on whom I should be able to rely for support.

He remembered Napoleon's phrase 'You can always trust the enemy.' As if to justify the axiom, his Aide de Camp entered his quarters with a despatch.

'It's from General Loison.'

'Give the order to the advance party to prepare to move on at once,' he replied without even opening it.

-100-

Tuesday, July 25ᵗʰ 1854

I gained permission from the company commandant to sketch inside the ruined palace. I was particularly impressed by the ogee windows, which I had seen on our first day, and which gave every reason to presume that this had been the chapel of the palace. Inside the patio, a line of rebates clearly showed where the floor level had once been. Decades, nay centuries, of abandon and vandalism had reduced it to the sad state which I witnessed, although even in this state of dilapidation it had not lost its majesty.

Architectural drawing was not my forte, but I felt moved to make some simple line drawing to register the nobility of this ancient structure. It was not long after I had seated myself that I became aware of an old man, who was slowly but deliberately making his way towards me. I hoped that I was mistaken, for interruption is the enemy of artistic activity. Unfortunately, I was not wrong, since, as soon as he stood before me, he directed an accusing finger at me without any formalities and politeness and said, 'You were with the sandy-haired one, the owner of the strange contraption.' By his references, I perceived he was referring to Flower and his camera obscura. I had to admit the truth of the observation and found myself obliged to give a brief description of the principles of photography.

The old man seemed to be far from convinced and as soon as I had finished, immediately enquired why I didn't use it. I told him that the process was complicated and cumbersome and that I preferred the simplicity of direct transcription by hand.

The answer seemed to satisfy him better, and his tone towards me mellowed slightly, asking me if I was a compatriot of MacDonnel. The name signified nothing, but I presumed him to be British and therefore concurred. He made a gesture by closing his hand and jerking his thumb in the direction of his mouth. 'Conhaque,' he said. 'More conhaque,' and broke into a toothless cackle. I deduced from this pantomime that in his opinion the said MacDonnel was incommensurately fond of the bottle.

Having imparted this confidence, he felt sufficiently emboldened to reveal something of his own life, directing the thumb towards himself, saying, 'Soldier, man and boy; all my life, soldier.' So as to leave no doubt, he extended one arm in front of him and brought the other up to his shoulder in the classic pose of the rifleman. 'French,' he said, aiming down the imaginary barrel, and to replace the report from the muzzle he spat venomously on the ground. 'Liberals,' he spat again. 'Maria da Fonte.' A fresh expectoration. 'Patuleia,' and another gob of phlegm struck the ground. Indeed, the man was so well provisioned with mucous that with the same fire power in powder and bullets he would make an invincible enemy.

I could see that any chance of finishing the sketch was dwindling rapidly, so I began to assemble my materials. 'Aren't you going to finish your drawing?' he asked, and then *observed that I had not yet rendered the chimneys, so I set about concluding the sketch as rapidly as possible. The old man, however, was disappointed with the results. 'No good,' he said, shaking a bony finger. I hurried to put the sheet back into the portfolio and arose, saying that it was time for lunch, at which he jumped to attention. 'Severino Pimenta,' he said saluting stiffly. 'Sergeant of the 9th Infantry at your orders.' I could think of no other reply apart from, 'At ease, soldier.' He asked me if I was staying with Dr Joaquim, and, without waiting for confirmation, continued, 'Good man, very good man, a true gentleman, like yourself.' He would not leave my side, escorting me all way to the Doctor's house, saying, 'I'm only a simple soldier, but I've served crown and country without fail, man and boy, a lifetime of faithful devotion.' And then he began to recount all the various companies and regiments in which he had served.*

-101-

Soult faced the man who had deliberately disobeyed his express orders, who had placed all their lives at risk, by invalidating the plan for withdrawal, who had conducted treasonable communication with the enemy, and knew there was absolutely nothing he could do. The harm was done, and Loison was totally unrepentant. Fortune, however, had favoured his suit. He had been able to intercept Loison's division, and, now that the two corps were reunited, Loison could not openly defy him. The Emperor could choose to believe or not in what had taken place behind closed doors, but an open defiance of his commander-in-chief, in front of the assembled troops, not even someone as barefaced as Loison could disguise.

'General Loison, you may rest your men here for a while. As you still have your cannon intact, I would like your division to take up the rear guard. In the meantime, we shall move ahead as far as Guimarães, where we can prepare to spend the night and take stock of our situation.'

'In Guimarães we shall be but a few leagues from Braga.'

'Quite so; right under the lion's nose.'

'You don't think he will detect our presence?'

'I'm sure he will!'

'And how do you mean to fight him?'

'Who says I mean to fight him?'

'So you will surrender to Wellesley?'

'As I said, I shall review the situation in Guimarães.'

'Do you not think it better if I were to form the advance party? After all, my men have not marched as far as yours. You could give your men some extra rest while I go ahead at the front.'

Soult knew very well that Loison never offered to do anything unless it served his own interests.

'No, that won't be necessary. As Commander-in-Chief it is better that the men see me take the lead.'

'As you consider best,' said Loison, as he left Soult's presence.

Soult called General Lefevre to his side.

'Apart from Tholozé, you're the only one I can trust. I wish Loison to think that I am minded to surrender. At least that way he will follow us as far as Guimarães. Tomorrow I shall leave first, leading the vanguard. I will leave orders for Loison to destroy his train and baggage. We have some difficult terrain ahead of us and speed is of the essence. You will assume command of the rear guard. Loison will oversee the train. That way we can be reasonably sure that he won't act independently.'

'So you don't mean to surrender?'

'Of course not.'

'How, then, are we to leave the country?'

'By the same way we entered.'

'But we cannot retrace our steps. Braga is almost certainly in the hands of Wellesley.'

'That is true, but as yet we have not made contact with their scouts. They still don't know exactly where we are or what we intend to do.'

'What do we intend to do?'

'Give them the slip.'

'How?'

'From Guimarães we proceed northeast: São Torcato, Póvoa de Lanhoso and finally Salamonde. Once in the upper Cavado valley, it will be virtually impossible to impede our march. There is simply nowhere to mount an offensive against us. We will make a virtue of our own shortcomings and turn their advantage against them.'

Lefevre absorbed the implications of Soult's words. 'That means crossing the Serra de Cabreira as well as that of Barroso!'

'It's going to be a long walk back to Spain, but it's the only alternative left open to us.'

'What about Silveira?'

'Silveira is almost certainly in Vila Real, probably awaiting the arrival of Beresford to receive new orders. Beresford is probably in Régua, exchanging despatches with Wellesley to co-ordinate their movements. Wellesley won't move until he knows the operation is properly articulated. If we move and move quickly, we can still slip through their fingers.'

'It's going to be a close-run call.'

'If it fails, it will fail at the beginning. As time goes by, the more we distance ourselves from the enemy, the less chance they have of barring our passage.'

'Very well. Write the orders and I will transmit then to our friend tomorrow.'

Meanwhile, Loison returned to his men, who were taking their rest in the abandoned monastery of Pombeiro.

Colimaçon recognised the look of displeasure on his general's countenance.

'What are our orders, sir?'

'Our orders are to take up the rear.'

'Very well, sir! And what shall we do while we are waiting for the rest of the army to move out?' he asked, hoping that the General would allow them time to set up the cook pots.

Loison looked around at the blue tiled panels on the cloister walls and the coffered ceiling in chestnut wood. 'Burn it down!' he replied. 'Burn it to the ground!' And then added, as an afterthought, 'After Soult has left.'

-102-

'Very well; today we shall look at replying to a letter. Let us image that the letter was dated 13 July. How do we begin?'

Isaura began to write in her carefully measured script. 'Dear Sir.'

'Very good; now let us continue,' he said, beginning to dictate. 'In reply to your letter of the thirteenth instance... Thirteenth not thirtieth... Not third: thirteenth. Say "thirteenth".'

'Tur-tint.'

'Yes, well, let us continue.'

With her head bowed over her work, her brows furrowed in concentration, Horace's gaze fell upon that portion of her neck which lay exposed between the lace frill that finished the neck of her dress and where her hair was pulled upward and held in a pile by an ivory comb. The sunlight played on some downy wisps that grew on her nape, too short to be caught up by the coiffure. This small area of her person so absorbed his attention that it expanded to fill his consciousness. When she had finished writing, he would say, 'Very well, do me the honour of reading the text please,' and would sink once again into reverie as he listened to her sweet voice struggling with impure vowels, diphthongs and consonant clusters. He would not need to consult the watch he no longer possessed, for the passage of each hour was struck in the belfry of the Colegiada.

'I believe that is all we have time for today,' he said regretfully, as the final stroke died away. Isaura would meet the news with impassive indifference, simply collecting together her effects, and, clutching her gloves and the book, would rise gracefully from her seat, and, with a polite 'Good afternoon,' would leave the room.

With half an hour to recompose his thoughts, Grimpil would join his hostess and Isaura's mother for afternoon tea, which Eugênia served beautifully in the finest porcelain, accompanied by freshly baked cakes. While the two ladies made polite conversation,

Grimpil could hardly divert his gaze from Isaura, who sipped her tea in silence while apparently making a detailed study of the carpet. This did not pass unnoticed by the two matriarchs, although they saved any commentary on the subject for their own private tête-à-têtes.

'You know that it was the Portuguese who introduced afternoon tea into England.' Eugênia smiled her most beguiling smile. 'When your King Charles married our Catarina of Bragança, she took to England some of the courtly habits that the Portuguese had acquired through their contacts with the Far East.'

Grimpil suspected that this was the sum total of the woman's historical knowledge.

'Quite so,' he rejoined. 'Indeed, many people were so confused by the new habit that they did not know whether to drink the liquid or to eat the leaves.'

'*Que horror*! she said, offering Grimpil another slice of cake lest he fall into the same error as his ancestors. 'I made it myself,' she announced. Translated this meant that she had mercilessly cajoled the kitchen maid while she attempted to follow her instructions, occasionally having to intervene personally to show how it should be done. Like the wife of Louis XVI Dona Eugenia believed that all problems could be remedied by a slice of cake. When the maid came to remove the tea tray, Grimpil would rise to take his leave of the ladies. His relief at escaping the paralysis of his hostess was tinged by his disappointment at separating from Isaura, a melancholy at least tempered by the knowledge that tomorrow the ritual would be renewed.

-103-

Amélia sat staring moodily at Alfredo while he ate his breakfast. As the English gentleman had settled into a routine, he went about his daily business requiring progressively less assistance from Alfredo. Although she had hoped that this would leave him free to spend more time with her, Alfredo was spending ever more time out and about, especially in the inn run by the horse-trader universally known as 'O Gaita'. Amélia was certain that there must be some strumpet there, who was working her charms on Alfredo, for him to spend so much time there. When he returned, he only spoke about business; the only way to make money was by moving goods from where they were abundant and cheap to where they were scarce and expensive. He was very excited by the idea that a bad year for the farmer was a good year for the trader, for by reducing the quantity of wine on sale, the price would increase.

'Just imagine if I had a little money to invest. I could buy goods in Oporto, like *bacalhau* for example, which my cousin could take up the Douro and sell in Tràs-os-Montes, where he could buy olive oil to sell in Gaia.'

Amélia listened and liked less and less what she heard. She had hoped that by getting the mistress to agree to let her visit the annual fair in Campo da Feira, she would be able to promenade with Alfredo through the stalls as if they were a soon-to-be-married couple, buying essentials for their nuptial home. Alfredo had been laying plans to accompany the driver of the Póvoa de Lanhoso stagecoach, for which he had already obtained permission from his master to undertake.

'Póvoa, what is there in Póvoa that's worth going to see?'

'I won't know till I've been there,' he replied, giving her his winning smile. At the beginning he had found her attentions flattering, but now he was beginning to tire of her affections. Besides that, he was on the track of some interesting information and was not going to let a recalcitrant wench deter him from his objectives.

'I'll be back by the day after tomorrow.'

Amélia got up grumpily and pretended to be busy in the cupboards. She vented her spleen on the china, until the sound attracted an admonition from Jorge.

She closed the crockery cupboard door resignedly. 'If you're going on today's stage you'd better take something with you to eat.' She began to make busy with a large cloth, into which she put bread and cooked meat.

'Hurry up, then; it'll be leaving any minute.'

Swinging the pack over his shoulder, Alfredo gave a broad grin at Jorge and bade farewell.

-104-

Grimpil now realised that whenever he set foot outside the house he could expect Sergeant Pimenta to appear within seconds. They were descending the Rua dos Fornos together when they were confronted by a meagre-looking woman with a child hiding in her skirts. At first, Grimpil expected an outstretched hand, begging for charity, but the woman fixed him in the eye and then spat at his feet, before returning to her abode. He was perplexed and turned to Severino for an explanation. The latter shrugged his shoulders. 'Widow of the disgraced town assayer; can't be right in the head,' was all he said in reply.

'Disgraced how?'

'How? How should I know? I'm but a humble foot soldier, all my life, man and boy…'

'Yes, I know, loyally serving your country,' Grimpil interrupted. 'But she spat at me; on purpose.'

'José António Fernandes de Sousa.' Severino's thoughts were already marching off in a different direction. 'Dead, of course. They're all dead: colonels, captains and corporals; all dead except for me. Everybody wants a good life, but nobody worries about a good death. They all think death is something that only happens to other people, and then one day, when they're least expecting it, it's their turn and they just can't believe it. Do you know the first person I saw killed in a real pitched battle?' It was of course a purely rhetorical question. 'He was a flag sergeant. But do you know what? He was surprised. Can you imagine walking in the front line of battle, directly towards the waiting muzzles of the enemy, waving a flag to boot, and being surprised at getting shot? He looked down at the hole in his chest in complete disbelief, as if it was the last thing he expected to happen. And then he looked up as if he wanted to blame somebody for having spoilt his jacket. Then his eyes rolled back and he fell stone dead. It was only then I remembered that I had to reload my musket.'

'Quite so,' Grimpil replied abstractedly, still troubled by the contempt shown by a complete stranger. He was minded to paint a panorama of the town as seen from the flanks of Costa, from where one had a full view of Guimarães, from the castle mount all the way down to the water meadows of Creixomil. He wanted something he could offer Isaura as a gift, something that would oblige her to regard him differently, something that would establish his worth in her eyes. If he had been musical, he could woo her with song, but much as he liked listening to a concert his own musical education had never advanced beyond a few failed attempts to master the keyboard. Poetry would be the normal route for a gentleman to express his tender emotions, but he was certain that Isaura's command of English was too fragile to deal with poetic language, while he doubted his own capacity to produce winning verse in Portuguese. He didn't have any books of poetry with him, otherwise he could have set a particularly appropriate verse for her to study in the hope that it might awaken some faint echoes in her own breast, although he was uncertain of Isaura's own emotions. She was always so contained; perhaps offering his gift might cause her to reveal her feelings towards him. He would spend the morning painting and then, after lunch, he would be in her presence again.

-105-

At the end of the lesson, after she had gone, the chair where she had sat appeared like an empty throne. Horace sank to his knees as if in an attitude of prayer and rested his head on the seat. A very faint scent came to his nostrils, like the odour of some timid forest creature, almost masked by the smell of damp earth of an autumn wood. A picture came to Horace's mind: a medieval tapestry, a lady and a unicorn '*À mon seul désir*'.

An idea sprang to mind of such simplicity, which appealed to him to such a degree, that he decided to act immediately. What he needed was a cushion, a small flat cushion whose presence would go undetected. He considered the various parts of the house he knew and their respective upholstery but could not recall anything suitable. It was only later that day that his eyes fell upon the piano stool with its shallow padded top. In a moment when the drawing room was vacant, he investigated closer. It was easily removable, and so without further ado he took it up to his room for safekeeping.

Although Amélia, the lady's maid, was not the most assiduous of servants, she had a quick eye. Despite the fact that the drawing room was amply furnished, she noticed the lack of the cushion on the piano stool the following morning and immediately saw the possibility of getting Francisca into trouble. Once her mistress had finished her breakfast, she enquired casually if she had ordered the cushions to be cleaned. Dona Eugenia was never completely surprised by the strange questions that Amélia was capable of asking, but she did wish to know why.

'The cushion from the piano stool has disappeared.'

She would never take for granted what the servants told her without verifying for herself the truth of the situation. Standing at the piano, she could refute the veracity of the fact.

'Cushions do not simply disappear; someone must have removed it.'

'Who?' asked Amélia.

'I don't know. Send for Francisca.'

Francisca was summoned, but she denied all knowledge of the occurrence.

'Come now, 'said Dona Eugenia suspecting some connivance on the part of the servants. 'Someone must know something.' She sent for Jorge. But he was not able to throw any further light on the matter, and the four of them stood looking at the missing cushion as if their collective disbelief at its disappearance might make it return.

It was in this moment of distraction that she gave permission to Francisca's request to go out in the evening, something she never would have done otherwise without first questioning her closely.

-106-

Grimpil stood back to assess his labours, not entirely satisfied with the results. Perhaps it would have worked better in watercolours, although he had opted for the more difficult task of rendering the landscape in Indian ink.

'He was here, you know!'

'Who?' enquired Grimpil distractedly.

'The devil incarnate.'

'The devil was here in Guimarães?'

'When God made him, he created him without a heart.'

'Without a heart? What are saying, man?'

'Without a human heart,' Severino explained. 'He had the heart of a tiger.'

'Who, damn you!'

'O Maneta.'

'Loison.'

'Loison in Guimarães.'

'But I thought you said you saw him off. You told me you chased him as far as Lamego.'

'Ah, but that was the first time. This was the second time.'

'Are you sure?'

'Sure as my eyes are in my head. Both of them – Loison and Soult.'

'Soult and Loison? What were they doing in Guimarães?'

'Running away – after they were forced to retreat from Oporto. Soult was a gentleman, but Loison was the devil incarnate.'

'Nonsense! Such notions are pure propaganda. Fear itself is also a weapon of great value, sometimes more effective than a squadron of dragoons.'

'They were here, too. La Hussaye and 4,000 dragoons.'

'4,000 dragoons? Impossible!'

Severino spat ferociously on the ground.

'4,000! I counted them as they rode past.'

Grimpil washed his brush with a sigh. Some people were beyond the access of reason.

'He was never more content than watching a town being devoured by flames. Work of the devil, sure as my ass is split down the middle. You know what the whores used to say about him?'

'No, of course I don't know what the whores used to say about him,' responded Grimpil somewhat testily, thinking to himself, but I've got a feeling you're going to tell me.

'Big Bess told me once that when he came, his fluid was stone cold, and she made me swear on my mother's grave I'd keep it a secret.'

'Big Bess!' retorted Grimpil. 'An impeccable witness.'

'No, mad as a bedbug; disease of Venus,' Severino said, tapping his temple. Grimpil closed his eyes to regain his patience. 'Used to feed the horses on consecrated hosts.'

'Big Bess or General Loison?'

'No, French soldiers in general.'

'Not a very substantial diet.'

'They fed them maize as well. They used St Peter's on the Toural as their barracks. You know them little seats all around the altar, like armchairs all joined together?'

'You mean the choir stalls?'

'Aye, that would be about right. Well, they used them as mangers. Filled the seats with hay and each horse had its own box. Canny, eh?'

'Indeed.'

'And then the altar was like their kitchen. No shortage of wood for cooking, either.'

'Quite so.'

'Of course by that time anything worth lifting was already long gone. And what they had with them they had to leave behind. It's quite surprising what objects soldiers will try and take home when the fancy takes them. I remember an infantryman lugging a writing desk with him, and he didn't even know how to dip a quill in an ink pot. Burnt it all, of course; if they couldn't have it they weren't going to let any one else get the benefit of it.

They made a big bonfire in the Toural; everything went up – baggage, wagons, gun carriages. Made quite a fire, but not enough to satisfy Loison, so he set fire to the Couros as well. You see, all the factories, sheds and buildings were wooden. Went up like dream! Like I said, devil incarnate; only wanted to see everything burn like hell! So off they went in the direction of São Torcato; only this time they never came back, thank God. But the Brits were hot on their heels, because later the same day a detachment of cavalry rode in to town on the Braga road, like the devil was chasing them. Only it was them that was chasing the devil!'

-107-

That afternoon Grimpil went to the library earlier than usual, in order to make ready his plan. It was still the hour of the siesta, and he calculated that no one would see him smuggling the piano stool cushion into the library tucked under his jacket. He was just about to place it on the chair, when he was surprised to hear the voice of Dr Joaquim behind him. He hastily rebuttoned his jacket.

'I apologise for startling you,' said the Doctor, looking quizzically at Grimpil's fully buttoned jacket, 'but I only wished to advise you that the outbreak of cholera has reached alarming proportions in the more populous quarters, and therefore you should take care in your wanderings about town.'

'Very well, Doctor. I shall not drink from any public fountains.'

The Doctor continued to wear a puzzled expression.

'My dear Grimpil, you seem to have put on weight recently.'

'Portuguese cooking,' Grimpil replied with a faint smile.

After the Doctor had left, he completed the task, sitting on the chair with and without the cushion, before coming to the conclusion that its presence would go undetected. Nevertheless, he felt a certain anxiety when Isaura came in, but she maintained her calm routine, performing her usual ritual. Grimpil, on the other hand, could hardly contain his mounting nervousness and had never waited so anxiously for a lesson to end.

Finally, at the end of the hour, he could hardly wait for her to leave before taking up his precious treasure and drink in the strangely disturbing scent imprinted on the cushion. He had accomplished a stroke of genius, as clearly registered on the Venetian flame-pattern needlework was the essence of the young woman, just as surely as Flower's heliography could register images. Forgetting caution, he triumphantly carried his prize upstairs.

In the sitting room, Dona Eugenia was waiting for him to join the ladies for tea. Turning to her companion, Dona Constância voiced her astonishment. 'I do believe I have just seen Mr Grimpil going upstairs carrying the piano stool cushion,' she said.

-108-

The *Comendador* stood looking out of the window with his back to the room, listening to his nephew's report. It was a technique he had developed while Intendant of Police, and one which was very effective. He could listen detachedly, without being distracted by the speaker's appearance and without betraying any reaction to the information being imparted. At the moment of his choice, he would turn to face his interlocutor. This was the moment of truth, when he would directly fix the speaker with his penetrating gaze and fire a question at point-blank range. But after his nephew had finished, he turned to him not with a broadside but with a confession.

'I'm afraid that I may have been wrong.'

He had never doubted his intuition before, but now he was less certain. Nothing had contributed to substantiate his insight, but since his interview with Doctor Joaquim, he had been troubled by the sensation he was chasing after the shades of the long-gone. Needless to say, he had had no news from the Doctor. However, it had been a long time since he had been in contact with an individual of such honest goodwill, who had dedicated his life to the well-being of those less fortunate than himself, notwithstanding the daily risk of infection from the most vile diseases. It served to throw his own hardness of heart in to sharp contrast, and he felt diminished by the comparison. All that was noble in his spirit had been degraded; his aspirations had turned to rancour; his magnanimity for the sake of the cause now only fuelled private revenge.

Rodrigo was surprised. He had never heard his uncle express anything but the firmest conviction, the most unshakable faith. He did not want his uncle to sink back into apathy.

'Let us review the options,' he stated, taking one of the old man's stock phrases when faced with an intractable problem 'Option one: Grimpil senior is not in Portugal. End of story.'

He studied his uncle's face for any trace of reaction but found none.

'Option two: Grimpil senior is in Portugal; therefore, why hasn't he made contact with his son?'

The question hung in the air while Rodrigo collected his ideas on the subject, during which time the *Comendador* remained silent. He continued.

'A: he is unaware of his son's presence. B: he is aware but does not wish to contact his son. If not, why not? Because he is aware of the risk involved in revealing his whereabouts?'

It was his uncle's turn to speak.

'If the old fox is here, I think we can safely assume that he is aware of the fact that the pup is here. That he has many enemies in this country he certainly knows, and if he is here he has kept his presence a well-guarded secret. That he would not wish to expose himself now, after so many years, is more than logical – but at the expense of not meeting his son, who has grown to manhood since they last saw each other? That is why, on balance, I must regretfully draw the conclusion that our man is not here. Nor can we rule out definitely some communication between father and son, directly or indirectly, in England. After all, our network is not as good as it once was. There is only one thing that leaves me uncertain: it is Grimpil's behaviour itself. Everything points to the reason for his presence here to be unattained: the pointless journeys; his prolonged stay in Guimarães. It is as if he is still waiting for contact to be made. We must be patient if we are to catch the old fox when he comes out of his hide. However, we can play our trump card while we are waiting.'

'Our trump card – what is that?' enquired Rodrigo.

'Why, my dear boy, it is you. He believes you to be a friend, his saviour. You must go and be with him. Seek an opportunity to tackle him directly on the issue. Perhaps he will let the mask slip. Who knows?'

'But won't he become suspicious if I suddenly appear without good reason?'

'Let me think... Did you not mention that Francisco Sarmento had been in Flower's company during his visit to Guimarães?'

'Indeed; he dined at the Doctor's house.'

'And how well did you know him at Coimbra?'

'Not very much, I was in my final year when he came up. Me, struggling to finish mine, and him, starting his at sixteen, damned intellectual. I understand from Cuzelhas that he spends all his time writing poetry.'

'Poetry, eh! You don't happen to have penned any verses, do you?'

'Uncle, please!' replied Rodrigo, deeply offended at the suggestion.

'I only ask because, if you had, you could ask him for advice; one poet to another; that kind of thing.'

'Who would seriously believe in my being a poet?'

'You're quite right, but I have a better idea: tell him you have a project to publish contemporary poetry, or a literary review or something of that nature. You're looking for contributors, and his name was suggested by a mutual acquaintance. The important thing is to get invited to stay there for a few days so that you can engineer a meeting with Grimpil. He'll be overjoyed to see you again; take my word for it. After several weeks of mouldering in Guimarães, he'll be most anxious to open his heart to an old and trusted friend, believe me!'

'Very well, Uncle, I shall do as you say, but it might take a while to bring about.'

'Time is all we have, my son.'

-109-

The mountain air was invigorating, and in the morning as fresh and crisp as a green apple. Soult felt restored to his former self; he was the leader of an army again. A strange sort of army, resembling a Spartan phalanx of a classical simplicity that Napoleon would surely admire. And as for its leader? He felt he had messianic powers, a Moses leading his people through the wilderness to the promised land. Even if Spain was not exactly the promised land, this was as much of a wilderness as one could wish. On every side, the gaunt flanks of the mountains rose in rocky crags. Every now and then, the stone bulwarks were cut by a tumbling cascade, from which the men eagerly refreshed themselves. Curiously, morale was high. In his heart, each soldier had secretly resigned himself to being captured, a fate worse than defeat, because to fight and lose was honourable, while losing without fighting was emasculating. Instead, almost miraculously, by tortuous routes through a seemingly endless succession of mountain ranges, the defenceless army had made its way without so much as a distant glimpse of the enemy.

Many hundred feet below, the waters of the River Cavado foamed in the rock-strewn bed on their passage towards the distant ocean. Soult had decided to keep to the right bank. Above Salamonde, the Braga road forks, one road heading in the direction of Montalegre and the other in the direction of Chaves. It was natural that the road to Chaves would be the first to be intercepted by the enemy, and there was information that Ponte Nova, upstream of Ruivães, was heavily defended by a body of militia. The road to Montalegre, however, was not without difficulties. The path was sometimes little better than a goat trail, and the scarps fell precipitously into the ravine carved by the River Saltadouro. The French gained possession of the right bank, driving off a loosely organised group of armed resistors and enabling them to cross the narrow bridge. The hostility of the terrain was superior even to the hostility of the natives, but in these inhospitable crags, where even sparse broom and gorse had difficulty in gaining root, inhabitants were few and far between.

Less than a league further on, they came up against another deep ravine, this time the gorge cut by the River Rabagão. Progress once again halted, amidst the scenery of awe-inspiring grandeur. Whether crafted by the hand of God or Mother Nature, the breathtaking splendour could not leave the spectator indifferent. Craggy granite peaks clawed the sky above, the rocky outcrops descending almost perpendicular into the gorge. The canyon was so narrow and steep, with so many tortured windings, that much of the river valley lay in dense shadow. However, it was possible to discern a narrow humpback bridge, springing in a single arch to span the gorge. The Misarela Bridge, made from local stone and covered in ivy, blended into the landscape in such a way that it seemed to be more a natural feature than the work of the hand of man. Indeed, the godforsaken locale and the horse-shoe bridge were the subject of diabolic legends that earned the bridge the name 'Devil's Bridge' in popular parlance. A rapid onslaught dislodged its defenders, and once again the army continued its march in the direction of Spain, now only a half a dozen leagues away.

Soult became aware of an unfamiliar agitation among his men. They were whistling and gesticulating, laughing and making obscene gestures. On the far side of the gorge, out of range of musket or cannon, even out of earshot, was an expeditionary force of the Anglo-Portuguese army, marching in the opposite direction from Chaves to Braga, no doubt in the hope of cutting off their retreat. Soult smiled for the first time in many months. The men were jubilant at this strange victory for a strange army in an unfamiliar form of warfare, and were anxious to display their triumph at the incredulous enemy, who could only watch them pass as if a military parade.

Soult turned to Tholozé.

'Now I know what I should have called my palace!'

'Indeed?' replied the Aide de Camp.

'*Palais de la Gloire*! Gloria Palace!'

-110-

Francisca placed the coiled hair on the table.

'My dear!' exclaimed the old woman. 'I see you are most expert. You could not have chosen better.'

Francisca didn't understand the import of her remark but wished to proceed as rapidly as possible. 'What should I do next?'

'Patience, my dear; first we must make the necessary preparations. Go fetch some brushwood from outside and a few logs of olive wood.'

Francisca obeyed, and, when she returned, the old woman had already brought the kneading trough closer to the fire and was kneading, stretching and folding the white mass of dough.

'Stoke up the fire, my dear. We need a little flame, and put that knuckle of olive wood in the middle.'

The temperature in the small dwelling soon rose, and Francisca had to remove her shawl.

'Take this dough and mould it into an image of your man.'

Francisca closed her eyes and let her fingers blindly manipulate the dough into shape. When she opened them, she had fashioned a crude doll.

'What's that?' said the old woman, somewhat derisively. 'If that's your man he's hardly worth wishing for!'

Francisca felt defensive about her creation. 'All his members are here.'

The old woman realised that Francisca's innocence was more complete than she suspected. Brought up in the absence of any brothers, she was completely ignorant of male anatomy.

'The most important part is missing,' she said, throwing Francisca another piece of dough. 'Mould something that looks like a sausage, and then add a pompom on either side.'

Francisca completed the arrangement.

'Fix it to your man at the point where his legs meet. Oh no, ignorant creature! Not pointing downwards! That's no good. Pointing upwards.'

Francisca failed to see the difference, but it was obviously a very important one. The old woman took an iron bar and struck the knotted olive wood, which broke into pieces, emitting fiery sparks. Taking a shovel, she scooped up the embers and cast them into the mouth of the oven, where she spread them over the bed-stone.

'Go wash me some cabbage leaves,' she instructed, and, while Francisca set about the task, she began to divide the dough into lumps, marking each with a cross. When Francisca returned, she placed each loaf in the oven on a cabbage leaf and told Francisca to do the same with her figurine. Francisca placed it as gently on the cabbage leaf as if she was laying a baby in its cradle. The flesh was soft and springy, already swollen in the heat of the room. She unfastened her bodice.

'Don't uncover yourself yet, my girl. You still need to go to the cattle shed and fetch me a cowpat.'

Francisca looked incredulous.

'Don't just stand and stare at me, girl! Do as I bid: fetch me a fresh cowpat.'

When she returned with the requested material, the old woman was raking the glowing embers to the side of the oven, leaving the floor free to place the bread. In went Francisca's homunculus alongside the old woman's bread, and she pressed the wooden hatch up against the aperture, her still nimble fingers pressing the dung into the crevices around the mouth of the oven until the aperture was completely sealed.

While Francisca gazed abstractedly into the fire, mesmerised by the tiny flames while the old woman scrubbed down the kneeling trough until every trace of dough and flour had disappeared.

'Now we deserve a little rest,' she said to Francisca. 'Fetch me that flagon.'

She poured the purple liquid into a small white bowl and produced a pinch of sugar, which fizzled on contact with the liquid. The old woman drank from the bowl and offered it to Francisca, who had never drunk wine before in her life. Finally, the old woman took a draught and swilled it around in her mouth, then spat it forcibly into the fire. The wood squealed; the fire sighed and exhaled coils of acrid smoke.

'Your man is a stranger?' she asked.

'Yes.'

'Gallego.'

'No.'

'His name is Spanish.'

'No.'

'Strange!'

The old woman refilled the bowl and pondered the question. She thought she had perceived a name, not Portuguese, and obviously not Spanish. It had sounded like *de Ath*. There were many things in the world both visible and invisible. They all issued from the hand of God, but that did not necessarily mean that He was the last person to touch them.

She struck the wooden door to loosen the now baked dung, which fell away from all sides. With a heave she pulled the wooden door free, and at once the hovel was filled the smell of freshly baked bread.

'Come and reclaim what is yours,' she said, giving Francisca a cloth.

The girl gingerly picked up the baked figure. It was now golden brown in colour and firm to the touch. More marvellous still was the way that the little sausage she had placed between his legs had grown to impressive proportions.

'Pretty, ain't it!' smiled the old woman. 'From a pan to a snake, everything has a way of taking hold of it. If you know how to grasp things and keep hold of them, the world is for the taking. Some people will tell you that getting a man is difficult, but in truth there isn't anything simpler. This is where a man has his handle,' she said, and, taking hold of the spike of dough, she broke it off with a snap. She presented it to Francisca's mouth.

'If you want to possess a man, this is where you start. Eat it!'

Francisca obeyed, although halfway through she began to choke. It was the hair. The woman thrust the bowl of wine in to her hands. 'Knock it back, all in one,' she insisted. 'In life we have to swallow a lot of things. If everything was as easy to swallow as this you will have nothing to complain about.'

-111-

Monday, July 31st, 1854

The trip to São Estevão was the first that I had been out together with Alfredo since our fateful trip to São Torcato. The events of that day were something that I wished to exclude from my mind, but every now and then, much to my discomfort, I recalled the scene of the moonlight tryst. What disturbed me most was the knowledge that my parents must have performed the same act in order to bring me into the world. Had my mother shown the same wanton delight in the transaction as the unknown woman in the field? I comfort myself with the notion that she must certainly only have allowed herself to be so used in order to fulfil her duty as a Christian wife and become a mother, without taking any pleasure in the process. Of my father I have my doubts. They say sea captains have a wife in every port. Does this mean that I have a series of half-brothers scattered along the Atlantic shipping lanes? Then I remembered Isaura. Was this bestiality what I wished to do with her? The fact that she would be there had played a large part in my accepting the invitation to the picnic. Rodrigo, my saviour from Oporto, would also be there. The menace in the eyes of my pursuers brought to mind once again the sad end to my visit to São Torcato, and I did not wish the outing to be clouded by these memories.

Indeed, it would be difficult to imagine a more

perfect summer's day. Crossing a humpback bridge, the horses' hooves rang out against the metalled surface of the Braga road as we quickly passed by the water meadows and fields on our way to Taipas, where we stopped at the spa to take refreshments. It was here that I parted company with Alfredo, who was going on to Braga, although at the time it did not occur to me to enquire into the purpose of his sojourn. We made our final farewells and I continued alone in the carriage as it set out on the Póvoa de Lanhoso road, before climbing in the direction of São Estevão.

-112-

The house of Senhor Martins Sarmento was a wide, low mansion, with a sweeping staircase rising to the main entrance. Another carriage was already waiting in the driveway, on to which the servants were loading hampers and baskets of all sorts. Sarmento came down the steps briskly to greet the newcomers.

'I have chosen São Romão for our picnic; a finer place cannot be found in all the Minho.'

They greeted each other.

'Any news from Flower?' he enquired genially. Grimpil felt that Sarmento compared him unfavourably to Flower, but his courtesy and attention was faultless and his spirit gay.

'I have not been in touch with him,' replied Grimpil as he watched Isaura descending the staircase on the arm of Rodrigo, a sight that could not fail to cause his heart to flutter. She was as beautiful as ever in a pale blue dress, her face hidden by the shade of her parasol. She detached herself from Rodrigo, greeted Grimpil somewhat formally, and joined Sarmento, who handed her into the carriage.

Rodrigo, meanwhile, gave Grimpil a hearty slap on the back.

'Grimpil, old bean, good to see you in one piece. I hear you've been in scrapes again. Fear not: I'm here to protect you! No harm shall befall you today.'

He jumped into the carriage with a chortle, taking the reins. Further mention of Grimpil's tribulations only served to disrupt his well-being, already disturbed by the sight of Isaura climbing into Sarmento's carriage. He had hoped the seating arrangements might be different.

'Let us go, then,' said Rodrigo, shaking the reins and putting the horses in motion.

The carriages lurched uphill in the shade of the overhanging trees. Rodrigo was in an expansive mood. Everything he saw filled him with admiration and pleasure, while Grimpil was feeling taciturn.

'They tell me your mother was Portuguese; is that right?'
'Yes, quite right. She was born in Vila do Conde.'
'Have you been there?'
'Yes, I paid a visit.'
'Do you know anyone there?' asked Rodrigo, trying to lead the conversation in the direction he wanted it to go.

'No, no one,' came the unhelpful reply. The sense of isolation provoked by the visit only deepened Grimpil's reticence to speak on the matter. Talk of his mother brought back childhood memories of her sewing basket, a treasure chest profuse with coloured yarns. He remembered combining and recombining the pastel hues of the glossy silks in endless symphonies of harmonious or dissonant chords. How many hours had he spent thus entertained at his mother's feet, while her nimble fingers sewed the snowy white linen field with myriad points of colour, which, as if by magic, grew into garlands of flowers.

Rodrigo looked at the abstract expression on his interlocutor's face. It was not going to be an easy task drawing water from this particular well.

'If I had known, I could have given you an introduction to an aunt of mine,' he said, by way of re-launching the conversation. 'So how did your mother come to abandon these sunny shores for the nook-shotten isle of Albion?'

'I beg your pardon?'

'Shakespeare – nook-shotten isle of Albion.' Grimpil was obviously not up on his Henry V. 'England.'

'Oh! It was at the time of the war.'

'Now, which one would that be? We've had so many recently!'

'Napoleon's.'

'Ah, yes, I've heard my grandfather speak on that subject. Many Portuguese took refuge in England. It was there that they organised the *Leal Legião Portuguesa*, to organise and arm refugees to return and fight the invader.'

'Indeed!' Grimpil's usual interest in these matters was dampened by his melancholy. After his mother's death, time had closed around her existence like water after the passage of a ship. He had not stopped to reconsider who was the person who had departed from his life.

'And did she go with her family?'

'No, she went with her husband; that is to say, with my father.'

'Ah, and what was he doing in Portugal? Carrying off our women, like some latter day Paris?'

'He was a navy man. Indeed, it was his intention to name me Horatio, after the hero of the Nile and the victor of Trafalgar. By my mother's intervention I was transformed into Horace. To the disillusion of both, I lacked the boldness of the Lord High Admiral or the inspiration of the great Roman poet.'

'Sons can rarely live up to their fathers' expectations, and, if the truth be known, fathers rarely live up to their sons'.'

Grimpil recalled a bitter altercation between his parents in which his father had accused his mother of mollycoddling him.

'You've spoilt the child rotten! What he needs is a bit of discipline to knock him into shape.'

He couldn't remember when he saw his father again, for shortly after that he had been sent to boarding school. School was a place where no shortage of knocking took place, on the part of both school fellows and teachers. The opportunistic bullying of his colleagues was easier to sustain than the systematic and institutionalised violence of the masters, but none of it contributed positively to the formation of his character; much to the contrary. It had only taught him to hide, to camouflage, to deny. The only place he had found refuge was in his studies, with the result that, at the end of his schooling, he was able to exchange one all-male institution for another, where at least brute force was replaced by intellectual superiority.

Rodrigo also reflected on the subject of sons and fathers. His mother always spoke of his father as a dead hero, but quite how and why, he never had the courage to ask. In fact, but for the portrait of the handsome cavalier that hung in the study, he had no recollection of the person. In the sunshine of his talented and comfortable youth, the question was too troubling to be raised. His uncle had assumed the place of a guardian and mentor; one day he would have to ask him to explain the matter in full. Thinking of his uncle reminded him of his mission.

'When did you last see your father?' he asked, unable to find a more subtle approach.

'He came to visit once, during the summer holidays, when I was about ten. He wanted to put me into cadet college. My mother was dead set against the idea, naturally. I think she was opposed to the idea in principle. By that time, my father's prolonged absence meant that he no longer had the moral authority that a parent should have.'

Grimpil told the story, but within he felt the complex emotions he had experienced at the stranger's appearance: an unwelcome intrusion from someone that not only did he not love, but could not. Someone, who by some right accrued prior to his own existence, was able to claim part of his mother's attention, if not affection.

'So if he was away from home for such long periods, where did he live?'

'I always presumed he was at sea.'

'All the time? Even sea captains spend time ashore.'

'I never really considered the question.'

'Did he not have contacts in Portugal?'

'I suppose he must have done.'

'With your grandparents, perhaps.'

'I really don't know. Portugal always seemed so remote.'

'He must certainly have had business relations.'

'Undoubtedly, but I can't see my father living in Portugal while my mother lived in England. It wouldn't make sense.'

'Maybe, maybe not,' said Rodrigo, guiding the horses into a clearing where Sarmento's carriage had already pulled up. 'This looks like our picnic stop.'

-113-

They proceeded to unpack the hampers. From the height of the mountain top, there was a tremendous view over the fertile valley floor, densely vegetated with cultivated crops and vines. Bathed in the brilliant sunshine, it shone like a precious stone, replete with the promise of an ample harvest. In the distance rose the sombre mountains.

Sarmento was in fine spirits. 'You know, whenever I come here, I remember the passage in the Bible. You know, the one in which Satan tries to tempt Jesus and he takes him to a high place where they can see all the world. I think it was a place just like this. From here, this rich river valley is the epitome of the land flowing with milk and honey. What more could one seek in life?'

'I'm afraid,' replied Rodrigo, 'that if I was to exchange my mortal soul I would require something more substantial than mere bucolic bliss.'

'Palaces with gilded mirrors, courtesans and ministers of state, no doubt,' jested Sarmento, with more than a grain of truth in his ironies. Junqueira was from a family in whose veins statecraft ran in equal measure with blood. 'Possibly we have here an idea for your literary gazette: latter-day Fausts. What would you ask for in exchange for your soul? We could ask for a contribution from our learned friend here,' he said, giving an affectionate slap on Grimpil's back. Grimpil had been lost in admiration of Isaura, and had Mephistopheles been present at that moment, this Faust would almost certainly have traded his soul on the spot for the amour of his fair beloved.

Rodrigo, contemplating the floodplain of the river, traced the road that ran from the hot springs in the direction of Braga.

'Sarmento, would you not say that there was a Roman hand in all of this?' he said gesticulating to the valley below. 'They held thermal baths in very high appreciation and a road as straight as that one was made for the legions to march from one outpost of the empire to another.'

'Braga was more than an outpost of the empire. It was the imperial city of Bracara Augusta, capital of the Northeast and a veritable hub of Roman administration and commerce.'

'It's not difficult to imagine the legions marching down below, nor our ancestors up here, watching them go by, maybe plotting some act of vengeance. History repeats itself: great armies march in the valleys, while bands of guerrillas lurk in the mountains.'

'I think the difference was more profound than that. Our ancestors forsook the lowlands in favour of the highlands. We have to suppose that the lowlands were densely wooded, subject to flooding and more vulnerable to attack from outsiders, whether Moor, Goth, Viking or rival tribesman. Up here they could organise their settlements along established patterns.'

'You mean to say they actually built towns on these heights.'

'Yes, I think it probable that they did, although, as yet, no one has made a systematic study of the pre-Roman peoples of the peninsula.'

'The Roman writers give the impression that they only found savage tribes or barbarians.'

'Quite so; how else could they justify their "civilising mission"? Certainly local culture did not have the same level of organisation as that of the Romans. After all, it was their civil, and especially military, organisation that enabled them to conquer most of the known world.'

'So who was here before them?'

'There were settlements founded by Greek and Phoenician colonists, although they came to exploit natural resources and to trade, not to conquer. They would have kept mainly to the coast. Their relations with the indigenous people would have been peaceful and culturally enriching, even if they did move in different spheres.'

'And who were these indigenous people?'

'That also, my friend, is not yet fully understood. In common with the greater part of Europe, a Celtic people probably. Pre-history is a difficult area of study, precisely because of the lack of written records.'

'So how can we know of the existence of pre-historic peoples?'

'By their artefacts. Their records almost entirely consist of stone, which is the only material that lasts the thousands of years that separate us from them.'

'And can stones tell stories?'

'Through the developing science of archaeology, they can.'

-114-

Grimpil had been listening to the discussion with only half an ear, the greater part of his attention being directed towards Isaura. She, too, had become uninterested in following their conversation, and, taken by the beauty of the flora, had distanced herself as she gathered the natural blooms. Seeing the opportunity that he had long awaited, Grimpil also stole away from the picnic site, leaving Rodrigo and Sarmento deep in conversation.

When Isaura saw Grimpil approaching, she stood upright, clutching her bouquet of wild flowers to her breast, crimson patches against the pale blue bodice of her dress. 'What do you want of me?'

'Oh, Isaura, don't try to hide your sentiments. Can you honestly not say that in all the time we have spent in each other's company, you have not nourished certain feelings towards me?'

'Sir, I have every respect for your learning, as I hope you have respect for my sex and station.'

'No, that isn't what I meant. I was referring to more tender emotions.'

'It is neither the time nor the place to be discussing such matters, Mr Grimpil. I must remind you that I am from a good family, and I cannot be importuned as if I were the serving wench in some wayside inn.'

'My darling creature, I should be quite unable to treat you so miserably,' said Grimpil, taking her hands in his, 'for you are queen of my heart, the very empress of my soul.'

'Your soul, Mr Grimpil, belongs to God and not to me,' she replied, freeing herself. 'If there is something that afflicts your heart, you would be better consulting Dr Joaquim; he is an excellent physician.'

'No, my dear, you are all the balm my heart requires,' he replied, drawing near to her again.

She turned her back on him. 'Mr Grimpil, if you do not desist from this conversation I shall have to become vexed with you.'

'You should not, for I am no more master of my destiny than a moth before a flame.'

'And is it on this basis that I should deliver myself into your hands? How may I know if I can trust you? Is what you say true or mere passing fancy?' She turned to face him again, her cheeks aflame with unknown emotions.

'You may trust me, for my intentions are the most noble, inspired by the highest code of honour,' Grimpil rejoined, somewhat taken aback by the demonstration of such fervour.

'In that case, it is not I you should be speaking to,' she continued, more mildly. 'You should be addressing my father.'

The very idea of expressing such tender emotions to a man so dominated by material concerns filled him with aversion.

'Oh, Isaura! How can you be so cruel?'

'It would be cruel for me to nurture false hopes. I cannot associate myself with any man without the permission of my parents.'

'But my love for you is too strong to remain silent within my breast!'

'I say that it is my father who shall decide to whom I shall be wed. Therefore, if your intentions are honourable, it is to him you will make such protestations.'

'Will you not give me any sign that my affection is reciprocated?'

'That would be most improper of me. You are my tutor; it would be a grave error on my part to see you as anything else. It would break the bond of trust between me and my father, not to mention the confidence he has placed in you.'

'Then you feel nothing for me?'

'Mr Grimpil, I will not have my sentiments cross-examined. If I were to speak, you would call me a stupid girl, whose inexperience is appropriate to her age. You, however, who are a man, must respect one who is not yet a woman and who has preserved her innocence.'

'Isaura, I have seen you in the company of gallants, your avowals exceed the facts.'

'I will not declare myself indifferent to the attentions I have received. A woman, Mr Grimpil, is like a painting: to be valued she must be admired. However, you must understand my position. I cannot bestow upon you any more than the courtesies that society permits, otherwise I should lose the good name that my parents have given me, and I would not inflict such injury upon them. I suggest we join the rest of the party at once.'

-115-

They rejoined the two others, who were in high spirits.

'It has been decided,' announced Rodrigo grandly. 'I shall become the King's High Councillor so that I may persuade the state to award Sarmento a subsidy to perform the inestimable service of discovering the origins of the Portuguese people.'

'And to whom should I award this fine bouquet of flowers?' said Isaura, joining in their game. 'To the man of state or the man of science? An impossible decision. I shall divide it in two and offer half to each.'

Rodrigo bowed deeply. 'On behalf of the Portuguese nation, I humbly accept the many gifts Mother Nature has bestowed on us: this superb view and this delightful bouquet. However, I cannot let the moment pass without saying that the beauty of these tender blossoms,' he declared, cradling the flowers, 'is only surpassed by the beauty of the hand that offers them, but with one great difference. The flowers that bloom today shall fade tomorrow, whereas tomorrow Isaura will be even more beautiful than she is today.'

'I am deeply honoured by such praises,' replied Isaura, barely able to hide the colour that rose to her cheeks at such gallantry.

'And what of our English friend?' asked Sarmento, aware that Grimpil had largely been excluded from their exchange. 'What fine destiny awaits him?'

'That I can also answer,' replied Rodrigo gravely, 'for the fates have spoken to me!' He allowed a dramatic pause before continuing. 'Sarmento will discover our collective ancestors, while Grimpil here will discover the whereabouts of his father.'

'My father. But my father is dead!'

-116-

On the following day, Grimpil felt a certain reluctance in going to the library, like one awoken from a dream, who only seeks to return to sleep. He examined their exchange, the words, looks and gestures, to discover if in her behaviour there was anything that would reveal her inner feelings. After all, her words were perfectly correct and did her modesty great credit. On the other hand, did they stem from passion denied or from indifference? Whether this inner turmoil delayed his arrival, or whether Isaura had arrived earlier than usual, he did not know, but she was already seated at the escritoire. She had not heard him coming and was busily writing, a sight so familiar to him that he felt more closely bound to her than ever. He made a slight noise to advise her of his presence and entered the room. As if surprised in some illicit act, Isaura startled and instinctively shoved the page under the blotter to hide it from his sight.

Their physical proximity now caused him conflicting emotions. He felt awkward in his movements, and his voice sounded like that of another person. He felt like a man sentenced to death, living out the last hour of his life. Could it be that all his silent longings were no more substantial than a river mist, banished by the rising of the sun? He felt impelled to fall to his knees, to implore her, to plead with her, but he knew that this would only provoke her indignation; nor did he have the courage to confront her rejection. The hour that had once been balm to his soul was now a tortured infinity, minute dragging painfully after minute, like a wounded animal dragging itself towards its den in order to expire in obscurity. It was a passion play in which both were playing the roles ascribed to them, making the appropriate gestures like well-managed marionettes, waiting for the moment when the curtain would fall on their private drama, ending it once and for all.

When the clock struck the hour, Isaura collected her materials and left without saying a word, beyond a strained 'Good Afternoon'. In her hurry to leave, she forgot the sheet of paper under the blotter. When he was certain she would not return, he withdrew it from its hiding place and read:

Guimarães, August 14th, 1854

Dearest Cousin,

Greetings. My father's business keeps us all in town, despite the advanced season. It appears that we shall only be able to go to our farm later in the month, and therefore I have asked Mamma's permission for you to come and stay with us.

Do please make every effort to come, for I miss your company terribly and the city in August is so stifling, especially so since I am having lessons to improve my English, there being an academic of that nationality staying in the Doctor's house. Dona Eugenia has arranged for me to have lessons every afternoon. My dear Lucia, have pity on your poor cousin, for you cannot imagine what an imposition has been placed upon me. While I have every desire to be able to help Papa in his transactions, what benefit can compensate for such intolerable tedium? I can not imagine a soul so insensitive as to make a young lady suffer under the weight of such erudition. He so taxes my brain with meritorious learning that my head aches merely to think of it.

I only hope with all my heart that when my parents consider me ready for the sacrament of marriage they find a husband who in all respects bears no resemblance to this Englishman. I cannot imagine any greater purgatory on earth than being married to such a creature as this, devoid of all sensibility.

-117-

Grimpil read no further. Mechanically he returned the letter from whence it had come. Looking out of the window to the street below, he saw a funeral was taking place in front of one of the houses across the street. The pallbearers were carrying a coffin to the waiting hearse, the horses decked in black crepe, shaking their black feather headdresses nervously. Another victim of Cholera, or had the Angel of Death moved closer?

He left the house and, more by the force of gravity than by any resolution of his own, went downhill to the lower town. It was a now familiar trajectory to him, although he paid even less heed to his surroundings. Indeed, he was so absorbed in his inner turmoil that he was unaware of them until he found himself before a wayside shrine – a station of the cross. At this hour of the afternoon, a shaft of sunlight illuminated a prostrate Christ, bleeding profusely from the forehead, looking appealingly towards him in supplication beneath the crushing weight of the cross. The soldiers, with their fiercely tipped lances, pulled at the cord bound around his waist, as if seeking to control a wayward animal.

Grimpil gazed upon the Cavalry, but his mind continued in its previous mould. Along the course of time they had spent together, bonds of affection had grown between him and the young woman, a sort of relation he felt befitting for a man of his station with regard to a young female of good family of equal standing, a liaison that was correct from all moral or social standpoints. Her submission was no more than tolerance, her collaboration no more than obedience.

Crossing the Toural, Grimpil continued going downhill by the side of the ruined Dominican monastery. The street was narrow and the houses, with their wooden balconies, closed in from both sides. This was the more populous part of town, and he recalled the street from his arrival in Guimarães. In the heat of late afternoon, it was a canyon of shadow, nevertheless busy with the incessant passage of traffic. Grimpil stepped into an archway to allow a cart to lumber past. From behind came the clamour of beating and hammering. Drawn by the sound, he penetrated deeper into the gloomy courtyard.

The scene which greeted his eyes seemed to be Vulcan's forge, transposed from the underworld. The open mouths of small furnaces lit the scene with a dull orange glow, until they were roused by the bellows to an incandescent fury shooting out tongues of angry flame and spitting exploding embers in all directions. Hammers striking metal provoked a deafening chorus without compass or melody, accompanied by the shriek of blades against the rotating grindstone, not only sending out a tortured wail but also a cascade of sparks. Grimpil had inadvertently wandered into one of the many cutlery workshops which abounded in this quarter of the city. The assault on his senses by the infernal cacophony was accompanied by the stench of unguents of the lowest quality, used in the polishing, spread through the dust-laden air, provoking a profound nausea. He fled from the hellish uproar to the relative calm outside.

-118-

Grimpil had tired of keeping his journal and retired for the night, but the heat was too much for him to tolerate even a linen sheet. He lay on top of the bed, listening to the muffled sounds that occasionally entered by the open window. The night was still and the city quiet. In the silence it seemed he could hear footfalls approaching his room along the corridor. Did he hear someone opening the door? A waif-like figure slipped into the room, scarcely making a sound.

'I have come to you, as I knew I must, and as you knew I would,' said Francisca.

'What on earth are you doing?' he asked, but his question was answered by actions and not words. She extended her body alongside his, taking his hand and kissing it, as she lay down on the bed next to him as if they were a married couple of long standing. He made to rise from the bed, but his movement was interrupted halfway by the fact that she was lying on the tails of his nightgown.

'Are you out of your mind? Go back to your room at once.'

'You pretend not to care for me, but that is because you do not yet know how your life would be better if I were a part of it.'

'I can assure you I have no intention of letting you become part of my life,' he replied somewhat huffily.

Francisca lay her hand on his chest.

'Let there not be any impropriety,' he said.

'I think it's very appropriate,' Francisca replied.

'I didn't say inappropriate; I said improper,' corrected Grimpil, moving his body away from her hand.

'You can touch me wherever you wish.'

'I can assure you I have no desire to touch you.'

'Why not?'

'Why not? Why should I?'

'Because it's natural.' And she placed her hand where she

guessed that the difference between her and him must lie. Beneath the fabric of his nightshirt she could feel a soft protuberance, approximately a hand span in length.

Grimpil withdrew her hand. 'I fear that you're maybe harbouring lewd thoughts and intentions.'

'No,' she smiled at him, 'simply curious.' She slipped her hand under the hem of his nightgown.

'I must protest in the strongest terms,' he objected, for she was trespassing on territory that had been untouched by a female hand since the days of his infancy. Francisca let her hand lay still until he calmed down.

'Have you ever had congress with a woman?' she asked instead.

'My dear young woman, you really must learn to restrain your curiosity.'

'I take it that means no.'

'No, it means I think you are being untoward.'

'Un to what?'

'Oh! Do keep still.'

Francisca's wandering hand had finally come into contact with an appendage. The old woman was right. Men really did have a handle by which to take hold of them.

'Oh, please…' he protested, but he was unable to complete his sentence. Francisca understood the words to mean encouragement, and she ran her fingers along its length to discover more of its contours. It began to take shape in her hand, the soft amorphous tubularity acquiring new characteristics. She was no longer content to merely feel this curious object; she wanted to see it, too. Without letting go of her prize, she lifted the skirts of his nightgown to expose it to her gaze. Between the ring of her thumb and forefinger appeared a dark red fruit. Just like the bread stick she had made from the soft dough, it was growing in size and increasing in hardness. When she released it, it did not fall back into the dark mat of hair, but stood clear, raising itself with little convulsions into a more upright position. She was even more curious than ever at the sight of this transformation. Now that she had felt and seen it, she wondered what it would taste like.

-119-

Francisca arose from the bed where Grimpil lay sprawled motionless. She had not expected such an explosive end to her investigations; her plaything had shrunk to its former size. Walking to the commode, she looked into the mirror to detect any difference in herself but only noticed that her hair was seeded with liquid pearls that were difficult to remove. Meanwhile, Grimpil had begun to stir. She returned to his side.

'Where do you live?' she asked.

Grimpil drew in his breath and puffed his cheeks.

She had noticed him doing this before. It signified a complicated answer to a simple question.

He let out his breath slowly. 'I live in a great hall.'

This confirmed her imaginings. 'Do you live there alone?'

'No, we are about forty in number, not counting the servants, of course.'

Now the picture no longer fitted the frame.

'There are a lot of servants?'

'There must be – let me see – over a hundred.'

'Then it must be a palace.'

'No, it's a college.'

It was her turn to sit up abruptly. The only college she knew was the *Colegiado*, and now she saw her predicament in a new light. She feared that instead of merely transgressing social conventions, she had trespassed on forbidden territory.

'You're a priest,' she said wide-eyed in awe.

'No, I have no vocation for Holy Orders.'

'Then what type of college is it?' she asked distrustfully.

'It is an academic college, of course. Why? What else did you think?'

Francisca still feared being deceived. An academic college was beyond her experience.

'I thought it was a college like that of Oliveira.'

Grimpil laughed at her ingenuity. 'Well, it is true we are all bachelors.'

Francisca didn't like him making light of her innocence.

'So if you were to marry, you could no longer live there.'

'Well, there are married bachelors.'

Francisca was more distrustful still at this apparent contradiction.

'How is that possible? Either you are married or not. You cannot be both bachelor and married.'

Grimpil explained more about academic life, for her to understand better. The explanation displeased her; mention of monastic community further convinced her of the possibility of his disguising the truth.

'Next you will tell me that a man may be a priest and married.'

Grimpil laughed again. 'Which indeed, in my country, they can!'

Francisca was angry with him. Either he was lying to her or his country was more foreign than she had imagined.

'So if you took me with you as your wife, we would live together in your great hall with its hundred servants?'

'No,' he said firmly. 'I am not taking you as my wife. When I return to England, I shall do so alone. I shall return to my college and…' resorting to the fairy tale ending to conclude his description of academic bliss, 'live happily ever after.'

'But you are not a happy man, I can tell. There are some things that neither your books nor your paintings can give you; something only I can give you, a woman who loves you unreservedly.'

'In the first place, you are not yet a woman, and, in the second I will hear no talk of love.'

'You do not know, you cannot know what a woman feels,' she said resentfully. 'Your heart is shuttered and locked against affection; your mind is filled with sterile facts; your spirit wanders a waterless desert in search of refreshment.'

-120-

When he awoke, only a faint trace of lavender remained as a proof of her presence. He dressed quickly and went downstairs. It was early and the servants were just stirring. He passed by Amélia in the hall, who gave him a conspiratorial look.

'Sleep well, did you, sir?' she said with an ironic tone.

Grimpil stopped in his tracks.

'And what, pray, did you intend by that remark?'

'Only that sir has risen very early this morning. It is sometimes a sign of having been up during the night,' she replied blandly.

Grimpil scrutinised her face. He would have to accept her words at face value, but he doubted their proclaimed innocence.

'On the contrary, I slept extremely well and am keen to start the day,' he said stiffly.

'Indeed, sir, I can well imagine,' she said.

Their discourse was interrupted by the voice of Jorge, summoning Amélia to her duties. 'Mr Grimpil,' he added, 'you have a visitor waiting for you in the library.'

A visitor? For him? Who could it be? Unless it was the Consul with his documents. But it was an exceptionally early hour for such matters.

When he opened the library door he could not contain his surprise at seeing Alfredo standing by the fireplace. 'Good lord! What are you doing here?'

'Mr Grimpil, I came to bid you farewell, prior to my going to Régua.'

'Are you not returning to the service of Mr Woodhouse?'

'No, I intend to set myself up in business.'

'Set yourself up in business? But you don't have any capital.'

'Not as yet.'

'And how, pray tell me, do you intend to come by funds sufficient to start a business? Is some rich relative going to leave you an inheritance?'

'No, it is you who is going to provide me with the necessary sum.'

'I?' said Grimpil incredulously. 'For what possible motive should I give you anything at all?'

'Because I have something to sell, which you wish to buy.'

Although he was slightly disturbed by the calm certainty of the younger man, he pressed on. 'What do you have in your possession that could be of possible interest to me?'

'This,' said Alfredo, producing a battered ledger. The passage of many years had turned the leather cover a dirty brown but had not completely extinguished the gold embossed lettering. 'It is a diary,' he said, opening it at the first page of writing, revealing a calligraphy of a kind now fallen into disuse.

'I was not aware that you had turned antiquarian book seller,' commented Grimpil somewhat flippantly. 'What makes you think I should be interested in buying it?'

'Let me see... Does the name Porfirio Tibães mean anything to you?

'Tibães? Tibães was my mother's maiden name.'

Alfredo smiled and began reading.

'Since the sad loss of my beloved wife I have found myself without a living soul in whom to confide and have turned to the pages of my ledger to set down my innermost thoughts. These are troubled times, and never have I felt greater need to unburden myself, but there are concerns that a man may not disclose to his daughters, however dearly he may love them.'

Grimpil stretched out his hand to take the book, but Alfredo closed it with a definitive snap.

'May I enquire as to how this document entered your possession?' said Grimpil.

'Your grandfather passed his final years in Braga. When I passed through Braga, intending to return to Oporto I had the good fortune of encountering the former maid to your aunt, Dona Maria das Dores. Knowing that you would esteem such an important artefact and place high value upon it, I took the liberty of acquiring it on your behalf.'

'That was most considerate of you, Alfredo. And do you intend to restore it to its rightful owner?'

'Rightful owner? And who would that be?'

'The diary belongs to my family; it is rightfully mine.'

'Is that so, Mr Grimpil? At the moment, the journal happens to be in my possession.'

'Should I understand you mean to sell me my grandfather's diary?'

'Mr Grimpil, this journal has cost me a considerable investment in time and effort, not to mention a certain financial outlay. I consider myself more that justified in expecting some return on this investment.'

'And may I also enquire at what price you intend to part with this valuable artefact.'

'Given its undeniable sentimental and historical value, I would consider the price of twenty pounds sterling quite reasonable.'

'Twenty pounds! You rascal! You would sell me my grandfather's journal for twenty pounds?'

'Mr Grimpil, I would ask you to refrain from raising your voice, and also from making insulting remarks. After all, we are two gentleman negotiating terms for the purchase and sale of an antiquity and must conduct ourselves appropriately.'

'You are not a gentleman, sir, for a gentleman does not exploit an advantage for personal gain.'

'You may not, for your position affords you the luxury of refraining from doing so. I, however, as of yet, am not in that fortunate position, and therefore must regard the question as one of the law of supply and demand. I am offering you a unique opportunity in exchange for a modest reward for my labours in your interest.'

With this he opened the ledger at the page marked by the ribbon, and, as if no longer concerned with the business in hand, read aloud, ' "12 March 1808. I awoke this morning with my anxieties unstilled by sleep and confirmed by the news that reached us in the course of the morning on the progress of the French troops" ' and, turning to Grimpil, added innocently, 'I trust the price does not exceed your purse.'

'Of course not,' denied Grimpil hotly, only afterwards to realise he had not done himself any favours in the bargaining process.

'Very well, then; is our business concluded?' asked Alfredo, snapping the book shut with an ominous gesture. This was the critical moment; his fate depended on a positive outcome.

Grimpil pressed his lips together and expelled air from his rounded cheeks. On the one hand, the man was asking an exorbitant price. On the other, he held the trump card. He could not see how he could walk away without his grandfather's diary.

'Very well, ten guineas.'

'I'm afraid Mr Grimpil may not have fully understood my offer. I said my price was twenty pounds.'

'Come now, let's be reasonable. Ten guineas is more than a fair price.'

'It is the seller, Mr Grimpil, who sets the price.'

'Fifteen guineas then.'

'You do not do justice to yourself, nor to the value of your acquisition,' said Alfredo, tucking the volume under his arm. 'I had not expected to enter into this kind of bartering with a gentleman, but, if you prefer to negotiate in guineas, then let us say twenty guineas then.'

'This is sheer banditry,' said Grimpil gracelessly.

'Mr Grimpil, insults will only cause the price to rise further.'

'All right, all right. You shall have your twenty guineas.'

'And you shall have your grandfather's journal,' said Alfredo with a smile of triumph.

-121-

Outside in the hall, Jorge was reprimanding Amélia.

'You have no business conversing with our house guests. If you do not have work to do, I can always arrange some for you.'

Amélia was most dissatisfied with the course of recent events. Although Alfredo had returned to the house, he was completely uninterested in her. What was more, it appeared that Francisca had managed to get the better of her, with – and this was the strangest part – the Englishman. She allowed for a moment of dramatic silence before adding cryptically, 'At least I limit my intercourse to words.' She waited for the barb to sting.

Jorge seized her roughly by the arm.

'Explain yourself!'

'As I said,' she replied, removing her arm from his grasp, 'I did but exchange words with the gentleman, unlike other members of the female staff, who have gone much further in gaining intimacy with our esteemed visitor.'

Jorge was liking the tone of the conversation less and less.

'Whom might you be referring to?'

'I would not be so disloyal as to name names... but as adults we must allow a certain discount for indiscretions of our youngest brethren.'

Jorge rapidly calculated the age of the servants. 'Francisca!'

She left him with the observation that there are some who have never broken a plate who will yet break the whole dinner service, and he pondered what he had learned.

-122-

Rodrigo rode slowly along the dusty road that led to his uncle's house. He was in no hurry to give his report to the *Comendador*. He had so wanted to confirm his uncle's convictions, give the old man a reason to believe that the past could be rectified. Instead, he had only succeeded in strengthening his doubts. The old man would almost certainly be in his book-lined study, searching among the works of classical literature for the passage whose ancient wisdom might enlighten the obscurity of the present. How much longer would the family coat of arms, sculptured in granite, stand over the gateway to his uncle's mansion? So many sons had perished in combat, so much income had been spent on fighting causes. He himself had been born after these troubled times. He had been able to follow the chartered course without interruption or incursion: college, university, lawyer's office. Perhaps, after all, he might consider a career in politics, a distinguished marriage, possibly diplomacy, raise the family name again on new foundations, using law and legislation to re-establish the ancient rights of the house and the fortunes of his name.

The *Comendador*, looking down from above, saw his nephew's tardy progress and sensed that he was bearing ill tidings. So be it. By the time Rodrigo had climbed the steps of the tower which lodged his uncle's study, the *Comendador's* face was set in calm resignation before an open bible.

Rodrigo now carried the weight of his uncle's disappointment up the winding wooden staircase, arriving wearily at the halfway landing which gave on to his uncle's study. To his surprise, his uncle already seemed to know of the mission's failure.

'Come in and sit down, do not trouble yourself further with the stale leftovers of an old man's defeats. You who belong to the new generation must fight the battles anew with the weapons at your disposal. I thank you for your assistance in this my final quest, but now you must start out on your own. Go with my blessing!

'Have I failed you?'

'No, you have done me proud. But this affair is mine. You must leave now, for I do not wish you to be involved in what comes next. Do me the favour of sending Xavier up as you go.'

Rodrigo understood what the old man intended, and, kissing his hand, did his bidding, knowing that it was time for him to retire and leave the path free for others.

When Xavier slipped noiselessly into the room, the *Comendador* barely looked up from his reading, merely handing him a folded paper, which he carried with him back to his quarters. When he opened the message, the words 'Deuteronomy, Chapter 5, Verse 9' were written on the paper in the *Comendador's* scrawling hand. Xavier went to his black leather-covered Bible and looked up the reference.

> For I the Lord your God am a jealous God, visiting the iniquity of the fathers upon the sons to the third and fourth generation of those who hate Me.

Xavier smiled in understanding of the implied command. He would finally get the prey that had escaped from him before. Opening a drawer in the bedside table, he took out a shark-skin sheath, from which he drew a five-inch stiletto. Made from the finest Toledo steel, it was exactly the right length to sever an aorta when plunged in up to the hilt, but short enough to conveniently hide in a sleeve until required. He liked to work at close quarters to his victims, to have the physical contact that gave him the certainty that his victim had no chance of recovering from the wound inflicted, but time enough to reflect on the hand of divine justice in the few minutes prior to bleeding to death.

-123-

While having breakfast, Grimpil could not resist the temptation to delve into his grandfather's journal and began reading.

Tuesday, November 24th, 1807

Since the sad loss of my beloved wife, I have found myself without a living soul in whom to confide and have turned to the pages of my ledger to set down my innermost thoughts. These are troubled times, and never have I felt greater need to unburden myself, but there are concerns that a man may not disclose to his daughters, however dearly he may love them, for fear of disturbing their tender sensibilities. And in the worst of times? If I had ever suspected that these times would come to pass, I would rather have remained single and never brought children into the world to confront such tribulations, even though my dear wife and daughters are all the happiness I have known. My youngest has the heart of an angel, generous and kind, while her sister, Quitéria, has the face of an angel but a shallow spirit, quickly filled and as rapidly emptied. My eldest is made of sterner mettle and has rapidly taken command of the housekeeping, maintaining all under a strict discipline. As she is responsible for household expenditure, I have advised her of the perilous state of our finances since the departure of the English. When I think of Napoleon, it is well-nigh impossible to believe that one man can wield so much power as to make his will felt across thousands of leagues. Our own Prince Regent was obliged to sign the decree expelling British subjects from the national soil and closing our ports to their shipping, much to the disruption to our trade.

It is difficult to describe the confusion in Oporto, where their colony was so deeply implanted that many were considered as equally Portuguese as our own brethren. Much weeping and lamenting took place on the quays as families, business partnerships and friendships were torn asunder. The Alfândega was open day and night, on Sundays and saints' days, such was the volume of goods to be shipped, and, although many were the vessels of their own flag, many, too, were the ships of other nations, including over thirty of our own, hired to freight them abroad at excessive prices; over four silver pieces per pipe of cargo!

These chattels and movables could be transported; their real estate, however, was hurriedly passed into other hands, I myself being obliged to receive a number of properties in lieu of payments pending. While the business may be advantageous in the long term, it leaves me without capital. A cargo of woollen goods upon which I was counting to provide me with some liquidity arrived off the Bar of the Douro on the very day the prohibition came into effect, so that I was obliged to watch my investment and potential profits spread sail and return to England.

He stopped reading. He had not known what to expect from the journal, but he had entered a world were he felt he was an intruder and a foreigner. This glimpse into the inner secrets of another man's life, even if it were his grandfather's, disturbed his spirits. Taking the book with him, he stepped out for his morning constitutional.

-124-

Francisca, on her way down to the *feira de leite*, with an empty pitcher balanced on her hand, thought only of renewing her intimacy with Grimpil. She felt a strange glow in her body that was like the warmth that came to her cold skin after stepping out of icy water. Francisca was very conscientious in her ablutions, in contrast to Amélia, who often went weeks without washing, compensating her lack of hygiene with her mistress's French cologne. Whenever she passed the cows in the cattle market, with their fat udders and strong animal smell, it was always Amélia that came to mind.

Today, however, the world seemed strangely altered; familiar things looked strange, and the world seemed full of details she had never noticed before. On her return journey, as she went up the Rua dos Fornos, balancing the pitcher, now full of milk, on her head, as if in answer to her thoughts she passed him on his way down towards town. She smiled at him coyly but did not alter her pace for fear of upsetting her burden, nor did she say anything for fear of those who may be watching them from behind the wooden shutters.

Grimpil felt strangely ambivalent about the girl. On the one hand, everything about her was ridiculous, but, on the other, her disarmingly natural approach to him was refreshingly different from anything he had experienced before, disconcertingly frank in her naïve questioning, uncomfortably honest in response to his inhibitions. Would she return to his room that night? What would happen if she did?

He reached the centre of town to discover that it was the Feast Day of Our Lady and the town more animated than usual at this hour to make ready for the celebration, not only of *Nossa Senhora da Oliveira*, but also the solemn commemoration of the victory she awarded on this day to the heavily outnumbered forces of King John at the Battle of Aljubarrota. The church itself had been rebuilt by the grateful king in thanksgiving for the triumph awarded, a victory which not only consolidated the dynasty of the *Mestre d'Aviz* but also maintained the country's independence for another 200 years.

It was, therefore, a day of maximum importance for the chapter of the Royal College, when the Prior would lead the canons of the *Colegiado* in celebrating sung mass in the square before the assembled dignitaries from civic, military and corporate life. The acolytes were already setting out seats around the portable altar on which would be placed the most sumptuous relic of the Treasures of Our Lady – the gold and silver triptych depicting the life of the Virgin, which had been part of the donation of Good King John himself. Above the altar, a purple silk baldachin had been erected, extending from the *Padrão* so that the old market cross formed the backdrop to the place of worship.

On the north side of the square stood the council chambers, raised above ground level on a heavy stone arcade. At the top of the stone stairs that led up from the square, the beadle was just unlocking the door. Later, the civic leaders would assemble here, but until then Grimpil asked permission to sit and read at one of the windows looking down onto the square.

-125-

Sunday, December 13ᵗʰ 1807

Upon this day, at eight in the morning, General Taranco, the military governor of the province of Galicia, entered the city with an escort of little more than a hundred men and was installed in the Casa da Feitoria. During the afternoon, the troops of his division arrived without clamour or incident, the city being ungarrisoned and the people instructed by the Bishop to receive them as protectors and not as invaders. The independence that our ancestors regained with such sacrifice, after many years of armed struggle, is undone without so much as a cry of protest. We are now subject to the King of Spain, who is nothing but a pawn in the hands of the Great Tyrant. Junot is installed in Lisbon. The Masons flock to his side and promise cooperation. The shepherd has abandoned his flock and the wolves have entered the sheep fold. We are delivered into the hands of our enemies.

Monday, December 14ᵗʰ, 1807

How shall we celebrate the Feast of the Nativity when there is so little to be had? Since the closure of the Bar of the Douro, no *bacalhau* has entered the city, and, this being the season for its consumption, stocks are diminishing and prices rising. There is talk that there may be some to be had in

Vigo, but who will risk going to fetch it hither? I have advised Doreteia to consider making a rabbit stew, since rabbit is both plentiful and inexpensive, but the girls are disappointed and say that rabbit is not worthy of a saint's day, let alone to celebrate the birth of Our Saviour. I reminded them that Christ Our Lord was born in a stable and that on the night in question his parents almost certainly went without. The silence which followed spoke volumes.

Tuesday, December 15th, 1807

Taranco has made a proclamation and calls us neighbours, telling us that we may rest assured that we are under the protection of the King of Spain. We will not be harmed in the peaceful pursuit of our lives and businesses, according to our laws and customs, as long as we do not raise arms against them. The city remains quiet and there have been no outrages practiced by the Spanish troops. Is it possible we may yet live in peace?

Thursday, December 17th, 1807

Seeing that all is quiet, I obtained a pass to travel as far as the property of my late wife. I returned on the same day with such comestibles as we shall need: potatoes, cabbage and chickens. I also cut some holly in berry and evergreen to give the house a more festive air, in the hope that it will be sufficient to enliven the spirits of the girls. It was evident there was much demanding my attention, but I returned as rapidly as possible. Although apparently calm, there is much suspicion outside of town. I would not dare venture abroad at night.

Saturday, December 19th, 1807

Yesterday General Carrafa arrived to billet his troops. He was preceded by a lengthy artillery train, and it is said by those who went to meet him in Vila Nova that he treated them with rudeness and arrogance. He refused the invitation to stay in the Feitoria and chose instead to lodge in the mansion of the Van Zellers. Two generals in the same city does not bode well, and they say that Carrafa is in league with Quesnel and together they have the ear of Junot. Our fate is in their hands.

In her innocence, Zezé asked me a question that I could not answer: if there is party in favour of the French, and another in favour of the British, why is there no party in favour of Portugal?

-126-

The priest descended the steps of the church, carrying the ancient statue of Our Lady of Oliveira, the painted wooden features decked out in the magnificent costume offered by King John V for the miraculous cure that the sacred image had bestowed on him. In one hand she held the Child Jesus, and in the other a sprig of the miraculous olive tree that was jealously guarded behind an iron railing from the stone polygon where it grew.

Behind the Prior came the thurifer, already sending up clouds of aromatic incense to mask the more earthly odours of the assembled populous, who, although washed and dressed for the occasion, could not fail to bring with them the smell of cow dung and chicken shit that formed the olfactory backdrop of the farms where they lived. Behind the canons came the choir, chanting plain song, while by the magnificently wrought processional cross donated by João das Regras preceded the procession, flanked by torch bearers.

The Feast of our Lady was the most ancient of pilgrimages. Even in the days of the legendary Countess Mumadona it had been celebrated. In more recent times it was the culmination of the Fair of St Gualter, the town's patron saint. Not only was all the town here, but the inhabitants of all the surrounding towns and villages as well, all joining together in an act of collective devotion that packed the square and surrounding streets with a pious throng. Those who were fortunate to have family living in the houses around the square could accompany the ceremony from the balconies, whose balustrades were hung with red and purples damasks.

Grimpil watched the scene from the balcony of the Senate House. Although his mother had been Catholic, he had been brought up in the prevailing Anglican faith. The differences in the celebration of the Eucharist were not very evident, except that he had never attended an act of worship of such pomp and ceremony.

His attention soon strayed from the altar to the faithful. There were a number of people he recognised, but when his gaze fell upon Isaura he became blind to the rest of the congregation. Apart from her mother, she was accompanied by a young woman of her own age. It must be her cousin, he thought, remembering the text of her letter. Although they followed the ritual, he was aware that it also was not the entire focus of their attention. From time to time they seemed to looking in a different direction. Grimpil followed the line of their gaze. It appeared to be directed at a handsome cavalry officer seated among the dignitaries. Behind their fans, Isaura and her cousin exchanged disguised whispers.

When the proceedings finally drew to their conclusion, the assembled multitude began to redistribute itself, congregating in small cluster of acquaintances. Before long, the apparently random movement of these groups brought the three women in contact with the circle of people which included the cavalry officer. Grimpil could see the tight black curls that decked his head when he removed his shako. His closely cut jacket, overflowing with gold braid, hugged his broad shoulders and terminated in a narrow waist. As he bowed deeply to kiss the hands of the newcomers, it was evident that the cut of his trousers left not an inch of slack, as the seat stretched tightly over his buttocks and clung to his thighs. From a distance, Grimpil followed the elaborate choreography of social etiquette, in which, during the politest of conversations many gestures and looks were exchanged, which would later be scrutinised in great detail by both parties.

He had seen enough and descended the stone staircase to disappear into the general confusion. He felt an impulse to declare his feelings to Isaura's father and ask for her hand in marriage. After all, if this was the shield that she employed to deflect his solicitations, then he would call her bluff. Would she accept his suit if it was her father's will? Reflecting on the scene, he recalled that the three women had not been accompanied by Senhor Gominhães. Where, then, was he? Grimpil followed the movement of the crowd in the general direction of the Toural. However, he would only go as far as the Largo da Misericordia, where Gominhães had an office. Was it possible that he would find him there, working even on a day of such consummate importance for the spiritual life of the town? His suspicions were confirmed when he passed by the shopfront. He perceived a single figure, lost in the shadows of the premises, working over his account books by the light of a single candle. He realised then the impossibility of the task. How could he speak of rarefied emotions to a man who could only calculate transactions in terms of profit and loss? Was she a commodity to be bought and sold on the open market? How would his market value be assessed? He allowed the ebbing tide of humanity to carry him on towards the Toural, where he could lose himself in the ever changing flux of social encounter, endlessly repeated in new and unpredictable combinations.

-127-

Wednesday, January 27th, 1808

The city is greatly perplexed by the news of the death of Taranco and sorrows as if he were one of our own. Despite everything, he maintained his promise to the people and did much to alleviate the difficulties caused by the blockade.

It is widely rumoured that Quesnel had a hand in the matter, for not only was Taranco's death unexpected but also occurred under highly suspicious circumstances, having dined at the house of Salabert, a French merchant, on the night of the twenty-fifth. I learned from 'O Bicho' that he returned to Porto in the early hours of the morning, complaining of a colic. Although it passed, during the afternoon he suffered severe stomach cramps and died the same evening. Everyone is of the opinion that he was poisoned. If Carrafa thought he would thereby advance his career, he was disappointed, for, before expiring, Taranco named Balestá as his successor.

Thursday, January 28th, 1808

General Taranco went this day to his final resting place amidst great pomp and ceremony. We goldsmiths received his mortal remains in the church of our patron saint, after a funeral cortège composed of all the brotherhoods and religious orders of the city, headed by his personal guard - the

Grenadiers – as well as a company of cavalry, playing muted trumpets, and four pieces of artillery. The roads were lined with three rows of soldiers all the way from the Rua dos Inglezes as far as the Church of Santo Eloi, and behind them the populace, bareheaded and silent in reverence for their fallen protector. Many now fear the worst.

-128-

Distant thunder rumbled in the surrounding hills. Francisca lay silently on her narrow bed, looking up at the skylight, expecting her room to be illuminated at any moment by a flash of lightning. She was also certain that at any moment her prince would come. She strained her ears for the slightest sound that might announce his arrival. How long should she wait if he didn't appear? Then she heard something that sounded like a soft footfall on the stairs that lead to her garret. Yes! Surreptitiously, someone was climbing up to the door of her room. They paused. How like him this uncertainty was, poised at her door, reticent to take the final step. It seemed she could hear his breathing. The silence was disturbed by a fumbling at the latch. Should she open the door for him? Obviously he had not brought a lamp. Then the sound changed, metal turning against metal. Francisca sat up in bed. The steps were going back down the stairs. She ran to pull open the door, but it refused to move. It had been locked from the outside.

–129–

Saturday, February 6th, 1808

There is little reason to stir abroad. Business is virtually non-existent. I would attend to matters on our farm, but the price of a passport to travel outside the city has reached such proportions that only the highest imperative justifies such expense. However, we are tranquil within the walls of our house and spend our time indoors as profitably as we can. Quitéria is fractious and no doubt feels most keenly being deprived of the visits by our British naval gentleman. It is now some five months since we bid farewell to our English friend, and one of his visits now, so rich in entertaining stories, full of courtesy and attention to myself and my daughters, would greatly enliven our spirits. What prospects have we of ever meeting again? The French tighten their hold over our country. Yesterday came the news from Lisbon of the decree abolishing the House of Bragança. All their property is confiscated, but it is a mere formality to legalise acts already consummated. The Royal Arms have long since been removed from public buildings or covered by the French flag. The people are divided over the withdrawal of the royal family but most of all are resentful of the tax that Napoleon will levy, although reduced to forty million cruzados. It is a heavy burden for our impoverished country to bear.

Grimpil put his grandfather's journal aside. He was too agitated to concentrate on these long past events. Instead he paced the room between the bed and the open window. He would have to be firm; if she came to his room again, he would send her away with a rebuff. He could not let this illicit liaison continue for any longer.

Suddenly he perceived a ray of light from under the door, which opened without so much as a knock. In the darkness stood a white-robed figure, holding a candle. It was not the slight frame of Francisca. It was the figure of a full-bodied woman, whose breasts weighed against the lace of her bodice.

'It was almost as if you were expecting me,' she said without further introduction. It was Amélia, the parlour maid.

'What are you doing here? Leave at once!'

She ignored his command, placing the candle on the dressing table and adjusting her appearance in the mirror. She pushed her locks forward, cascading in oiled locks over the lace collar of her nightdress. She studied her plump features from various angles and asked, 'Well, don't you like what you see?' with a coquettish smile.

As if to answer her own question, she ran her hands over her ample hips, spreading her gown in appreciation of the generosity with which nature had treated her.

'I must again ask you to leave. Your presence here is most indecorous.'

'Come now, sir. There's no need to pretend. I understand you gentlemen are all the same. Take away the top hats and starched shirts, and what are they underneath?'

Grimpil took a step away towards the window. Her shamelessly forthright manner suggested that the question was not entirely rhetorical and that she intended to discover for herself.

'Personally, I thought a true gentleman would be more courteous in receiving a lady,' she said haughtily, as she draped herself along his bed.

'Now look here…' he was beginning to find her persistence rather tiring. 'Your behaviour does not allow me to extend to you the respect due to a lady.'

'So what do you want to extend to me, then?' she said, and

then, changing her tone, added, 'I know what went on here last night. There's no need to pretend; although I'm not surprised you should find Francisca less than satisfying. She's a mere girl after all, and even when she can no longer use that excuse she will never be anything more than a scrawny creature, all skin and bone.'

As if to add emphasis to the difference, she allowed one side of her neckline to fall, revealing a fleshy shoulder that would have done credit to Rubens.

'I can assure you that with me you will find no need for hesitation or half measures,' she said, extending a plump calf from under the lacy hemline. 'There's meat here to satisfy the hunger of any man. Come; come to my side so that I can show you what a real woman is like.'

Grimpil did not move, regarding the intruder with distaste.

'So that's it, is it? You only like little girls?' she insinuated, adding as a sly afterthought, 'Or is it little boys?'

The words stung his ears, and all the repressed resentment burst in his head in a blinding, bitter tide of fury.

'You vixen!' He spat the words from between clenched teeth and raised his hand to strike her.

Her eyes radiated defiance and her words stung.

'Violence is the last resort of the weak... and the impotent!

He could no longer restrain his rage, bringing his hand down against her face with such force as to knock her sprawling over the bed. An intense flash of lightning vividly illuminated the look of contempt that she directed towards him as he stood immobile like a statue, his arm poised to deliver a second blow. She opened her mouth to scream, but the sound that issued from her mouth was eclipsed by an almighty peal of thunder that rent the heavens from east to west. Temporarily blinded by the brilliance of the lightning flash, he rained blows upon her in rapid succession, mindless of where or how he struck. 'No, no, no,' she sobbed in a suffocated voice, desperately trying to protect her face from each successive clout.

-130-

When Grimpil entered the dining room the following morning, the Doctor was already seated at the table, although there was no sign of him having partaken of breakfast, nor of it having been served. He gave Grimpil a penetrating glance and enquired blandly how he had passed the night.

Grimpil could not recall having read in any manual of etiquette a polite phrase for informing your host that you had practised physical violence against his wife's housemaid.

'A troubled night!'

'Quite so,' commented the Doctor dryly. 'Certainly a storm worse than any other this house has ever experienced.'

Grimpil looked at the empty table in front of them. He was feeling hungrier than usual and there was no sign of breakfast. He was not sure if he should say anything; however, the Doctor read his thoughts, saying by means of explanation, with heavy irony, 'You must forgive the lack of hospitality. My wife left early this morning for her country estate in the company of her maid.' And, after a short pause, he added, 'And Francisca was unable to go to the market this morning because someone locked her in her room last night!'

'Who on earth would do such a thing as that?" asked Grimpil incredulously.

'And why! However, in the light of these circumstances, I am no longer in a position to maintain my house open to guests. It is for this reason that I have taken the liberty to arrange matters on your behalf. I trust you will not take it amiss, but I have spoken to my colleague, the Count, who is putting a carriage at your disposal. He expressed his satisfaction in being able to avail you of this means of transport to convey you to Oporto, where the cooling sea breezes may suit your temperament better than the heat of the interior. I was so certain that you would accept his generosity that I have already asked Jorge to prepare your trunk.

That only leaves you with your personal possessions to organise, and as soon as you are ready you may leave.'

The Doctor's tone of voice was so even, and his manner so polite, that Grimpil could but acquiesce.

'Very well, the matter is settled. I must also apologise if I am unable to see you off; the hour is late and matters at the hospital require my attention. Therefore, I shall wish you *bon voyage* now, and assure you that your visit here shall not be quickly forgotten.'

Rising to pick up his hat and cane, he called his manservant.

'Jorge, see to it that our English guest is put safely aboard the carriage.'

Bidding them both good day, he went about his business.

-131-

There seemed nothing further to be done except complete his preparations to leave.

'I'm going to my room to pack the last of my possessions,' he called to Jorge. 'As soon as I am done, you may send word for the carriage.'

Indeed, there were few personal effects that needed to be put into a leather travelling bag. Putting on his jacket, he felt something in his pocket, a single sheet of paper carefully folded in three. It appeared to be a letter, but it bore nothing on the outside, so he opened it. There was nothing on the inside either; both sides of the page were perfectly blank. Curious, he thought, and, folding it, returned it to his inside jacket pocket. Once ready, he went downstairs and handed his travelling bag to Jorge.

'Tell the footman to have the carriage waiting in Santa Luzia. I shall wait in the garden until they send word.'

Grimpil stepped outside. The morning sky was washed clear by the overnight rain, and the smell of moist earth filled the garden, vegetation bursting forth with renewed vigour. He felt refreshed, although still anxious for his breakfast, which he would have to take at the coaching inn. There was a slight chill to the air, although the temperature would certainly rise throughout the day. He calculated that he might be in Santo Tirso for lunch and Oporto for dinner.

It was already August, and he had allowed himself to be diverted from his purpose. He had stayed far too long in Guimarães and achieved very little. He had not gone to Amarante, nor to Braga. He chastised himself for his lack of resolve in these matters. The inertia and somnolence of the town had overtaken him. Even his business in Oporto remained to be decided.

Turning these considerations over in his mind, he aimlessly followed the garden path along a walkway overhung with vines.

Bunches of grapes hung heavy among the broad leaves, darkening their swollen skins. He remembered the paper in his pocket and took it out, turning it in his hands in case there was some indication of its purpose that had escaped his first scrutiny.

'It is from me,' he heard a familiar voice say. He looked up to find himself before a great stone tank, filled from a stream of water whose overflow ran into a conduit, watering the kitchen garden. Leaning over it was Francisca, up to her elbows in the icy water as she pulled a mass of washing up to a small inclined stone ledge where she rubbed soap into the linen, before pushing it back down, agitating it vigorously in the water. As she leaned forward, the loose neck of her blouse revealed the silhouette of her barely developed breasts, coming to a hard rosy point where they rubbed against the coarse woven linen.

'You see, sir, it is a letter from one who does not know how to write. If I did, I would write to tell you how no woman could serve you better than me, that I would care and tend for you, and you would want for nothing, neither for your person nor your household.'

'But you are no more than a mere girl,' he interrupted.

Her gaze was steady and her voice even. 'If you would accept my love and let me love you, you would discover the truth of my words. Reject it, and you are throwing away a thing of great value. He who refuses once may never be so fortunate as to receive the same offer again.'

She returned to scrubbing the washing. He realised that these were the sheets from his bed. A stain was still vividly evident, a livid carmine patch that spoke eloquently of his crime. Her small hands rubbed the hard cake of soap insistently at the spot, without seeming to diminish its hue.

'At least you would not have needed to do this,' she said, holding up the stained sheet as if she were Veronica holding up the Holy Shroud. 'You know I would have given myself to you without you having to beat me!'

'That wasn't the way it was,' Grimpil interrupted angrily.

'How was it then? What did she offer? What did she withhold?

'Amélia was a saucy wench and got what she deserved. Let it be a lesson to her in the future.'

'And as for locking me in my room…'

'Locking you in your room? What are you talking about?'

'Don't tell me you would deny it.'

Of course I do. I didn't lock you in your room.'

Francisca sighed, resigned to never hearing the truth from him.

'This is not going to come out easily,' she said, voicing her thoughts as if Grimpil was remotely interested in the progress of her laundry. 'I shall have to get some ashes and cure it the sun.'

And so saying she stood up on the edge of tank to reach up to the washing line stretched above. She had wrapped the linen sheets, now heavy with water, over her shoulders and reached upwards for the line. Whether her wooden clogs slipped on the soapy stone, or whether she overbalanced, he did not know. All he knew was that one moment she was standing above the tank, and the next she was in the water, her gaping mouth shrouded by the waterlogged linen. Grimpil was transfixed by the drama unfolding before him, leaving him incapable of movement. The water was deep and cold, and the coils of fabric wound around the shrouded figure. Some air bubbles rose to the surface, but he could detect no movement from below.

He heard Jorge calling from the garden door that the carriage was ready. He turned his back on the scene and walked briskly towards the house. The waters of the tank stilled, the stained fabric slowly fanning out in the water, shrouding the inert form of the young girl who floated beneath. Passing out of the house and on to the sunlit street, he bade adieu to the butler and strode vigorously downhill.

Before Grimpil departed, he took a less than satisfactory breakfast at the coaching inn, owned by the horse trader whom everyone referred to as 'O Gaita'.

Later that same day, the stage from Oporto was to disembark a singular passenger, a saturnine gentleman, who did not utter a single word to his fellow travellers.

-132-

After lunch, while waiting for the horses to be readied, Grimpil continued his reading.

Friday, March 20th, 1808

Today was unquestionably the darkest day of my life. As treasurer of the Confraternity of the Holy Trinity, I weighed the pieces of silver in the possession of the brotherhood, which we were obliged to surrender to the French authorities under the decree of 27 February. Our votive lamps so recently substituted, the processional cross donated by the Deacon and our own tipstaffs: all had to be relinquished. As I held them in my hands for the last time, I could but reflect that while Napoleon had extracted his war indemnity he robbed us of our material wealth. To remove our religious artefacts was to add insult to injury; to wrench the very soul from the body politic. The total weight came to sixty-seven pounds and four ounces of plain and wrought silver. It was inventoried and handed over to the Official Receiver for surrender to the authorities. If it was painful to reflect on the sacrifice made by our own brotherhood, how much more distressing it is to contemplate the same forfeit multiplied by all the brotherhoods, churches, chapters and congregations of the city, repeated in all the towns and cities of all the provinces, the length and breadth of the kingdom. Today is indeed a day of national mourning on a scale that exceeds any grief that has gone before.

Grimpil had still found nothing that had direct bearing on his father, and therefore passed over several pages in order to move ahead in the account of events.

Sunday, April 3rd, 1808

The weather being clear and bright, I ventured forth with the intention of visiting 'O Carapito', for, if we are not to be reduced to a state of poverty, we must find a way to generate some income. When I got as far as Rua São João, however, I found my way barred by a contingent of Spanish troops, from whom I learnt of the arrival of General Quesnel.

He finally passed by at the head of an escort of thirty dragoons. He has a military bearing and apparently a long record of service in the field. It is clear that the French mean to assume direct administration of the province, for he arrived with a staff of officers to man the apparatus of state. Quesnel has been installed in the house of Melo's widow, which the town council has richly decorated to receive him. His acolytes have been lodged in other houses belonging to merchants: Taboreau in the mansion of the brothers Morais e Castro, Picoteau in Hortas, Prigny in Vitoria and Perron in the house of 'Bolas'. It is not wise to be associated with these occasions. The people see all but say nothing. It is not good to be remembered as a Francophile.

-133-

It seemed like an entire lifetime since Grimpil had first climbed the stone staircase leading to the chambers of Smith & Woodhouse. Dressed in his mayoral robes, the deceased founder continued to impassively survey his domain from the gilt frame of his portrait.

Exceptionally, neither Senhor Fernandes nor the other clerks were at their desks by the window; only Woodhouse and Chapel were waiting for him.

'We must conclude our business, Mr Grimpil,' Woodhouse said. 'I have received this from the Bursar of St Botolph's.' He gave him a page to read, 'If you agree, I shall ask Captain Chapel to sign the bill of lading, for the shipment is already on the quay and he is anxious to get the cargo stowed aboard. I, for my part, shall also be leaving town, once this transaction is completed. I am most anxious to visit the quintas upstream. The season is advanced, and I do not wish to tarry any longer than necessary.'

'It is agreed, then,' replied Grimpil, who in the meantime had scanned the Master's letter. 'I, too, must now arrange for my return passage. When do you sail?' he asked Captain Chapel.

'The *Flora* will sail on tomorrow morning's tide, although she shall be putting into Bordeaux and La Rochelle on her return journey. If you wish a shorter voyage, you may find another vessel which arrives ahead of me,' advised Chapel, 'but if you wish to sail with me, don't arrive any later than tomorrow night, for I intend to sail on the tide at first light.'

'Perhaps I might make a suggestion,' interpolated Woodhouse. 'Would it not be a good idea, Mr Grimpil, to take advantage of the opportunity to load your baggage, for even if you do not sail with Captain Chapel, you will at least be free from their encumbrance and can choose when you travel at will, safe in the knowledge that your luggage is already under way.'

'Excellent thinking, Mr Woodhouse. Would you expedite matters, Captain Chapel?'

'At your orders, sir,' replied the Captain. 'It appears our business here is concluded.'

'Most satisfactory,' said Woodhouse, and, addressing Grimpil, continued, 'I'm afraid I cannot extend my hospitality. We are at this moment closing my town house for our trip to São João. Perhaps if we were to pass by the house of Mr Flower, he would be kind enough to lodge you for a day or two.'

−134−

Xavier whipped the horse into a gallop. He must give his master the news before the day was out. The frustration of his own schemes was nothing compared to the imminent collapse of the whole enterprise. Never had he been so fretful at the passing of every second. He was filled with a frantic sense of urgency at the prospect of his prey, who had gained two days' advance over him, slipping through his hands once again. No one knew where he was, and at that very moment he could be about to embark for England, to escape definitively from the destiny that had been reserved for him.

The horse was lathered with sweat, foaming at the bit, but the great house, standing at the end of the avenue, was now in sight. The *Comendador* was still awake; a light shone in his study window. He spurred his horse to one final effort, the faster to arrive at his master's door.

The *Comendador*, startled at the sound of galloping hooves approaching and looking down from his window, saw Xavier's cloak flying behind the speeding mount as he galloped towards the house. Something was seriously wrong: hurry was something he had never seen Xavier do. He was a man who husbanded his resources with the greatest economy. Taking a key from a drawer in the desk, he rushed down the stairs so that he was already in the great hall when Xavier rushed in. The servant was highly agitated, and the *Comendador* made him drink a glass of water before starting to interrogate him.

'Grimpil?' he asked, and Xavier nodded.

'Dead?'

Xavier shook his head. The son was proving as elusive as the father.

'Where?'

Xavier rolled his eyes to heaven.

Damnation, he didn't know! The situation was worse than he

expected. He rang the bell to summon a servant and ordered his carriage to be made ready. Turning to Xavier, he said, 'You can explain further once we are on our way,' and, taking the key from his waistcoat pocket, unlocked a panel in the coffered wall. He withdrew two pistols, one of which he gave to Xavier and the other he kept for himself. Then he withdrew two rifles, which he placed on the table, throwing his great coat over the top to hide them from sight.

'Let's arrange some supper to eat in the carriage. You must be hungry.'

-135-

Ensconced in a tiny room vacated by Flower's eldest daughter, Horace Grimpil opened the leather attaché case that contained the two diaries. Oblivious to the fact that he had little more space than that occupied by a narrow cot, he started to read the spidery copperplate writing that was now familiar.

Monday, June 6th, 1808

All the city is abuzz with word that Balestá has arrested Quesnel and means to return to Spain with the French as prisoners. The revolt in Spain has finally had its effects here. There is no news from Lisbon.

Tuesday, June 7th, 1808

It is confirmed: Balestá has restored to freedom the city of Oporto. The fort of São João is in the hands of Major Pinheiro, who has proclaimed the Prince Regent restored to the throne of Portugal, unfurled the royal arms in the place of the French banner and declared the Bar of the Douro open to shipping of all nations. This was communicated to a British brig, which responded with a twenty-one gun salute. Our fortress replied in kind. Quitéria immediately rushed down to the quay to see if she could receive news of her beau, but it is still early days yet. I trust he will be in contact with us soon, now that communication is restored. Balestá shall withdraw today to Galicia, taking the French as prisoners of war. How the mighty are fallen!

Thursday, June 9th, 1808

We are undone. While news reaches our ears that the restoration is afoot in Braga, Luis de Oliveira has ordered the French flag to be flown from all public buildings as a sign of the continued loyalty of the province to the French authorities. He has dismissed the Junta and requests a new military governor from the French.

Saturday, June 11th, 1808

We are to be sent another French general to govern the city and province. The rumour is widespread that it shall be Loison. No one has heard of him, but I fail to see how he can impose his will without a large contingent of troops.

Tuesday, June 14th, 1808

The revolt spreads. Now it is the turn of Bragança to embrace the cause. God be praised.

Thursday, June 16th, 1808

The city is tense and the streets awash with seditious literature and pamphlets inciting rebellion. There has been much reticence on the part of the authorities to allow the traditional Corpus Christi procession, but it will take place nonetheless. They fear that to ban it would be an admission of weakness and provoke a popular outburst. Without their Spanish allies, the French will have difficulty in suppressing a general uprising. The corporations are nervous for their fear is that the apprentices will take advantage of the occasion to declare the House of Bragança *restored, and the wardens of all the companies have been advised to be extremely vigilant for any members carrying symbols of the old monarchy. I must assume my responsibilities in the cortège and terminate this entry here.*

-136-

The *Comendador's* carriage pulled up in front of the Woodhouse residence, and he waited while his lackey went to announce him. It was a dwelling which declared its owner's wealth and social status. His musings on the injustice of fortune were interrupted by the return of his servant. Woodhouse was not at home, he reported, added to which there were evident signs of the house being closed up, presumably for an impending journey. The *Comendador* nodded silently, absorbing the import of the news.

'Rua Nova dos Inglezes,' was his only reply.

When he arrived at this thoroughfare, he alighted from the carriage and bade Xavier to remain out of sight. He was in the very heart of enemy territory. It was here that the infidel had managed to appropriate the trade in Portuguese wines and create the wealth that enabled them to become the arbiters of the nation's destiny. It was not a place where he could move freely. He would need an intermediary, one who could ask the right questions of the right people, without arousing suspicion. A few coins would be sufficient to arrange the information he required from the poorly paid underlings who worked on the fringes of business.

-137-

Saturday, June 18th, 1808

We are experiencing tumultuous days. Not only do we have news of the adherence of Guimarães to the restoration, but word also comes of the departure of Loison at the head of an infantry division. He has orders to enter Oporto by the twenty-fourth - Feast of St John.

In the late afternoon, the church bells across the city began to sound the tocsin, and shots filled the air. It was the signal that the city had risen to take up arms to restore liberty and legitimate rule. The streets were soon filled with armed partisans of all rank and station, from all over the city and suburbs, waving flags bearing the royal arms of the House of Bragança and shouting, 'Long live Portugal, death to the French.'

Good to their word, they proceeded to all the houses where the French and the adherents to their cause had been lodged, although most had fled at the first sign of the uprising. The turmoil continued throughout the night so that sleep was impossible, although no injury was caused to person or property, except those who had espoused the cause of the invader. It is said that the arsenal has been emptied and arms distributed to 30,000 men, but I have no idea who is at the head of the movement.

Sunday, June 19th, 1808

We start a new day with rejoicing. Gone is the apathy and repression. Everywhere is resolution and defiance. A new regency has been declared, presided over by the Bishop, with eight ministers elected from the religious, secular and military, and two representatives of the people. Luiz de Oliveira has been dismissed and is replaced by Jozé Cardoso. The people, however remain distrustful. The mail for Lisbon was intercepted on the bridge and all the letters taken to be opened and scrutinised, despite direct orders from His Excellency the Bishop to allow it to proceed. He was threatened by the mob and had no option but to acquiesce. How quickly the mob loses respect for its superiors once it has power in its hands! They attacked the coach of Brigadier Oliveira, killed its horse and arrested his servants.

News comes from all quarters of the kingdom that other cities are rising against the tyrant and declaring the House of Bragança restored. All of the Minho takes up arms. There is not a city, town or village that is not preparing to defend its soil against the invader.

Monday, June 20th, 1808

The blockade is lifted. Today three ships left the Bar and seven entered, flying the flags of various nations. The patrols of public safety continue, and the crews of the newly arrived vessels were not spared, although they are all in favour of our cause.

Monsieur Perron was apprehended boarding an English vessel and sought asylum from the captain, otherwise he would certainly have been *thrown into the river, there being much odium against him. The house of Jozé de Sousa Mello was attacked for the second time. Not finding the master at home, the mob vented its rage on the furniture and windows, all of which were smashed to pieces. The same night they seized the Governor, who was beaten and suffered injury and insult, for what cause I know not. He now lies in the dungeon of Matozinhos, next to the hangman's cell. It is a great affront to one of the most distinct families of the city.*

The Junta has asked for assistance from England, but even if granted it cannot arrive in time to protect us from the French wrath. They will not be merciful to those who have defied their authority. Our individual lives are suspended. Our only concern is to learn more of the fate of the nation. There is much gossip and rumour; anybody arriving from outside the city is immediately bombarded with a thousand enquiries to glean what information can be had.

Wednesday, June 22nd, 1808

God has bestowed a miracle on the Portuguese. Loison has been turned back from the Douro and retreats south in confusion. News comes from Guimarães that the General himself was wounded in an attack and his personal belongings captured. One of his finest gold-braided uniforms was received by the Junta as proof positive of the veracity of these achievements, and the people flock to see it as if it was the captured General himself. Praise to the Lord and the Blessed Virgin Mary, protectress of the nation, for we have been delivered from the maw of the great beast. There shall be rejoicing in the streets on the twenty-fourth as has never been seen in living memory.

Thursday, June 23rd, 1808

We are much amused to read in the Lisbon Gazette of Loison's victory and pacification of the northern provinces. We await the arrival of the British army to put an end to their postures and impostures.

-138-

The *Comendador* leaned back against the seats of his carriage and thought aloud for the benefit of Xavier.

'Grimpil has put his baggage aboard the *Flora*. It is a reasonable assumption that he will also sail on her. She is due to embark tomorrow on the morning tide. We believe that Grimpil is lodged with Flower in Gaia. To go aboard the *Flora* he must depart from the Gaia waterfront, so it is there that we must await our prey. Successful hunting is about patience. We have established the point where our game must pass. Now we must wait for him to appear.'

-139-

Thursday, September 1st, 1808

A combined British-Portuguese army has repelled the French on all fronts and obliged them to retreat. Now we shall see the invader pay the price of their countless extortions, crimes, abominations and inhumanities. From the length and breadth of the kingdom, fatherless children, widowed mothers and all the innumerable victims of French oppression cry out to avenge the estates expropriated, the commonwealth despoiled, the churches defiled.

Friday, September 2nd, 1808

The people are outraged. The peace is more unjust than the war. The British have more regard for the defeated enemy than their oppressed allies. The French are to return home with all that they have plundered and looted, as if the army habitually marched with its knapsacks full of gold and silver, and the train customarily hauled furniture. In case of disputed ownership, their claims will prevail over our own rightful assertion of property. The British legitimise the sack of our country by allowing the perpetrators to go unpunished. It is bad diplomacy and even worse warfare, for they take with them all their war material and officers to return to fight another day. Even our own horses they claim as their cavalry. The

British are deaf to our protestations and do not even insist on the return of the Legião Lusitana. They will live to regret such generosity bestowed on their enemies and so little respect shown to their allies.

Monday, September 5th, 1808

We are pleased to receive news from Quitéria's young beau, who has requested leave to visit us.

Grimpil paused in his reading. Finally he had come across something which bore more direct interest on him personally. 'Quitéria's beau' could be none other than his own father.

I know he shall ask for her hand and I am minded to accept. He appears to be as worthy as any other suitor, of good health and sound character, although of limited prospects. This does not concern me greatly, for I can provide her with a substantial dowry. Most important is that he carries her off to England, where she will be safely out of harm's way.

Napoleon will not accept this reverse and shall return no sooner than the British reduce their numbers in the field. Except that the next time they come, it will not be as wolves in sheep's clothing. They will come as wolves upon the fold, and vengeful ones at that, seeking to assuage their wounded pride.

One daughter married and in England will at least be one daughter less to worry over. I would feel happier if I could arrange a husband for Zezé. Now that our ports are open again, it may be that I can find the means to send her to join the court in Brazil.

As for Doroteia, I am sure she will end her

days as an old maid, and I believe she is of the same opinion. There are some feminine wiles that she simply does not possess. Men find her too forthright, which is a shame, for she is a woman of many fine qualities, unfortunately none of those which men find attractive. In many respects she is superior to both of her sisters, but I know that it is she who has filled the place of their mother and will not put her happiness above mine. I pray that a lasting peace may come so that I might find a man for her among the sons of my fellow goldsmiths; not only to repay her loyalty to me, but to give continuity to my profession through a son-in-law. I fear, however, that a lasting peace can only come through the final victory of Napoleon, who will place one of his cousins on our throne and permanently put an end to British ambitions for our independence as a British protectorate. Until then we will be the bone of contention, disputed by two dogs.

Thursday, September 8th, 1808

My future son-in-law has communicated a date for his arrival. In anticipation of his visit I have advised Father Bernardo to make the necessary preparations, although Quitéria is quite unaware of these steps. It is better that young people believe they are making their own decisions, especially one as capricious as her. The bans can be published as soon as they have expressed their acceptance.

-140-

The hours passed slowly in the motionless carriage. From time to time Xavier would descend to prowl round the quays, in case their quarry was slipping past them without them being aware. The *Comendador* was more firm in his convictions. He knew that Grimpil would appear openly, suspecting nothing. He did not want to show his face. It was more prudent that no one should know he was here. There could still be someone who would recognise his countenance. To wait patiently, that was the key.

-141-

As soon as Flower returned home, his wife related the events of the day.

'Something happened today which left me perplexed, my husband.'

'Speak your mind, woman, so that I may know what troubles you.'

'A man called at the house today, asking for you.'

'Who was he?'

'I don't know. He didn't leave a card.'

'What was he like?'

'An elderly Portuguese gentleman, very well dressed and extremely well-spoken.'

'I see no reason for you to trouble yourself; it must have been a client.'

'I don't think so. When I told him you weren't present, he asked after Mr Grimpil... by name.'

'Indeed!' Now Flower shared her concern. 'How did you reply?'

'I told him that this was the residence of Mr Flower and that no Mr Grimpil lived here; after all, it was no more than the truth!'

'You did very well, my dear, but this does not bode well for Mr Grimpil. I'm afraid this means I must go out again.'

'But you will have dinner first, will you not?'

'Of course, my Dear. In fact I feel unusually hungry tonight.'

-142-

Tuesday, February 13ᵗʰ, 1809

Incessant and heavy rain. The wolf prowls but cannot enter the sheep fold. Soult, at the head of an army of 40,000, has not succeeded in crossing the River Minho. It appears that the measures taken by Bernadim Freire to defend our borders are bearing fruit. We do not have the men to stand alone. When will the British send reinforcements? Wellesley remains in England. How typical of the British to punish their generals when victorious, instead of pressing home their advantage. If the Treaty of Sintra was iniquitous, it was the Portuguese who suffered thereby. Dalrymple and Burrard, however, have also suffered the consequences in England, and only Wellesley has survived with his reputation intact, but remains without a command. He is the only general who has shown capacity to equal or surpass the French. Would that he were here now! His energy and leadership alone would be sufficient to give us hope. Beresford and Forjaz are busy in Lisbon. Together they will reorganise our army, but many of our squires find the place to which they aspired occupied by British officers. It is inevitable that there is resentment.

Wednesday, February 14th, 1809

It is inevitable that the girls feel the absence of their sister. They have never been parted before. Without the presence of Quitéria, Doroteia is more imperious, Zezé more fractious than ever. All my attempts to convince her to join her sister in England have been in vain. Although Quitéria's letters are full of details about her new life in England, I suspect she has not adapted well to her change of environment. Even though she has the company of many Portuguese emigrées, she, too, must be missing the intimacy of our family life and the fellowship of her sisters. She has always been gifted at disguising her true emotions, and I believe she hides her own solitude behind a façade of social intercourse. It is difficult to be newly wed and have a husband away from home. As long as the war lasts, it will not be easy for my son-in-law to spend much time at home. It is a poor start to a marriage.

Friday, February 16th, 1809

I have spoken to Doroteia of my plan and she has agreed. We shall avail ourselves of a property that I received in lieu of payment from an English merchant, which lies in the parish of Oliveira, close to Avintes. Being on the south side of the river, it will be safer than my wife's estate, which lies to the north, a direction from which the French must inevitably come. Doroteia will organise the gradual removal of our valuables in the most discrete fashion. It is best that as few people as possible know of our intentions; I have not even said anything as yet to Zezé. In the meantime, I have a suitable hiding place already prepared and will start my journeys to Oliveira de Douro forthwith. It would be unwise to make more than two journeys per week, as trade is almost non-existent, and I must find some suitable pretexts for these absences.

Saturday, February 17th, 1809

The French have been repelled at Vila Nova. It is a great victory for Portuguese arms. Where will they strike next?

-143-

Flower took a cab along his familiar path to the wine lodges but, once at the waterfront, continued along the river front as far as the sand banks at the estuary. A fishermen's village, constituted by a cluster of houses, stood at the bend where the road curved inland; the broad strand covered by extended nets and other fishing tackle. He told the cab driver to wait for him and entered a tavern in which gentlemen of his class were not usually expected to enter.

Inside, a single lamp scarcely illuminated the fog of tobacco smoke. In a corner, a man picked a tune from the strings of a guitar the likes of which Flower had never seen before. Groups of men sat around drinking and playing cards, some of them even listening to the staccato verses with which the guitarist accompanied his halting melody. The sight of Flower caused a lull in conversation, but, as he was known to the proprietor, he was ushered into an inner parlour. Those in the saloon resumed their activity as if nothing had happened. It was an establishment only frequented by fishermen. Undoubtedly there were some present who occasionally netted a case of French brandy or a batch of Scottish woollens.

In a corner of the back parlour was a curtained alcove, in which Flower found the person he sought. He was a robust man; only the greyness of the hairs on his barrel chest announced his age. When he spoke, his voice was firm and rich.

'If you've come for me at this hour, the news is not good.'

'Quite so; we must act with some urgency.'

'Let me guess: we must put the lad aboard the *Flora* afore she sails.'

'Exactly.'

'He's at your house?'

'Indeed.'

'Then go and fetch him. By the time you get to Cais Novo, I shall be waiting there for you with a skiff.'

-144-

Wednesday, March 15th, 1809

It is evident that the British do not intend to come to our aid and have abandoned their allies. Cradock is an old woman and will not stir from Lisbon to come to our aid. Wellesley is still in England, and there is no sign of the much vaunted expeditionary force. After the defeat and death of Moore, they dare not set foot in Spain again. Chaves has fallen; the French march on Braga. Our turn will come next. There is nothing more that can be done but remove ourselves from their path.

Zezere is extremely nervous. It is not in her good nature to imagine the barbarity that is war. Doroteia is more pragmatic and has organised the despatch of our valuables so that even our neighbours are unaware of our preparations. Everyone speaks of armed defiance, and it is better to pay lip service to the foolhardy notion rather than try to argue reason.

I have had to deceive my brothers of the Confraternity as to my true intentions. Although we are not obliged to perform militia duties, it is expected of every able-bodied man to bear arms. My participation in the military preparations has only strengthened my belief in the futility of our endeavour. I do not doubt the convictions of my fellow citizens, but we lack the materials of war, and, even more so, experienced officers. In the end it is not just gold and silver that Napoleon has stolen from us, but also our trained and able fighting men. The Napoleonic mechanism of war uproots men from one extreme of the Empire in order to impose his will on the other. Our best are fighting his battles in Germany, while to defend our own hearths we must rely on lads and old men armed with antique muskets and rusting cannon.

The worst of it is that we are the last to oppose his will, now that the Spanish revolt has been crushed and his brother sits on the Spanish throne. If his enterprise succeeds, the hope of a Europe not subject to the will of the Emperor is extinguished. England is now closed out and, much as she may fulminate behind her wooden walls, cannot prevail against a united continent. Little difference will it make whether we be Portuguese or Polish by birth. We will all be citizens of the Empire, subject to the same law and will of the same emperor. We have returned to the days of Caesar Augustus.

-145-

The long hours of waiting extended into the night. All movement on the waterfront ceased, apart from the silent ebb and flow of the mist. Across the river, the mass of the city formed a dark shadow against the hurrying clouds. Xavier gazed at his master, his eyes transmitting all his mute anxiety.

'Fear not; our prey has not escaped us. He must arrive at any moment now. Stay vigilant and he will yet be ours.'

-146-

Monday, March 27th, 1809

The populace remains all astir with war-like preparations. Earthworks have been thrown up, houses loopholed, trees felled to barricade the streets, all in the belief that it is possible to prevent the French from entering the city. They lie beyond the range of guns around the outer line of fortifications. This, however, has not prevented the artillery from discharging round after round throughout the day, without inflicting the slightest injury on the enemy. Tomorrow, when the French attack in earnest, they will have no munitions left! All is in the greatest disorder. There are no officers to direct the militias, and even when there are they pay scant respect to them. They spend their time shouting themselves hoarse in defiance of the French, but God preserve them when they really find themselves face to face with the invader. Much of their bravado is of the type found in a bottle, and their objective seems to be to empty the cellars before the French do. There is much tumult, with the firing of rockets and the ringing of bells, but I'm afraid it is all sound and fury, signifying little.

The Bishop has refused the terms of surrender offered by Soult. Having experienced French friendship under Taboreau, I shudder to think how they will treat us if we offer armed resistance. At least I had the foresight to anticipate events. Our house here in town is now void of valuables, and we have but to lock and bar the doors before we leave. The weather is not promising; we shall set forth early so as not to be caught by rain.

Tuesday, March 28th, 1809

Today began bright and clear after the torrential rain of the night before. Our repose was interrupted by the most frightful confusion from the city. In the middle of the night, a fearsome cannonade erupted from the artillery, which seemed to have mistaken the thunder and lightning for a French attack. The guns on the Serra replied in kind, creating a deafening roar. It is but a foretaste of what shall elapse today.

It is a relief to be in the relative safety of Oliveira. As we left by the water gate, we were abused by the populace, who called us traitors and accused us of being rats abandoning a sinking ship. Some hurled stones as well as insults. We were not the only ones, however. There was a steady stream of people crossing the pontoon bridge, but none spoke in their own defence. Each was more concerned to distance himself from the impending tragedy. My own life is not my greatest concern. Given the circumstances, I cannot expose my daughters to so imminent a risk.

-147-

As he climbed the stairs to his daughter's bedroom, Flower reflected on Grimpil's wilder tales and considered that there was likely to be a greater measure of truth in them than he had previously appreciated. Despite the lateness of the hour, he would have to wake him. However, on entering his daughter's room, he found Grimpil in bed, reading.

'I apologise for disturbing you, but I think it would be advisable for you to sail tonight with Captain Chapel.'

'What are talking about? I had decided to wait for the *Endeavour*.'

'I know, but events lead me to believe it would be better if you were to depart immediately. Get dressed and I'll explain as we go. Hurry man! It could be a case of life or death.'

'What the devil are saying, man! Whose life or death?'

'Yours.'

-148-

As the carriage clattered downhill towards the Gaia waterfront, Grimpil continued to complain bitterly.

'Explain yourself! What has happened to make you take such extreme measures?'

'I believe your life may be in danger.'

'In danger? But from whom? I don't know anybody here.'

'No, but your father had enemies here.'

'My father? But my father is dead.'

'Your father may be dead, but there are some animosities that last beyond the grave.'

'I still fail to understand.'

'Your father supported the Liberal cause at the time of the civil war. There are still those who have not accepted the defeat of Dom Miguel.'

'Absolutists.'

'Quite so. There are many who believe their cause was betrayed by foreign intervention, foreign gold and foreign ideals.'

'But Oporto was the capital of Liberalism.'

'Quite so, but Braga was the stronghold of the *Miguelistas* in the north.'

'But why does that make you think that I may be at risk?'

'Because a man called at my house today and asked for you directly.'

'So why is that so alarming?'

'Because, apart from myself and Woodhouse, no one else knows where you are.'

'Someone obviously does.'

'Exactly. Someone who is following your movements.'

'You mean spying on me?'

'Yes, I do. From the description that my wife gave me, I think there are very strong grounds for suspecting that is the Count of Alforello himself.'

'The Count of what?'

'The Count of Alforello was one of the principal *Miguelistas*, a fervent royalist. Don't underestimate the power that these men still possess. They may have lost wealth and position, but they still command the loyalty of many.'

'It all seems very dramatic to me.'

'Better to be safe than sorry.'

They were already at the waterside. The two men alighted from the carriage.

'I apologise for such an indecorous parting. Take this storm lantern in order to be able to signal The *Flora*. Let the watchman see your face, or he might think you're a river pirate.'

'There are river pirates?'

'There are bandits everywhere, except that they are not obliged to wear a badge of office.'

Flower accompanied him to the water's edge and illuminated his descent to the waiting skiff. 'I'm sorry for having to take the precautions, but I do it in your best interest. Farewell! Mind how you go. God's speed.'

After he had alighted and the cab was already heading back up the narrow streets, he noticed that Grimpil's briefcase was still lying on the seat.

–149–

'It is he,' said the *Comendador*, as some one hundred yards ahead of them Flower raised the storm lantern high to illuminate the steps at the quayside for Grimpil to descend. 'God be praised!'

Xavier made towards the rifles, but the *Comendador* restrained him.

'Take the reins so as to advance as soon as the cab departs. It will be more prudent to wait until the other has gone.'

It was no easy matter handling the rifles inside the carriage, still less withdrawing the ramrod from its housing and inserting it cleanly in the thirty-nine-inch barrel, but the *Comendador* was calm and composed, delicately ramming home the powder like someone performing a well-practised ritual.

'Enfields' said the *Comendador* appreciatively. 'Can drive a bullet into 4"of timber at 1000 paces and with a steady shot kill a man beyond that distance. Finest rifle available! Rather appropriate, don't you think?'

-150-

The boatman pointed the skiff downstream towards Captain Chapel's brig, which lay moored midstream awaiting the tide. Grimpil, sitting in the transom, closed his greatcoat about him to keep out the chill air which circulated above the river. The swirling veils of mist covered and uncovered the façade of the wine lodges on the Gaia waterfront.

Rum business, thought Grimpil. He still didn't know what exactly to make of it all. He was too involved in his own thoughts to pay attention to the fact that, despite the late hour, another carriage was sliding past the colonnaded portico of Sandeman's. He was anxious to find and board the *Flora*. The size of the skiff seemed to offer little security against the immensity of the body of water stretched ahead of him.

'Look lively, laddie.' It was the boatman who spoke, resting on the oars. 'You've let the lamp go out.' He was surprised to be addressed by the boatman in perfect English. What's more, the rich voice seemed strangely familiar. He was more concerned, however, to catch the matchbox that the boatman tossed in his direction and relight the lamp. He ran the head of the match across the rough wood of the bench, but no sooner had he raised it to the lamp than it was blown out. He could now feel a steady sea breeze, which would make lighting the lantern difficult.

-151-

As the carriage slowly drew abreast of their target, the *Comendador* rested his weapon on the window ledge for greater accuracy and squinted down the long barrel towards their target. It was going to be a duck shoot.

'Take your time,' he said to Xavier. 'We only get one shot at the target, so only fire when you're certain.'

Xavier was too intent on sighting his prey to pay attention to the Count's advice. He had jumped down from the carriage and was in the kneeling position of a trained musketeer. It gave greater accuracy, but he would have much preferred to kill his victim at close quarters; it was more intimate and he could be certain of a job well done. Shooting someone at a distance was so impersonal. At that very moment, a fresh burst of light pinpointed their target, only to disappear as quickly.

'The Lord my God has sent a light to illuminate my path,' intoned the *Comendador*. 'Oh Lord, guide my hand to smite thine enemies.'

-152-

Grimpil bent double, cloaking the lamp against the wind with his greatcoat, and struck a third match. The boatman was resting on his oars, holding the craft steady in the current. He took advantage of the pause to speak again.

'Listen, son, there's something I'd like to tell you.'

But Grimpil's attention, now that the lamp was lit, was diverted to the river bank, where he saw two flashes of light issue from the direction of the carriage on the embankment. They were followed by a sound like that of a branch breaking twice in rapid succession. Something whistled past his ear at great speed. It was a bullet. Someone was shooting at them from the shore.

The boat suddenly dipped heavily to one side. The boatman was lying backwards, extended over the opposite gunwale, bleeding profusely from a wound in his chest. Grimpil tried to raise himself, but as soon as he moved the boat lurched dangerously because of its ill distributed load. He knelt on the base boards, water slopping over his knees. The ungoverned craft had been picked up by the current and began to rotate slowly about its axis as it gained speed.

He heard the sound of wood grating against wood. Looking to his left he saw the oar, free from its rowlock, sliding away along the gunwale. He made a lunge for it in vain: it had floated free. His desperate attempt, however, nearly capsized the skiff instead, taking on water which soaked his legs. The craft continued to be spun around by the current, it could be dashed against any of the hulls moored in the river. If it was going to be possible to dominate the craft, he needed to secure the other oar which the dead or dying boatman still held in his hand. Grimpil, however, could not move to the other side of the boat without running the risk of upsetting it. The weight of the inert boatman was still lying over the starboard gunwale, not only prejudicing its waterline but also aggravating its tendency to spin. He grabbed at the man's jacket and tried to pull him inwards. The boatman was corpulent, and the dead weight was more than he could shift. As he heaved, his foot made contact with something in the bilges. He searched the murky water with his hand and pulled up the boathook. Using the pole, he was able to hook the blade of the oar and bring it inboard, the boatman still clasping it with his immobile fingers. After considerable exertion, he was finally able to roll the boatman over using the leverage afforded by the oar, so that he lay face down in the prow. The man was certainly lifeless, and prising the oar from the dead man's clutch was no easy matter. In the midst of these tasks, Grimpil had little time to pay attention to the downstream career of the skiff. Barely had he time to free the oar when he saw the wooden walls of a hull loom ahead of him. He must avoid a head-on collision at all costs, for it would snap the flimsy craft like a dry twig. Instinctively he extended the oar to fend off the impending shock. The oar splintered in his hands like a jouster's lance, and the force threw him backwards. With one hand he clung desperately to the gunwale. Although his feet were still inside the boat, his torso was over the river, and only by forcing his head upwards could he keep it clear of the water. The skiff struck the side of the ship with a resounding thud.

-153-

Aboard the *Flora* the watchman was roused by something that sounded like a barrel being dropped. His persistent ringing of the ship's bell summoned his shipmates from between decks, already awoken from their slumbers by the impact even before the alarm had been sounded. Within seconds, all hands were on deck, peering over the port rail at the river below.

Captain Chapel was already giving orders to lower the ship's longboat, and the deckhands heaved on the hawsers at the same time as the current dragged the skiff's keel along the length of *Flora's* hull in an ominous drum roll of death. Before the little craft finally turned turtle, the men at the rail distinctly heard an anguished cry for help. Not only was there a life at risk, it was the life of a fellow countryman.

-154-

The current dragged the keel of the skiff, now clear of the water, along the planking of the vessel. It reduced its speed in the water, but the angle increased dangerously as Grimpil desperately struggled to lift his body clear of the water and back into the boat. He could hear alarmed voices coming from the deck and had enough strength to cry for help before the lifeless body of the boatman, responding to the angle of the skiff, began to roll over. The skiff followed the motion of his slowly shifting weight, plunging Grimpil's head below the water. He made a final exertion to lift himself above the waves, but instead the boat overturned, tipping the boatman into his outstretched arms. He found himself in a macabre embrace with the lifeless boatman, whose dead weight bore down on him, carrying him deeper underwater.

-155-

The six-man crew of the long boat held their oars upright as it was lowered towards water level. The captain, already at the prow, could see the upturned keel of the skiff. The splintered planks could be clearly seen, although he couldn't tell if the ribs had been damaged. In any case, it appeared to have fouled a mooring line and was being held against the current at least temporarily. 'Ahoy!' he shouted down at the swirling water, but there was no reply.

The upturned skiff was slowly swinging round in the current. It would soon free itself from the restraints of the mooring cables. The *Flora* was at the head of the anchored ships, and there was nothing more to prevent if from being carried out to sea. A splash from astern told him that the longboat was in the water. He could hear the boatswain calling to the oarsman, 'Pull. Pull. Port side only. Pull. Pull.' The boat was manoeuvring in the current to come around alongside the upturned skiff on the downstream side.

'Look sharp!' the Captain called down. 'She's drifting loose.'

The men braced themselves against the oars to bring the nose of the longboat in against the current. Just as she was perpendicular to the *Flora* the skiff broke free, now on a collision course with the longboat. The men scarcely had time to raise the oars on the starboard side to prevent them from being fouled, before the skiff struck her broadside. It did not resist this last impact and started breaking up, wood from the crippled boat being stripped away by the current and carried off into the darkness.

-156-

Grimpil longed to open his mouth and fill his lungs with air. He could see a brightening expanse before his eyes, like a blank page; a moving canvas depicting scenes from his own life as if seen from above, a kind of mute pageant of him standing on the deck of the *Flora*, walking along the river front, dancing with Flávia, taking tea with Dona Eugenia, sketching the *Paço dos Duques,* sitting alone in a carriage being jolted over cobblestones, a book in his lap. The images were dissolving like ink in water, but the book was drawing closer, open at an empty page on which an unseen hand was writing. One by one the words appeared: *I wish to possess her love as much as my love for her possesses me.*

Why not enjoy the next book in the Grimpil series?

GRIMPIL'S RETROGRESS: INVICTA

In the second part of Grimpil's Retrogress we return to places already familiar to the readers of *Grimpil's Retrogress* – Oporto and Guimarães, although this time seen through the eyes of Horace Grimpil's father, Captain Alexander Grimpil.

Grimpil's Retrogress: Invicta accompanies the last day of his life while he revisits the haunts of his youth and is haunted by his youthful adventures at the time of the Civil War and the siege of Oporto. Most of all, he recalls his confrontation with the fearsome Count of Alforelo, and the reasons for which the *Comendador* later seeks to extract his final revenge on father and son.

Printed in the United States
123936LV00001B/31-39/P